COOPER'S MOON

COOPER'S MOON

A Cooper Mystery

Richard C. Conrath

GULF SHORE PRESS
St. Petersburg, Florida

Cooper's Moon

Published by Gulf Shore Press 2018
St. Petersburg, Florida

FIRST EDITION

Library of Congress Control Number: 2018901973

ISBN 978-1-946937-00-1

Book design (cover and interior) by Cathleen Elliott

Cover photos: iStock.com/OSTILL, Jasmina007, ParkerDeen, THEPALMER, parameter, cloki, aleksandarvelasevic

～

Dedicated to my wife, Karyn.

We made it!

～

Prologue

It was August when our seven-year-old son went missing. On a Tuesday morning in Muskingum, Ohio, trees still green under the punishing late summer sun. I was teaching a class in metaphysics, that part of the course that asks about the nature of the world; you know, the tree falling in the forest, does it really fall or is it only falling in our minds? The kind of discussion that made my students think I was smoking.

The Dean knocked on my door and motioned me into the hall.

"Cooper," he said, hesitating, "you need to go home...your wife..."

"She's been in an accident?" I said.

"...called me," he added quickly.

"About?" I said, starting to turn down the hall, but he was holding my arm.

"It's about your son..." he said, trying to stop me.

"He's hurt!" I could picture it. I pulled away.

"No, she can't find him," he said, as I headed down the hall. Then I thought about my class and turned back to him.

"Go. I'll cover," he said, turning and disappearing into the classroom.

I hurried through the exit at the end of the hall, taking the concrete steps in a leap and hit the parking lot running. I could see my house from there—the roof that is—over the tops of trees that crowded the woods separating my home from the college. I hurried past the cars parked in the lot and then into the woods, hoping to see my son on the way—surely he was hiding there, chasing a ball maybe, just hanging out like a seven-year-old would. But I broke through the trees without finding him, then I was facing a field, about a hundred yards of overgrown weeds, and beyond the field my house, and I saw Jillie standing there, watching me as I began to cross the field, not hurrying now, I saw no reason to—I don't know, something in her demeanor told me to approach cautiously—and I sensed that something bad had happened to Maxie...that he wasn't just missing...that perhaps he was really gone, and I hesitated for a moment, but she began to scream out my name, so I ran as hard as I could across the few yards left of the wild grass and blackberry bushes that pulled at my pants, and up the porch stairs where she stood with her arms folded over her breasts, as if protecting herself, and she said, "I can't find him! He's gone!" and she threw herself into my arms and began to sob, so hard that she shook, and I found it hard not to do the same myself, as I looked out over the field and across the highway that runs in front of our home, Old Route 40, hoping to see him come bounding back, recklessly, not paying attention to the traffic, yellow hair and all, maybe bringing back whatever it was that he had been chasing.

But he didn't. And my heart was in my throat.

Seven Years Later

PART ONE

TOGETHER

CHAPTER 1

The Call

Friday, October 1

The call came in on a late Friday afternoon. A lady said someone shot her twelve-year-old son. *A drive-by maybe,* the dispatcher said. Maybe one of those random shootings that happens in Miami. Some crazy guy in a Chevrolet driving I-95, shoving a shotgun out the window and blasting away. It happened in the summer of '82. That's the way it goes in this city, especially in the summer when the sun heats up and everyone becomes a potential crazy.

This shooting was on Northeast 36th Street, that's Route 27. I knew the address. It's near Little Haiti. A dangerous part of Miami. Easy to get shot. Most cops don't like going there.

My partner, Anthony DeFelice, picked me up in an unmarked and we were out the door and on the road blowing our way through the afternoon traffic and scattering cars like leaves in autumn.

Anthony and I had grown up together on the near east side of Cleveland, a tough neighborhood even then. Now—well you don't walk through the near east side without protection. As one cop told me recently when I asked him if things were a little safer there now, *Hey this is Cleveland, Cooper. Same as when you was a kid.* Only back then Tony and I and another friend, Richie Marino, who's a mob enforcer now, handled the neighborhood. Richie used a baseball bat to set the rules. Tony and I had guns.

So now I'm a homicide cop with Miami PD. I used to teach philosophy in a small college in Ohio—imagine that—until somebody stole my son while I was teaching. And I almost killed myself—not really—almost though. And I was married to a good woman. She taught English at the same college. And she was home with Maxie when he disappeared. And then for a year we beat each other up about who was more to blame, forgetting, of course, that there was someone out there who had taken our son and that we should be blaming him. Not ourselves.

But as it usually goes, we blamed each other and then we split after a year. After a miserable year of fighting. And about then I got a call from Tony, now a homicide cop in Miami, that there was a gang in the city transporting kidnapped kids out of the country and that I should come down and check it out. I was thirty years old, split from Jillie, and so depressed that I really couldn't teach, so—you guessed it—I tossed it all and went to Miami. Tony talked me into taking the police officer's exam—which I did—and I passed it and became a street cop, then when a spot opened for a promotion to detective, I took that exam and that's where I am now. A homicide cop. Six years after I left Muskingum, Ohio. An idyllic town in middle America where bad things are not supposed to happen to people. But they do.

It took us sixteen minutes to get there. The area was already cleared and lined with yellow tape, cop cars and fire-rescue trucks painting the street blue and red. Near the back door of one of the emergency vehicles, a woman was crying over the body of someone being hoisted on board.

A cop cleared the tape for us and we pulled in near the ER truck. I could hear the woman talking to the person on the gurney.

"Don't worry, honey, you're gonna to be jus' fine. Don't you worry your pretty little sweet head."

It was a boy they were loading onto the ambulance. And he wasn't moving.

"He's just twelve years old," she said to the men loading him.

And then she turned—to some gangbangers hanging out across the street by a red brick building that looked like it had just been bombed.

"He's just twelve years old!" She screamed loud enough for them to hear.

They didn't move. Just leaned against the building, the one that looked bombed out, the one that had bars on its windows, the one that had a sign hanging over the street that read, 'Groceries'.

"Talk to her," I told DeFelice. "I'm gonna see if I can find the cop who was first on the scene."

I asked the cop next to me if anyone saw the shooting. He looked to be about thirty-five or forty, large arms—a lifter—and the stiff face of a marine.

He said, *No.*

"The mother?" I said.

"No," he said.

"No one saw anything?" I said.

"No."

"Uh huh," I said.

"Anyone talk to those guys over there?" I said, pointing to the gangbangers the mother had just yelled at. They were still hanging out on the corner near the vacant store.

"No," he said, "nobody talked to them yet. Saved that for you, detective."

"Uh huh," I said, and *Fucking thanks for that* under my breath as I headed for the mother.

DeFelice was already talking to her, his large body bent over her small frame, nodding sympathetically as she shook her head and cried. He looked up at me and then at the boys on the corner. She had the look of a woman who knew her son was as good as dead. I told her that the doctors would do all they could for him and leave it in their hands.

But she wrung her hands and told me *Them doctors not God, mister*—chiding me for being so foolish—*they just men with men's hands.*

I nodded. She watched her son being loaded into the emergency vehicle. She was getting ready to climb in with him. I touched her on the shoulder—gently. She turned to me. I asked her if she saw the shooter. She was angry—not with me—but with the gangbangers standing across the street.

She turned to them as she shouted, "I don't have to see no shooter, I knows who shot little Darly. It was one of them boys over there," and she pointed to the gangbangers. They just stared, like *What the fuck's your problem.* No fear. I nudged DeFelice to go with me and have a talk.

There were about six in all. As I got closer I spotted the tats on the arm of one of the bangers. The Latin King symbol, black and gold markings on a 5-star crown. I didn't see the LK in the tat but I saw the colors. Then, suddenly, all six turned and disappeared into the alley that ran between two buildings. The space between the buildings was narrow. No sunshine would penetrate there. There were trash bins, but they weren't much use since most of the trash was on the ground. And the stench—I needed a gas mask.

Some rats crawled out of a heap of cans and paper and old tires and left-over food. They scurried past like I was coming for them, then disappeared into a hole in the building—all that was left of a door. Ironically, the whole place is known as the Hole. And part of it is in the Magic City, which is why DeFelice and I were here, and part is in Oceanside. And, as its name implies, the Hole is a cesspool of drugs and random killings—like Darly's—and rapes and every kind of bad stuff you could imagine. And, as I said, part of the Hole is in Oceanside, a city south of Miami that stretches from the Bay of Biscayne to the Everglades. Part is in Miami.

So about halfway into the building, DeFelice and I would be in another jurisdiction. And Rodriquez, our commanding officer, would be pissed as hell about that. As I was soon to find out.

As I was adjusting my bulletproof vest, I happened to look up and saw a head appear over the top of a rusted out fire escape. I would remember that face in the future. Then I saw fire erupt from his hand and something hit me in the chest like a sledgehammer, knocking me against a waste container. I lay there for a moment figuring I was shot. Blood was running down my neck.

"You're okay, partner. You ain't shot," said DeFelice who was standing over me now. "You just got a nasty cut on your head," he said, kneeling down and fooling around with the back of my head. "Just got to stop this bleeding," and he pulled out a large handkerchief that he kept in the lapel of his coat, stretched it over the wound, then pulled the ends around my head and tied it off. "That should do it," he said, starting to get up. Then, "What's this?" pointing to the tear in my vest. I looked down. "Looks like you got hit, buddy," he added. "This is your lucky day." He paused, "You okay?"

I nodded. I figured being dizzy didn't count.

DeFelice studied me for a few moments, then, "Okay, let's go get this dumb fuck," and we headed for the hole in the wall.

There was a flight of stairs just inside the doorway. And as I passed the hole and into the hallway, noxious odors hit me like a tidal wave, and I fell back choking and covering my nose. There was garbage in the hall, and dead rats and food rotting in torn MacDonald's bags, and feces, and urine. That was the worst.

"Christ," said DeFelice. "These people live like animals."

"It's why we never come down here," I said. "It's why the garbage men call it the Hole."

He nodded and we both moved toward the stairway. I pulled the slide back on my Glock to load a shell into the chamber, the sound echoing through the hall. Nothing like the sound of a shell being pumped into the smokestack to make someone nervous. I headed up the stairs. They were simply constructed. Each stairway consisted of ten steps and ended at a landing halfway between the next floor and the one below it. From there we would do a one-eighty and head up the next flight, which would bring us to the second floor—where I figured they would be waiting for us. Maybe. At least no one would be able to hear creaking steps. They were made of concrete.

Two cops had followed us into the building. They stayed well behind us—about twenty feet or so. It's always good to keep space. It makes a harder target for the bad guys. I was almost at the first landing when I heard a noise above me, then shells ricocheted off the stairs and walls driving me to the floor. I yelled for DeFelice to go back but it was too late. I heard him grunt.

"Hey pendejos," someone yelled—and bullets sprayed the landing again and I scrambled down the stairs stumbling against DeFelice who was slumped against a wall about halfway down. I grabbed onto him. Then another round of shells and I felt sharp stings in my shoulder and legs and then both of us tumbled down the rest of the stairs onto the landing below and hands pulled us out of the building, dragging as fast as they could and yelling, "Officer down!" and things went dark after that and I heard sirens—they seemed far off—and I wondered who was going to the hospital.

CHAPTER 2

Miami General

Sunday, October 3

"Probably an initiation killing, Coop," said Rodriquez as he leaned over my bed to look at my shoulder dressing.

"How do you feel?" he said, straightening up.

"Shot," I said.

"Uh huh," he said. "Same wise ass."

John Rodriquez is the Lieutenant in charge of homicide—I was ready for his lecture.

"You look like shit, Coop," he said. "Why the hell did you go in there without backup?"

"Had backup. DeFelice and two cops," I said.

"I'm talking about guys with armor. You don't go into the Hole like you did, chasing gangbangers without serious firepower. See what happens?"

I didn't say anything. That was the lecture. I gotta let him have that.

Rodriguez stared out the window.

"The Kings must have ordered the killing," almost like he was talking to himself. "You want to be a King," he continued, gesturing like it was all happening below him, "you go across the street and shoot some homeboy," pointing through the window as if there was somebody down there, "which is what it appears they did. No random car this time, just a walkover and a shoot," looking back at me from whatever it was he saw out there. The only view I had was of another rooftop and some rusty AC units staring back at me.

"How's Tony?" I said.

"He's doing fine. He got shot up like you did, amigo. He asked about you. Looks like you two are gonna be here a while. Make sure you take a coupla days when you get released."

It's funny how cops see everything in terms of getting released.

"I'll swing by DeFelice's room on the way out," he added, like it was his exit line. Then, "Take care of yourself." Like I could do anything else.

"Tell Tony I'll be down as soon as they unwire me here," I yelled at his back. He waved without turning.

If you pull out your computer and check out the Latin Kings on the web, you can read all about them. They got started in Chicago in the 40s by some Hispanic males with the aim of fighting racism. But they must have needed money because they soon became criminalized, selling street level drugs, like crack and heroin. And now the way to join the Kings, or for that matter most any gang, is to kill someone or at the very least diss a member of a rival gang which usually results in a killing anyway—and so, the murder of the little Haitian boy, Darly. He was just such a victim—probably.

I forgot to mention. He died on the way to the hospital. That mother. She would remember I had given her hope and she would probably hate me for it. I had reason to hunt down his killers. And I would, as soon as I got out. One face stood out in my mind. A young Latino. I noticed him when we crossed the street to *chat* with the gangbangers. A baby face. I wondered if he was the new member.

There was another face I will never forget. The face of the kid who shot me from the rooftop outside the building.

Thirteen Days Later

CHAPTER 3

The Cemetery

Saturday, October 16

A cop had called in a DOA to the station and asked for an officer in charge around 12:55 a.m. Dispatch woke me up a few minutes later. My body still ached from the past weeks. I called DeFelice and told him I would pick him up. This is the bad part about being a cop. These early mornings, no warning, just a call, an address and get down there ASAP. Chance to get shot again. Thanks a lot.

No time for a shower, too early for breakfast, just time for some coffee and out the door. I drove from my house in Oceanside which is about ten miles south of Miami at the edge of the Everglades into South Miami and picked up DeFelice. We got to the scene around 1:55 a.m. and checked in with the patrolman who had secured the scene. The ME was already there and had established that the vic was DOA. Dr. Mantillo is an efficient and systematic son of a bitch, meticulous and finicky about everything. He was surrounded by gravestones—everywhere—mainly because this was a cemetery.

The victim was a twelve-year-old boy. The left side of his head was a mass of blood and tissue. I could see grey matter, actually more pink than grey. Another gang killing I figured. This is the 55th Street Boys' territory.

"Sucks doesn't it, Coop," said DeFelice.

"Yeah," I said. "Sucks."

The ME was checking the trunk of the boy's body then shifted to the head.

"Here's the locus of the death blow, fellas," said the doc, pointing to an area at the back of the boy's head—where the gray matter had oozed out.

"Uh huh," I said. I wondered if he was putting me on.

"Is he fucking kidding?" whispered DeFelice.

"So anything else, Doc?" I said, hoping the doc didn't hear.

"Not yet," he said, curt, and went back to work.

The ME is in charge of the crime scene once he arrives. That means even the OIC—that's me, the Officer In Charge—reports to him. But, he's supposed to let me know immediately about his findings. Nothing in the book about being nice.

"We got an ID on the vic?" I asked, turning to the young cop standing behind me, the one who had secured the crime scene.

"Yes sir. Miller, Ethan. Lives on Woodworth Street, ten blocks south of here. ID's in his pocket. Wallet, picture, name, address, age, phone number."

"Anyone talk to the parents?"

"No sir," the young cop replied, looking like he was just out of the Academy. Nervous.

I asked DeFelice to call the Duty Officer at the station, fill him in on the case, and see who's going to notify the family. He said fine and jumped on his cell. I could hear him talking to the DO and getting pissed. *No sir, we're tied up at the scene right now.* He looked at me like what do they think we can do, leave the scene and visit people? *Yeah, a woman officer would be good to accompany. Yes sir, we're planning to visit once the parents have been notified. And yeah, we would appreciate a follow-up call after the visit.*

"Jeez," he said when he got off, "it's like these guys never did this before. All they gotta do is follow the damn protocol!"

I nodded and turned back to the young cop.

"Who discovered the body?" I asked.

"Coupla kids cutting through the cemetery on the way home from a basketball game. Used their cell phones, called 911, Unit 837 responded and called it in."

"Where are the kids?"

"I let 'em call their parents and go home. Got their names, addresses, phone numbers," said the young cop. He handed me his written notes.

"What's your name, officer," I asked the patrolman.

"Jesus Diaz, sir."

"In the future, Diaz, don't let witnesses leave a crime scene until the OIC arrives. Okay?" I said, pissed.

"Uh, okay. Sorry about that, sir. You want I should call 'em back?"

"No, forget it," I said, feeling the anger rise up. I knew where it was coming from. It was the same anger I felt when the cops made mistakes in my own son's case. I was glaring at the cop without realizing it. I turned away when I saw him look at me nervously.

"Okay, Tony, we'll catch up with the kids later," I said with an undercurrent of irritation.

"What the hell's wrong with you this morning, Cooper?" he said.

I told him I was sorry; I just didn't get enough sleep. He said, yeah, I know, same with him. It didn't make me feel any better, apologizing for anger that's always there, ready to rise up at the right moment, like when we have a case like this one: young kid, murdered, no apparent reason. My son was seven when he disappeared. That was almost seven years ago. So today he would be just a little older than Ethan Miller. So sure I was mad. I looked at DeFelice and shrugged as if to say, sorry—again. He waved me off.

The only lights that were burning now were the street lamps and the lights from the crime scene. The techs moved in and out of shadows cast from the trees and the gravestones. And overhead the late October moon, a Hunter's Moon, hung low and big over the cemetery. It's a good time to take in the crops when the moon sits low over the fields. It's also a good time to hunt. You don't need a torch to find your prey on those nights. The fields are clearly lit.

Native Americans had a different name for this moon: the Blood Moon. They said the fields of autumn ran with the blood of slain animals, that the moon had a tinge of red in it on those nights. I turned to see if the moon in the sky tonight showed any signs of red. It did. Perhaps it arose from the emanations of red flashing from a police car pulling away. Perhaps it was just in my mind. Perhaps it was because it really was a Blood Moon.

CHAPTER 4

Memories of...

The killing of Ethan Miller bore a striking resemblance to a killing in Oceanside about three weeks ago. A young girl, a year older than Ethan, was found dead in a cemetery on County Line Road that runs along the border of South Miami and Oceanside. Only about three miles or so from the cemetery where Ethan was found. Her killer had slammed what appeared to be a metal bar into her head, crushing one side of her skull. According to the ME's report, the blow to her head was the immediate cause of death. There was no suspect as yet.

There's nothing worse. The death of one of your kids. No parents should outlive their kid. I should know. Sometimes married couples can't stand the sight of each other after losing a child. All the blaming, finger pointing. *What do you mean you didn't see him go out the door? Weren't you watching!* Or *What do you mean you couldn't pick her up on time? Look what's happened!* In other words you killed your child. It's no way to live a life. And so they split up. It happens all the time. Even when you try to avoid it. It happens.

It happened to me. So I know how it is. I could feel the same thing in the air tonight. It would happen to the parents of this kid. It was just a matter of time.

I have friends who lost a child to cancer. There was no one to blame there. So they just stayed together and fought through the grief. There was no way to tell one another, *What did you do to cause our kid to have cancer?* No way.

But here, now that's a different story. I hated to think about how it would go. Watching the ME examine Ethan brought it all back to me. About Maxie's disappearance. I went home directly from class, found my wife, Jillie waiting for me on the front porch, and she had that—how can I put it?—lost and helpless look—and I had told her, *No problem, we would find him—he's just hiding in the woods*—some crazy thing like that—every kid does that—and we began looking— all the rest of that morning—all through the afternoon—and the sun burned more fiercely as the day approached mid-afternoon— no breeze—I remembered it clearly. Me wearing out my voice from the calling and Jillie wearing out her spirit—she was too nervous to join the search: *I need to be here in case he comes home,* she said, and that made sense. And we continued the search through the late afternoon. Then, I decided to call the police—again. The first time I called—it was late morning—they were reluctant: *Probably hiding. Maybe went to a friend's house,* was all they would offer. *Let us know if he doesn't show.* I wanted to believe them.

And so we searched some more—me, Jillie and some of my friends from the university. Some maintenance people joined us in the late afternoon. Even the President. But no Maxie. So I called the police again in the early evening. They finally sent out two detectives to help organize the search—thanks a lot. Some people from the town had joined us by that time and a TV 3 news truck pulled into our drive. All I needed. Jillie and I trying to find our son. And I'm trying to stay calm and a woman with a mike is trying to talk to me. I wanted to tell her to go to hell. But I didn't.

And so we searched the field, consuming desperate hours, and we searched the woods and the back streets, Jillie and I both now, the police and everybody else calling out and beating through every bush high enough to conceal a seven-year-old, Jillie and I getting more anxious as the hours turned into darkness. And I began to panic and so did Jillie, but I hid mine from her, and it got so dark that we couldn't see anymore and the cops handed out flashlights turning the fields and the woods into an eerie scene, like from a horror movie, lights flashing in the darkness, moving back and forth across the night, fireflies looking for a place to light, and the voices of the searchers murmured through the silence, and I strained to hear news but knew that if there were any they would scream it out, and we searched until my bones got weary and I suggested we take a break—it was around three in the morning—get some coffee—and Jillie whispered *No!* but it seemed more like a scream though it might have just registered in my brain like that, and so we kept on and the sun began to rise in the East, over the campus, and a feeling of dread that I didn't want to share with Jillie, came over me, like this is it. Our son is gone. Gone. Oh God, gone.

The Mother

Saturday Morning, October 16

We wrapped up the crime scene around 5:00 a.m. The techs had finished their work and the medical examiner had released the body for transfer to the morgue. I needed coffee. I grabbed DeFelice and we headed for an all-night donut shop in Oceanside. They serve breakfast for $6.95 that includes two eggs, bacon, ham and sausage, coffee, grits, choice of donuts and orange juice. A little much for early in the morning, but we weren't going to get much sleep anyway.

I ordered the $6.95 special. DeFelice got the same. We pulled out our notes and went over them. What we had to do was to stop by the station, fill out the paperwork, and then head out to see Ethan's mother, Hannah Miller.

It took several hours to fill out the paperwork, talk to Rodriquez, and get a rundown from the two cops who visited the family. They were in newly pressed blues. The woman, a young Hispanic, looked like she was just out of the Academy. She appeared shaken. Not the greatest first experience for a new cop. Victor, on the other hand, had the cool appearance of a veteran. No affect. The kind of police officer who is all, "Yes, ma'am," and "Yes, sir." The woman, Ivette,

24

summed things up for us: "The mother, Hannah Miller, is divorced, has three boys," she hesitated, "one of them now being deceased," she added. "She's thirty five years old and works as a secretary for a construction company in Oceanside. Her ex, Jack, is a salesman. He's always on the road. The mother doesn't know where he is currently."

I asked how the mother was doing. She said not well. Victor nodded in agreement. Rodriquez asked if they learned anything new about the case. Victor, jumping in, said "Yeah, the husband was supposed to have his son, Ethan, over the weekend. Never picked him up."

"Any other relatives in the area to notify?" asked Rodriquez.

"Just the grandmother. Lives next door. Mrs. Miller said she would tell her," Victor added.

Ivette asked if she could join DeFelice and me when we visited the mother. "She's having a bad time," she said. "Real bad," she added.

Rodriquez said, "Yeah, good idea. Stay for as long as you need. Might be a good idea anyway 'til we see what happened—make sure the family's safe." He paused and looked at us. "Anything more, amigos?" Then, "If no, then let's get to work." Turning toward me and Tony, "Cooper and DeFelice, get on over and revisit the Miller woman. See what the hell that kid was doing in the cemetery so late at night."

Ethan's mother lived on the southern edge of South Miami between Highway 874, the southern extension of I-75, and Route 1

as it swings southwest from the city of Miami proper and becomes Dixie Highway. The house was a small bungalow, sitting about sixty feet back from a newly tarred street that didn't do much to improve the overall appearance of the neighborhood. Several palms, weighed down with dead branches, stood over grass, brown from a long dry spell. Otherwise the landscaping was non-existent.

We pulled into the drive trying to avoid a neighbor's sprinkler. It was watering everything but the grass.

A news truck was parked in the street. A reporter talking to a camera on the lawn in front of the house was pointing to the front door. Someone had just shut it. Several neighbors were gathered on the street near the truck, probably trying to get their picture on TV, or maybe just plain curious. A few others stood on the other side of the street like spectators at a lynching.

The reporter must have recognized our car because she hurried over and asked if we had a suspect as yet in the case. I told her no. She stood there waiting like I was going to say something more.

We headed up the walk toward the house. There was a small overhang that covered the door and one of the side windows, providing some protection from the sun. No whole house air conditioning. Just some units hanging over the windowsills on the front porch, running loud, trying to crank cold air into the house.

I knocked. The neighbors looked on. I stared back at them while I waited for the door to open. When it did, a young boy peeked out. He must have been about eleven. Another boy hung back in the shadows. He looked a lot younger. The boy glanced around nervously at the minor circus that was gathering around the house. It had grown since we arrived.

"Yeah?" the boy said, his hair hanging over part of his face.

I told him who we were. He asked for our badges. A good kid.

"Mom said we always have to ask for ID before we talk to strangers at the door," he said.

We showed him our badges.

"The police lady who was here this morning is here again," I told him pointing to Ivette.

He nodded.

"Is your mom at home?" I said.

"Yeah, but she don't want to be disturbed now."

DeFelice edged by me. "We don't want to bother your mom, son. Just want to ask her a few questions about your brother, okay?"

"What's your name, son?" said DeFelice.

"Aaron."

"Aaron, would you please ask your mom if we can come in and talk with her? Tell her who we are," I said.

He stood there for a while. It looked like he was thinking about it. I let him think. Then Aaron disappeared into the house, leaving the door open and the other kid staring at us from the gloom inside. He reappeared after several minutes.

"She said to come on in," he said.

We followed him into a living room to the right of the entryway. To the left was a dining room, the kind no one ever uses. We had our choice of seating in the living room: Two beige couches sat at an angle to each other. The rest of the space was filled with two recliners and a few straight-back chairs pulled in from the dining room. One of the recliners was leaning on its haunches like it was about to fall backwards if someone sat on it. A blanket and pillow were arranged on the other one. Someone's bed for the last few hours. Light entered the room from a large bay window framed by floor to ceiling sheers. Heavy ecru drapes hung down the sides and spread over the top like a makeshift valence. I noticed a large portrait over the couch. It was a photo of a blonde woman with three boys. They were walking on a beach. A happier time. The older boy looked like Ethan.

I was staring at it when Aaron interrupted, "You can sit here," he said, motioning to the couch. Ivette sat on the couch. DeFelice and I took the dining room chairs.

The woman who emerged from the hall beyond the dining room was not the woman in the portrait; she was a shell of a body. An older woman, who bore a striking resemblance to the mother, was holding her arm, guiding her around the dining room tables and chairs. A tall man with a salt and pepper beard and pure white hair followed them. He walked with a slight stoop, the kind that comes with age. He stepped around the two women and introduced himself as Rabbi Wortzman. The older woman said she was Hannah's mother. That left just Hannah.

DeFelice and I introduced ourselves, told her how sorry we were about the death of her son. After we were all seated and a respectable period of silence passed, I told Hannah that we were familiar with most of the story from the police report, but just had a few more questions—if she didn't mind. She waited.

"How do you think Ethan happened to be in the vicinity of the cemetery last night?" I said. I wanted to ask, how did a fourteen-year-old boy happen to be out alone late at night? But I didn't.

She shook her head as if to say she didn't have any idea. I watched her moods change, like the tides under a full moon.

Ivette leaned in so she could face Hannah directly. "Mrs. Miller, you told the police earlier that your husband was supposed to pick up Ethan at the school. Have you been able to get hold of him?"

"No. He's not answering his phone," she whispered. "As usual," she added—to herself.

I asked for his phone number and she gave it to me.

"See if you can get hold of him, Tony," I said, turning to DeFelice. He left the room punching numbers into his cell.

We waited.

He came back into the room, shaking his head. "Guy don't answer. Tried him twice."

I asked Hannah if she could tell us anything more about Ethan that might give us a clue about what happened. Was he in trouble? Did he have problems at school? Who were his friends?

"He has nice friends. He's a good kid. He works as a volunteer at the student center over at the university," she added and then she hesitated. "I mean he worked," she said, correcting herself.

"At the Catholic student center?" I said, showing some surprise. I figured him for Jewish—I mean Rabbi Wortzman.

"Yes," she said, looking up at me, puzzled. "You mean because he's Jewish?"

"No," I said. "I was just clarifying."

"He's a good kid," she said again, a few tears forming around her eyes.

I needed to see Ethan's room before we left so I asked Hannah if she would show us. She nodded to her mother who got up and led us down a long corridor lined with bedrooms, like a shotgun house, two on each side, a half bath squeezed in between two rooms on the left. There was a den at the end of the corridor, with knotty pine walls halfway up to the ceiling and an old fireplace, ashes still there—a few remnants of burned logs.

"This is Ethan's bedroom," she said, pointing to the last room on the right.

There wasn't much in the room. Some posters of System of A Down and Linkin Park. Several film posters on the wall—*Memento*, *Shrek*. I recognized those two.

"Ethan really loves films. *Memento* was his favorite," the grandmother said.

"His dresser is there against the wall," she said, pointing to a small bureau, painted white, crowded between the bed and the wall, just under a window. Clothes were jammed in the two bottom drawers, no apparent order. The top drawers were filled with teenage stuff: several old watches—one a moon watch—change in a basket hidden in the back of the drawer, bubble gum cards, a yo-yo, comb, some old coins, a brochure from the student center, and a few boxes of matches.

"Your grandson smoke?" asked DeFelice.

"No, not that I ever saw. His father woulda kill...." She hesitated then stopped entirely.

"Killed him?" I finished.

"He didn't really mean it—just used to say it a lot. You know—when he got angry."

"Yeah, good reason not to say it, maybe. Makes you wonder if he meant it or not," muttered DeFelice.

She didn't say anything.

"Is this the tutoring program your grandson was in at the student center, Mrs. Miller?" I said, holding up the brochure.

"Actually my name is Kravitz. Yes, I think that's the program. You can ask Hannah."

We returned to the living room. I could see the street from the bay window. From where I stood I saw only the television truck, not the reporter, nor any neighbors. The afternoon sun was beginning to appear in the window as it dropped in the west. It didn't shed any light on our investigation.

The day was wearing on and darkness would crowd in before long. I get an uneasy feeling when the night comes and I'm working an unsolved case. The spirits of the those who are killed emerge in the night and haunt the dreams of people like me, investigators who are charged with being their avengers, even paid to do so. I don't mind that burden. But I feel the weight of it. I could feel it today. And the eyes of Hannah Miller burned into me. I didn't see them—I felt them. And the eyes of her two boys and of DeFelice, and of Ivette, and of the Rabbi, and of Hannah's mother, and of Maxie—of course, Maxie—It's been how long now? Seven years?—and the eyes of all those who were gathered outside the house. They were on me too. Making judgments.

I shook my head and stood up. I turned to DeFelice and said *Let's go.* I wanted to add *Let's get the hell out of here.* But I didn't. The moon wasn't up yet. We still had time.

CHAPTER 6

Time To Dream

Ivette stayed behind with the mother. Hannah was okay with that. So we headed out the door, past the neighbors—there were dozens now it seemed. Some had pulled up lounge chairs and were drinking beers and passing around chips. A tailgate party.

We got in our car and pulled out as the reporter caught up with us, yelling some last questions through the windows.

I yelled, "Why don't you write them down and fax them to the Chief," as DeFelice pulled away.

The drive back to the station through the traffic that was pouring out of Miami along Route1 isn't pleasant in the late afternoon. Everyone is a crazy driver at that time of day. As the evening wears on, the highway will turn into a steady stream of light moving against the ground like an endless ribbon of neon, winding its way in and out of the city in all directions.

I settled back in the seat and fell asleep, leaving the driving to DeFelice and dreaming of an earlier time.

CHAPTER 7

Walnuts

Maxie, Jillie and I had packed a picnic lunch, along with three empty bushel baskets, and headed for the dirt roads that connect the farms surrounding the towns in Muskingum County. We passed barns with signs painted in large yellow lettering, big red barns advertising Mail Pouch tobacco, or Camel cigarettes, or Coca Cola. We passed telephone poles, barbed wire fences, and high-tension lines that carried electricity to the farms.

Walnut trees lined most of the roads. That's what we were looking for. So we parked near several where we saw the nuts scattered along the road, pulled out our baskets, and began filling them, Maxie running ahead with a basket trailing behind, blond hair blowing, and grabbing nuts as he ran. It went like that through the late afternoon, Jillie calling out to Maxie as he got too close to a fence that was electrified, and Maxie running back and forth, his container a quarter-full of black treasure, and dumping it into a basket near the car. By the time we were done, we had two and a half baskets of nuts, jet black and smelling of country, our hands stained with the juice that comes from the skin of the nut. It's the devil to remove. Maxie held up his hands, stained yellowish-black, proud of his work.

We sat by the side of the road on a blanket near the wagon, drank Kool-Aid and shared egg-salad sandwiches and apples as the sun slowly disappeared. The hard work was still ahead—drying the nuts on the basement floor until the skin no longer bled and could easily be removed to get to the walnut. We would use hammers to break through the skin and then crack the hard shells and pull out the meat. But that would be later. For the time we enjoyed the sounds of cicadas as the evening drifted in. I'll never forget these days, I thought, as I sat and stared at the lights coming on in the farmhouse across the field. The darkness fell quickly and we still sat there—and the moon was like a vigil over us.

CHAPTER 8

Back Home

"We're here," said DeFelice, shaking me awake.

He climbed out, turned to look at me, shrugged his shoulders and said, "Nice fucking day, huh?"

"Yeah," I said, "nice fucking day."

"Maybe Rodriquez'll do his own dirty work next time. See what it's like," he said.

"Yeah, maybe so," I said.

"Screw it," he said and turned toward the station to collect his car.

"Yeah, screw it," I muttered. No one heard me.

I headed home, storm clouds gathering as they do almost every day in Florida in the rainy season. Only this time they seemed a little heavier, more menacing. The wind picked up as I pulled into my drive, if you could call it that. A gravel and dirt section carved out by tire tracks, mostly mine. The drive ended at the front door and an overhung porch with a six-by-six A-frame roof that I put on about four years ago. A single palm tree sits in the back yard, one oleander bush under a maple, and some seagrapes with branches bent on taking over the house.

It's a small house, only 1,705 square feet, on an acre that backs up to the Everglades. An old dock, with some boards that need replacing, sits behind mangroves and extends far enough into the swamp to be able to launch a small boat, my Boston Whaler to be exact. I bought the boat about six years ago from a guy who said the motor was no good. I had the motor fixed and have used it to explore the swamp and fish its waters.

There is nobody else around my house, no neighbors, just me and a cat that stays under the back porch. I feed him when I'm there in the evenings and on the weekends. When I am not out solving crimes.

I called the station immediately after coming through the door and asked the secretary for the number and address of the young girl, Tamara Thompson, who was found murdered in Oceanside about four weeks ago, the first of what the papers were calling 'The Cemetery Murders'. She went missing from school for several days, five to be exact, and then showed up dead in a cemetery near the Oceanside city limits. The disappearance of Tamara dominated the news as the Oceanside neighborhoods organized search parties. When her body was found, the ME said she had been dead for only a few hours. There were signs that she had been sexually assaulted. There were no leads so far, at least until now.

The secretary who had put me on hold with some elevator music to keep me occupied finally came back on the line.

"Number's 752-9504. And Detective DeFelice wants to talk with you," she said.

"Why didn't you tell me you was gonna see the Thompsons?" he said when he got on the phone.

"Thought you might be following up with the kids who reported the body in the cemetery," I said.

"Been there, bud. Nothin' so far. Called a coupla times and no answer. I don't think we're going to find anything there. And yeah, I'll go with you to the Thompsons," reading my mind.

"Good. Can you set it up?"

"Yeah. Pick me up at the station. Coupla hours."

I headed for the couch in the living room. It was only 5:25 when I fell asleep thinking of the boat, fishing, and the cool evenings in October, refreshing after the heat of July and August.

CHAPTER 9

The Thompsons

Saturday Evening, October 16

We headed for the Thompsons at 7:30. DeFelice was quiet. We were at the Thompson house in less than an hour. They live in a small, old, Florida-style ranch, probably built in the 50s. It was in a whole neighborhood of Florida-style ranches, one just like the other, distinguished only by minor differences in landscaping—one house might have two small palms in the front yard and another just one. It went like that, block after block. But the houses looked good in the night. They always do. The shadows dress them up.

There was a feeling of death here. You can't feel it. It lingers in the shadows, hovering over houses and peering through windows, keeping hideouts in alleyways and in the dark corners of buildings where streetlights can't penetrate.

I knocked. A short man appeared at the door.

"Mr. Thompson?"

"Yes?" he said, wiping a handkerchief across his forehead.

"Detectives Cooper and DeFelice, Miami Police Department. We called earlier to talk to you about your daughter, Tamara. May we come in?"

"Oh, right," he replied. "You're the officer I talked to," he said.

"No sir, that was Detective DeFelice," I said. DeFelice nodded. Thompson motioned us in.

"Elizabeth, the detectives are here," he said to the back of the house.

His wife came from a bedroom on the left. She drifted in like a ghost in a white pajama gown.

She fumbled for words. "Can I fix you something to drink?" almost apologetically.

I said, no and then explained why we were there. They said they had told the Oceanside Police everything already and asked if we had any new information about their daughter's murder.

"Fact is," I said, "we were hoping you both might help us with another case." And I told them about Ethan Miller, how his body was found in a cemetery just like their daughter's and, coincidentally, not far from where their daughter's body was discovered. "Their injuries," I continued, "were similar as well."

"I see," Thompson said. "But we've told the police everything we know," he explained for the second time, his shoulders slumped like he was worn down.

"I'm sure," I said. I asked them if Tamara worked. I asked about her friends. About school.

"She didn't work. We wouldn't let her. She needed to concentrate on her studies. But friends?" Mrs. Thompson hesitated, then looked at her husband as if he had an answer to that question. "Tamara was a quiet girl. She enjoyed her alone time. So she didn't have a lot of friends. But the few she did have were loyal," she continued without any help from her husband.

I nodded. "Do you have any idea where Tamara was during the days she was missing," I said.

Thompson looked at his wife. They both shook their heads. "We don't have any idea where she was. No idea," and his eyes drifted away.

"Detective Cooper, please do what you can to find out what happened to our little girl, would you?" begged the wife, breaking through a silence that had settled over the room.

I told her that the Oceanside police were doing all they could.

"But you're working on the young boy's case" she said. "You can surely work on my daughter's."

"Different jurisdictions," I said, but added that I would do what I could. Her eyes begged me to try.

"Ma'am, we will do what we can," I said again as we rose to leave.

We were out of earshot when DeFelice began to hammer at me. "Shit, Coop, this ain't our case. Let her bug Oceanside about it. We can't get involved," he chided as we headed for the car.

We left the Thompsons about nine o'clock in the evening. The night was cool for this time of year in Florida—early fall. It should be in the 70s—it was about 60. I dropped DeFelice off at his house and headed for my home in Oceanside. I was beat.

CHAPTER 10

Jillie

The bond between us became more fragile as the days slipped by with no word about the fate of our son. We blamed each other, Jillie and I, until there was no more blame to go around. It's like we couldn't stand to see each other, the mere sight bringing on accusations and gut wrenching arguments. We never talked divorce, but I began to sleep on the couch. That's the way it begins. You can't face a problem. Who can face losing a kid? You drive it deep underground until you can't find it, deep into the cave of your unconscious, where the monsters in your life dwell, and you let it simmer there— out of sight. But it eats at you, like an incurable disease that's been there from day one, and that's the stuff of nightmares. They began in earnest that year. If I described it as hell, I would be downplaying it.

In my dreams I lived out the scenario time and again. One time I lost Maxie in the fairgrounds, another time he was being carried away while I watched, or with me and then gone. In each case the nightmares were better than the reality that I woke to. I've gotta tell you, I would rather dream them than live them.

Later that year I got a call from a friend that I grew up with in the Tremont area of Cleveland, Ohio, Tony DeFelice. Tony was a police officer in Miami. It was 1:05 a.m.

"Hey, Cooper, sorry for the late call. You doin' okay?"

"Yeah, I'm fine," I lied.

"How's Jillie?"

'Okay." I paused. "We're both hanging in there."

Silence. Like why you calling this time of night, old buddy.

"I know you wonder why I'm calling this late." ESP.

I didn't say anything. The line between Muskingum and Miami pretty quiet this time of night. I heard his breathing, trying to decide whether to talk.

"I gotta tell you somethin' I heard on the street. Your son—I mean, Maxie—I think I got somethin' for you."

He had my attention. I leaned over the phone.

"Yeah, go ahead," holding my breath but my heart was pounding on my ribs.

"Hey, I don't know anything for sure, just the word on the street. One of our CIs is talking about a child kidnapping ring operating out of Youngstown, bunch of perverts selling kids. Supposebly they ship 'em down this way before they go overseas."

"But nothing specifically about my son?" I said, my stomach now in my mouth.

Shit.

"Not exactly." He paused while I died inside. Then, "But I saw some photos of some kids," and he seemed to take a breath as he paused again, "I can't be sure, but..."

"One of them looked like Maxie," I finished, hardly able to say it.

"A little. Maybe."

"Okay. I'm coming down, Tony."

CHAPTER 11

Quitting Time

Sunday Morning, October 17

One Miami paper was already calling them the cemetery murders. Reporters love to generalize. You know, SERIAL KILLER ON THE LOOSE! Crap like that. Makes for good reading with a cup of coffee in an otherwise boring day. Who needs it?

But that was the headline in the *Miami Herald* this morning. I drank my coffee, but this was not going to be another boring day. I was going to quit my job.

This would be the second time I quit a job in six years. Keep this up, I might never make retirement. How can a person retire if he doesn't have a retirement income? Thing about being a cop, you have a good retirement plan. I know guys stay on the job just so they can keep their benefits: pension, insurance. But what the heck, I'm only thirty eight. Got a lot of time to build a nest egg for later.

I was thinking about that this morning. And I was thinking about what DeFelice told me last night. This case is killing me. And the nightmares are back. Not that they ever left entirely. But last night was bad. I dreamed about Maxie again. I watched my hand shake as I picked up my coffee. I came down to south Florida originally because I hoped I could get some leads on my own son's kidnapping. Here I was helping others with no time to look for Maxie. So I had made up my mind. DeFelice would think I was crazy. But it was time to do it.

I jumped on the 997, a two-lane highway that runs north and south from Florida City, the last town in southeast Florida before you enter the Keys, to the edge of Broward County in the North where it runs into US 27. I usually take the 997 because it follows the eastern edge of the Everglades that stretches out for hundreds of square miles, spanning almost the entire southern end of the Florida peninsula. It's a lonely road with dense mangroves lining the left side of the highway and forests of barren trees, protruding like giant sticks from the ground, stretching westward as far as you can see. That scene characterizes the wilderness that comprises the Great Swamp. It consumes all the land from Miami to Naples, some hundred and twenty miles to the west, making it one of the largest natural preserves in the world.

This is my scenic route to work each day. Scenic only in that it's remote and that it avoids the congestion of Miami with a metro area of over three million people all trying to get to work at the same time. And people in southeast Florida drive with their horns. I hate horns and I don't like people early in the morning. So I like the remoteness of the 997.

It took me fifteen minutes to reach Kendall, a city on the western edge of Miami and abutting the Everglades. I cut toward Miami at Kendall, crossing under 821, which is really an extension of

Florida's Turnpike and under several other freeways jammed with early morning traffic. I hit US 1 and took that into Miami, or at least almost into Miami, turned north on Southwest 22nd Ave and headed for the MPD Investigation Unit that DeFelice called home. Rodriguez is there as well.

The Unit is housed in a round multi-level building with glass covering the lower floors and crowned with a white cap of stone. It looks like a modern office building with a solid, tinted glass exterior to fight off the hot summer sun. It reminds me of a bank building in Clearwater, Florida where somebody discovered what he thought was an image of the Blessed Virgin running up the glass exterior on one side. My guess, the glass melted under the intensity of the Florida sun and *voila* — the picture of the Virgin Mary. People bring folding chairs and cameras there to keep a vigil of the miraculous event—and maybe get a pic if the Virgin Mary actually appears. Believe me, I've seen them. The banking business is long gone now. Just the structure remains. An object of worship.

I parked illegally and headed for DeFelice's desk.

"No Virgin Mary on your building yet, huh, Tony?" I said.

"What're you talkin' about Cooper?"

I told him what I was about to do. He just stared at me for a few moments and basically said, *What the*—? (Did you expect something less?) *Are you out of your mind?* And he went off on me for several minutes. I just listened.

We've been partners in the homicide division now for about two years and on the force together for six, not counting the fact that we grew up together, went to high school together, and even spent a couple of years in college together, until I went to Georgetown to work on a doctorate in philosophy.

Anyway, that's where we were now. DeFelice about to lose his partner. I felt bad for him. He got me to come down here. I did it, left my teaching job and applied for a position on the MPD. I attended the police academy, passed my qualifying exams, became a patrolman and then went over to homicide. The rest is history and here I am, about to start all over again.

You may wonder why I would do it—quit that is. You lose a kid though, you wouldn't be asking me that question. DeFelice never asked me. He knew. He just looked completely beaten and shook his head. I got up. He followed me to Rodriquez's office. I had my letter in hand.

"What's this, Cooper?" asked Rodriquez, as I came through the door, holding out the white envelope with the letter inside.

"My resignation."

He looked at me in disbelief.

"Why?"

"This case. It…I can't do it any more," I said, shrugging off the face he pulled.

I could feel DeFelice behind me. I would have bet he was shrugging too. I turned around. He was looking at the Lieutenant and shaking his head.

"Cooper, I can't tell you what to do. But I *can* tell you you're making a big mistake. You can accomplish more here than you will on your own. Believe me. Think about this," he said softly. "I'm gonna take this, cause it's your right," reaching for the envelope, "but I'm gonna leave it in my desk for a while," pulling out the center drawer and tossing the letter inside, like it was an invisible thing. "You might be sick in the head. Who knows?" Then, "Me? I say you're gonna change your mind."

He paused. "No, don't say anything, Cooper. Just get the hell outta here. The letter's in my desk. You got a leave of absence. Now get out of here." I had never heard the Lieutenant say that much at one time in all my years on the force. He was really upset. Was he tearing up? Then, "Come on, Coop, get out of here for Christ's sake. Just get out," he said, motioning toward the door.

I reached for Rodriguez's hand. He took mine, reluctantly. Then he turned away. That was it. Just like that. Six years on the force. A new life—no pay—no retirement—was I crazy?

So DeFelice exited. Stage left. When we got to his desk, he grabbed me by my shoulders, looked into my eyes—for answers I guess—let go and shook his head again. I felt sad. I looked back as I reached the exit to the street, pushed it open and entered the Miami heat. There was no Blessed Virgin on the glass wall of the building this morning. Just the words, MPD Investigation Unit. Maybe I was hoping for a miracle.

PART TWO

ALONE

We enter the world alone,
and we depart in the same way.

CHAPTER 12

The City

It was late morning when I left Miami and headed east toward the beaches. I had lunch at a South Beach crab shanty overlooking the ocean. I drank a couple of beers and watched the water try to take over the land and then retreat again. I hung out there for the afternoon, until the staff let me know I had overstayed my time. So I went to the beach, took off my shoes and my jacket and sat in the sand. Time for meditation and somber thought. I suddenly felt depressed about what I had done and wondered about my decision. Stretching out in the hot sun, I pulled my Cleveland Indians ball cap over my face and sank into oblivion, exhausted from the tension of quitting—and too much beer.

In my dream I had returned to the Investigation Unit again and was going to ask Rodriquez for my letter back, when something hit me. I rose on one elbow and looked into the eyes of a young kid who was apologizing. He turned away carrying a volleyball back to a net where a bunch of guys and girls were waiting for him. "Sorry, dude," he said, turning around. And then he was off again. *Generation Y*, I thought. Nice kids. *No problem, dude*, I said to myself. It was about 7:00 p.m. when I climbed into my car and headed back to the city.

Miami is a dangerous city, but in another sense, a soothing one as well. As I followed I 95 north, I turned toward the darkening skyline of Miami's downtown. I'm always amazed at the colors of the night city. They're brilliant.

Miami shines at night. Its skyscrapers, crowned in neon, burn a hole into the darkness. Some buildings are dyed indigo, others crimson or spring-grass green, sharp against the blackness. But the dominant color of the Magic City is blue, a blue so deep and sharp that it looks like it's been etched into the night sky.

Miami is a city with crowded beach bars where women, pushing menus on the street in string bikinis, try to seduce the unlucky tourist to try the food. *It's cheap. Only $9.00 for any entrée!* Yeah, the meal is cheap but the prices of the drinks are so jacked up that a well-dressed man with a Caribbean accent stood up at a table next to mine one South Beach night and waved his bill shouting, "Don't eat here. I had four drinks and my bill is over two hundred!"

"Tell me about it," I said, looking at my own bill.

To the casual observer, Miami is a peaceful place on a summer night. But a careful watcher can catch the darkness of its spirit. Under the softness of the night there's another city.

It's a city clothed in black and under its velvet veneer is a world of drugs, and sex, and murder. But tonight Miami was bathing in its night colors, blue and green and crimson against a black sky. And I watched until the light show disappeared in my rearview mirror. I was somewhere between North Miami and Fort Lauderdale.

CHAPTER 13

Hannah

The moon was high in the sky when I dialed Hannah Miller's house. She answered on the first ring.

"Hello," she said.

I told her I had quit the department and then immediately wondered why I was telling her.

She said, "Oh," and a dead silence. I went on trying to fill the empty space, thinking this isn't the way you tell someone you're not going to help anymore. But anyway, water under the bridge. It weighed on me after I hung up. She was upset. Like a mother deserted, hugging her kids and still hanging on. I headed home with that picture in my mind.

Sometimes we do things we feel we need to do regardless of the consequences. I left my teaching job and my wife because I needed to, not thinking or caring about the effect it had, leaving bodies along the road. I wondered if this was the way it was going to be from now on. Take a job, do it for a few years, and then leave. But no matter; we never leave for good. There are always the reminders. If nothing else, they are what we dream about: back in the classroom, my son knocking on the door, the students thinking he was so cute—the girls always said that, the guys smiled; the blonde girl down the hall teaching English Lit—that was my wife. She smiled back then. Her smile, the thing that lingers in my mind even now. It stretched from cheek to cheek and wrinkled her brow.

I remembered the trees turning color then, first a slight tinge of a sunburn, then a deeper orange, with reds and purples thrown in as the autumn progressed. But it's just not the thoughts that come back. That would be bearable, it's the smells too. There's no release from those. And the sounds of summer. And the feel of her hand. And sometimes she still calls. And my heart drops each time. But I pick up the phone and we talk for a short time and the pain is renewed. She's dating, I think. I haven't done much of that. I went to bars for a while hoping to meet somebody. But no luck.

A friend of mine, Richie, said, "What you doing Coop. You ain't gonna meet no girls inna bar. Relax. You're a good lookin' guy. The girls'll come to you."

I followed his advice and met a nice girl at a Unitarian church. We dated for a while until she told me she was the Virgin Mary and I was Saint Joseph and we were going to have a baby. So I called Richie and told him that he should forget about Unitarian churches. But I have to confess, I still think mostly of Jillie.

I called DeFelice's cell. It was about 8:00 p.m. He answered on the first ring. He was always like that. Quick off the trigger—ready, fire, aim.

"Yeah, what's on your mind, Coop?" No time for small stuff.

"So I'm off the job and already you don't have time?"

"We're short-handed here today. Some asshole quit you know."

He sounded angry.

"You still at work? When are you going to go home?" I asked.

"Some of us ain't retired," he reminded me. "We gotta work. Where are you?"

"I'm on 41 heading west out of the downtown." I pulled over.

"That's great. I'll meet you in Kendall at the sports bar. You know the one? Just west of the turnpike. Be there in about a half hour. Order me a beer. Something dark. None of the lite shit, tastes like piss. Got that?"

I told him I got it and pulled back into traffic. Some guy honked at me. I looked to see if he was waving a gun. He wasn't. So I relaxed. Crazy city.

Kendall is west of Miami on the Tamiami Trail, otherwise known as Old Route 41. The name, Tamiami, comes from the two ends of the highway: Tampa on the west coast and Miami on the southeast coast. It was the main connector between those two cities in the old days, the 40s and 50s, before they built Alligator Alley, a super high-way through the Everglades. They really ought to call Old 41, Alligator Alley. Now that's a dangerous ride at night: a two-lane highway, with very little berm and hungry gators lurking on both sides of the road in case somebody breaks down. Not a pleasant thought. I'm scared of those creatures and don't mind admitting it.

I got to Flannigan's before DeFelice, ordered a beer, and located a booth in a dark corner away from the door. I took a seat where I could watch for him. Not many people there on a Sunday night. So I just drank and stared into the night, empty mind, empty feelings. Body follows mind.

"Where's my damn beer?" said DeFelice out of nowhere, putting his hand on my shoulder. He left it there for a brief time then dropped into the seat across from me. How'd I miss him?

"You doin' okay, pal?" looking steadily into my eyes. I looked down.

"Made a mistake, buddy. You should call Rodriquez, get your job back."

I just shook my head. Sometimes you make decisions that you know are right, but they really hurt deep down. Doesn't make the decision wrong. It just makes it harder to live with. It also becomes fodder for second-guessing and for restless nights.

I wondered if this decision would haunt me later. I could feel the tension on the surface of my skin, that burning sensation that feels like you're running a fever.

"What's up, Coop?" he said.

"When I first came down here, you mentioned a priest who works with young kids. Kids in trouble, you said. Remember?"

"Yeah. Why, you want to talk to him?"

"Yeah."

"He's at a church in south Dade."

"Hispanic?"

"Nah. Italian. Name's Ferrari."

He pulled out his cell phone and punched in a number.

"Hey, Padre. Toni DeFelice here." He looks at me, winks. "How you doin'? Oh, sorry about that. Hope your mother's okay. Yeah. I'll pray for her, Father" (he pronounced it 'Fadda'). Another wink. I didn't know he still went to church.

"Yeah, I know. I ain't had time to get to church lately. Chasin' bad guys. Friend of mine wants to get in touch with Father Ferrari. Used to work with kids, right? Yeah, that's right. I used to volunteer some too. Got a number?" DeFelice pulled out a pen and wrote.

"Yeah, I understand. This is police work, Father. I wouldn't ask if it wasn't important." He paused for a few moments, looking uncomfortable. "Yeah I'll try to get to church this week, Father. I know, my mother's there every week. She fills in for me."

Then, "Thanks and sure I'll see you one of these weeks and will bring my mother around to the rectory after church."

I could hear the priest over the phone saying her son ought to bring her to church every week and stop at the rectory after. "Don't be a stranger," he said, loud enough for me to hear. DeFelice shook his head as he hung up.

"Damn, every time I call I get the same thing." He paused and ran his hands through his hair. "It's why I don't call," he added. "Okay, the guy's in south Dade, like I said. Oceanside actually. He's assigned to St. Teresa's, but he don't work with kids no more. Apparently the bishop don't want him getting involved with all those young troubled boys. You know what I mean. All the crap goin' around about priests. But, trust me, he's one of the good guys. So here's the number," and he slid it across the table.

I thanked him, picked up the tab—beer and a sandwich—shook off his warnings and walked him to his car. I promised him I would keep him up-to-date, sure thing. He nodded like *I don't believe that one* and waved as he pulled out.

I headed down the last stretch of 997, past the little towns of Howard and Perrine, and crossed into Oceanside a little before 11:00 p.m. I was in bed by midnight, listening to the sounds of the swamp and Shark Valley just north of my house. I dozed off dreaming of gators and other predators.

Morning comes quietly in the Everglades. Not like in the city where you're awakened by the traffic or the roar of the garbage truck as it stuffs what you put out at the curb into its interior. I would probably still be sleeping if the phone hadn't rung.

"Detective Cooper?"

"Yeah. Who's this?"

"This is Hannah Miller." And then she went on before I could answer. "What you told to me last night really shook me up."

Then she went on to tell me how she couldn't sleep, worrying about— thinking about—her son's killer, then falling asleep and dreaming about him, waking up in a panic, living the whole thing through again, and couldn't I just stay on the case because she didn't trust the police, and *Couldn't I just do that for her?* because she knew I was a good man. She just knew it.

It was a lot to handle so early in the morning, but I could feel the tension, and the fear and the anxiety all wrapped up together, the kind that comes from losing a child, the kind that never sleeps, no matter how many pills you take, the kind that nightmares are made of and they don't go away even in the light of day, even after a year, or two, or more. But I didn't tell her that. What I told her was, okay, and not to worry, and don't lose any more sleep. And this is where I made my mistake. I told her I would work on the case and that I would find the bastard that killed her son, and she made me promise that I would do that. How dumb was that?

She said that she had five hundred and would that be good enough for a retainer? I told her that would be fine and that I would start right away. In reality Ethan had never left my thoughts ever since I met him in the cemetery just a few days ago.

I would continue to dig. And I knew just where that would be. I just never thought I would turn up what I did.

CHAPTER 14

The First Lead

Monday, October 18

Saint Teresa's is near Oceanside University, not far from a row of fraternity houses. Mass was letting out as people filed past a priest who stood on the front steps in his vestments, shaking hands. That's the latest thing in the church: Greet the people out front, don't just go back to the rectory for a cup of coffee or a glass of wine.

He was leaning over to talk with a lady who looked to be in her late seventies. She was about three feet shorter than he was and looking up at him like he was a skyscraper. He patted her on the back as he smiled, nodded, and turned slowly to leave. Then he noticed me approaching. He was still bent over.

"Father Ferrari?" I said.

"Yes?" And he straightened up.

"Any relation?"

"Nope. I wish," and I think he really did.

"I'm Cooper, a friend of Tony DeFelice. He talked with you about me last night."

"Oh yes. I thought you were going to call."

"It's easier for me in person, Father. You know, put a face to a name."

"Sure, that's fine. What can I do for you, Detective?"

"Tony said you worked with kids and might be able to help me with a case I'm working on."

"I see. But I'm no longer involved in that ministry. The only kids I deal with now are the children of university people. The college students go to the Catholic student center that's on the other side of the campus. This is a town church. Very few students come here," he said with a hint of sadness. I think he missed his work.

"The pastor there is young. You would like him. I understand that he also works with kids from the neighborhood. Street kids. Tell him you talked to me. Trujillo is his name."

He paused for a moment, pulled out his cell and turned it on.

"Here's his phone number."

I thanked him, turned down his offer for coffee and headed for the center, dialing the number on the way. A young female voice answered.

"Catholic student center." She sounded cheery.

I asked to speak to Father Trujillo.

"Just a minute, let me check. Can I tell him who is calling?"

"Yes, Detective Cooper. He doesn't know me."

"Please hold." Music.

Then, "Hello, this is Father Trujillo. Can I help you?"

"Hi, Father. My name is Cooper. I'm a friend of Tony DeFelice, Miami Police, Homicide. I got your name from Father Ferrari, the pastor at Saint Teresa's," and I hurried on before he could say anything. "He said that you do some work with kids in trouble. I'm hoping you can help me with a case I'm working involving the murder of a young boy."

"You're with Oceanside Police?"

"No."

"Father Ferrari said to call me, huh." A pause. "Okay. Give me about an hour. I have a few things to take care of first. How about 12:30?"

I'm always amazed how people respond when you don't fill in the silences and you just let them work it out in their own minds without offering to help. Silence is too uncomfortable for people to let it linger. I headed for a diner to kill about an hour. I was only about twenty minutes away.

CHAPTER 15

The Center

The student center is located on Midnight Drive, near the campus of Oceanside University, actually two streets south of the main campus near University Hospital. The center itself is a plain red-brick building surrounded by some run-down off-campus housing—cement block houses splashed with white paint to make them look better. What they really looked like were tenements with scruffy kids playing in the streets and mothers (probably all students) out on the lawns watching and talking with each other while their kids ran and screamed. I tried not to run into them when I parked.

It was exactly 12:30 when I slid into a spot in front of the center. I locked the car and found a doorbell. I pushed it. Nothing happened. I saw a young man approaching me from the street in a dirty tee shirt, black jeans, and unlaced tennis shoes.

"Cooper?" he called out.

"Yeah, that's me."

"Fr. Trujillo," he answered.

I looked at him, not believing it. He looked about twenty.

"Fr. Trujillo?" and almost added, Are you sure? but stopped myself. I couldn't picture him a priest, let alone someone with work to do before I got there. Maybe play some computer games with other kids.

"Come on in. We'll have more privacy in my office."

I followed the boy-priest into the center and into a sparsely decorated, dimly lighted corridor that led eventually into his office. He had a desk, a folding chair in front of his desk, a picture of who I guessed was Saint Teresa on one wall and his diplomas on the other—proof that he was really ordained. He saw the look on my face.

"I was ordained young, twenty five years old. Now I'm thirty two. I've been a priest for seven years. How can I help you?"

"This is a college student center, no?"

"Exactly."

"I understand you help younger kids too. How does that work?"

"This is a neighborhood where there are a lot of kids out in the streets. They survive by joining a gang. So we try to get them off the street, back into school, and into a job or college."

"You said we. Who's we?"

"That would be me. Plus anyone who wants to help out. Right now I have some students from the university helping out, Catholic kids who belong to the center. And the rector of the seminary here in Oceanside sends me students to help out. They call it their *Walk*. They have a lot of service opportunities, helping the poor, visiting hospitals, helping the speech and hearing impaired, and street kids. The volunteers are my biggest support."

I nodded.

"So, what can I do for you?"

"You heard about the two kids whose bodies were found in two cemeteries not far from here?"

He nodded, but looked puzzled. "You said you're not with Oceanside Police—"

"Right," I cut in. "The mother of one of the kids who was killed is my client."

"I see," he said. "So you're a private detective then," like *Aha!*

I ignored that and pulled out the pictures of Ethan and Tamara. I asked if he had seen them around the center.

He shook his head.

"The boy's mother said that Ethan worked here as a volunteer. You don't recognize him?" I pressed.

"You know, his face does look vaguely familiar. But we have a lot of kids who do volunteer work here. You might want to check with the seminarians. They coordinate the work of the volunteers."

"You work with kids in gangs. Do you think these could be gang killings?" I said.

"I mean there are gangs here. But they're into drugs, prostitution, protection, just about anything that makes money and controls territory. But they're not into killing kids. Killings down here are the result of gang wars mostly or from drug deals gone bad."

He said "down here" like it wasn't good.

"Miami is a big city, Cooper. Bad things happen here every day. But I guess you know that. I see things that make my stomach turn. He handed the pictures back to me. Do I know someone who could do this? Sure. Look around. A lot of people could have done it. But who? I don't have a clue."

CHAPTER 16

Murphy

Early Monday Afternoon, October 18
I left the center and headed for the seminary. It was located in a nice part of town, gray-stone buildings scattered along College Avenue, a main artery in Oceanside that runs east-west from Biscayne Bay to Midnight Drive. The main administration building is hidden behind a fence of sable palms planted so closely together that they effectively block out all light, the grounds a haven from everything secular. A stone gateway fronted the main building with the words *Pax Regnat* in large metallic letters overhead.

The grounds were quiet. Though the fall semester was in session, there was little sign of life on the campus. Several young men in black robes paced back and forth along the sidewalks that fronted the main building, reading from books with black leather jackets. Probably prayer books. I stopped one of them and asked where the rector's office was. "Over there," the young man said, pointing to a massive arched doorway in the center of a large, two-story stone building. And then he went back to pacing and reading. Good exercise.

There was no doorbell, so I walked in. I stepped into a dark hall, not a soul in sight. A door on my left, with the words, The Very

Reverend John Murphy, Rector, in gold lettering written across a nameplate, opened and a young man in black stepped out. We passed each other in silence. No nods. I caught the door before it closed.

"May I help you?" asked a white haired woman seated at a large, wooden desk. She was strategically positioned to block anyone trying to skirt around her and barge in on the rector.

"I would like to see the rector," I said.

She paused. "And you are—?"

"Detective Cooper," I said.

"Oh!" she said. "Is something wrong?"

"Yes," I said. The fewer words the better.

She said, "Oh" again and rose from her chair.

"Let's see if the monsignor is free. One moment please."

She disappeared through a door behind her, closed it quietly, and appeared again after a few minutes.

"The monsignor will see you," she whispered softly. I guess we didn't want to disturb anybody.

She led me into a large office, the size of a living room, with a sitting area to my left, two couches with a dark red plush covering, and several wooden chairs with matching red seats. How did I see all of this so quickly? The furniture stood out because it matched the black robe trimmed in scarlet that the rector was wearing. He stood in front of a dark, high gloss desk that fronted heavy drapes, dark red, like they had been dipped in a full-bodied cabernet, the same color as the couches and the chairs. A careful matching job. The drapes hung over each side of a bay window that overlooked the front lawn.

"How can I help you, Detective?" said the monsignor, smiling and extending his hand—sideways. A power play.

"Cooper," I said, turning my hand so that it met his. Try that sometime.

"So, Detective Cooper, I understand there's a problem?" he said, with a serious face now.

I nodded.

"I'm sorry. I didn't recognize your name. Are with the Oceanside Police Department?"

I told him I was a private investigator, looking into the murders of several children who were killed not far from the University and that maybe the seminarians who worked at the student center could help. The rector studied me closely, burying his fingers in his thick gray hair. He looked out over the campus, then back at me. "Mr. Cooper, we are a very closed community. Are you Catholic?" he said, his eyes fixed on mine.

I told him, not any more.

"Well then, you might not know how private we are. Our students spend most of their time in prayer and study. This kind of interruption would disrupt their schedules. I also don't want them involved in a police investigation."

I told him no problem. I would talk to them at the center. He stared at me. I thanked him and let myself out. I passed under the words, *Pax Regnat*, on the front gate and wondered how anybody could possibly know that.

CHAPTER 17

Jack

I called Hannah Miller on my way back to Oceanside. She answered immediately. I asked her if she had an address for her husband.

"He stays at a place in Key Largo called the Lazy Flamingo. When he's up here he stays at the Holiday Inn Express in Oceanside. But I already checked and he's not there. He works for Orange Grove Citrus on Powerline Road—if the place is still there," she said, hurrying on. "He's a salesman, but I don't have that number. Are you making any progress?" She never took a breath.

I lied and said yes. I didn't have the heart to tell her how slowly the case was progressing. I thanked her and called the Lazy Flamingo. I asked for Jack Miller. The man who answered had an accent. Indian, maybe. I mean American Indian. First Nation.

"Yeah," he replied to my question about Miller. "Somebody by that name here last week, but gone now."

"Was he there long?"

"Yeah, long time. Maybe two, three months. Lemme see. Yeah, two months and, lemme see," a pause, "thirteen days. That's it. You the police?"

"No, a friend. I've got a job for him. Let me know if you hear from him, would you?"

He grunted. I gave him my phone number and name. Big waste of time.

I looked up Orange Grove Citrus. No number. I wondered if the place ever existed. I found a number for wholesale orange dealers on the east coast and got a voice mail that said they were either out of the office or on another line. I hate that message. Neither alternative gives me any information. What do I care if they are out of the office or on another line. I get the message: They aren't there. So I left a message to give me a call. A woman called back a few minutes later. I gave her Jack's name and asked if she knew him. She said she did and last she heard he was working for a private broker on Powerline Road in Pompano. She gave me an address. It was 3:32. I was about a half-hour away.

Powerline Road is just like the name says, a road, a wide one, lined with power lines. Also known as SR 845, it runs from Lauderdale on the south and ends in Boca Raton on the north. Once in a while there is a shopping strip along the highway, but mostly it's light industry. I passed a deli on the way to Pompano Beach and stopped for a coffee, bagel, and lox.

It was 4:31 p.m. when I pulled into a small lot next to a building that looked more like a storage facility than a store. I found a good parking spot next to the front door. The smell of oranges gave away the place. I asked a woman tending the cash register for the manager.

"I'm about as close to a manager as you're going to get here, mister."

I was surprised she could fit behind the counter; she looked to be over 450 maybe 500 pounds. I thought she might do better working at Krispy Kreme Donuts. I didn't tell her that though.

"What do you need?" she said.

"I'm looking for a guy who works for you. Jack Miller."

"Hey, I am too. When you find him let me know."

I was running into blind alleys even on Powerline Road.

"Okay. Do you have a last address for him?" I said.

"Well that's a personnel matter, mister. What's your business with him?" She said *mister* like I was a foreigner.

"I'm a detective investigating a homicide. The victim is his son. I'd appreciate any help you can give me." That did it. She changed. "A detective! Oh, shoulda told me before. Lemme see what I can dig up," and she squeezed past the cash register and around the orange flavored soft serve ice cream machine that probably turned out nothing but sugared water with a little bit of milk and orange juice in it and was most likely pretty good on a hot day, like today. So I thought about it for a while and decided I would have a small cone if I got a phone number. She disappeared behind a door that was marked Employees Only. I stared at the ice cream machine. Maybe a cone would make its way to me.

She pushed open the door, breathlessly. A lot of work I guess, walking from one end of the store to another.

"I got an address 'cause I've gotta send Jack a check. He disappeared on me a couple weeks ago after he came back from a sales trip up in Georgia. Sold some good orders for oranges. He is a good salesman. All those kinda guys are good with sales and money," she says.

"What kind of guys is that?" I said.

"You know, Jews. Those people are just good with money—you

know what I mean," and she wiped her brow when she said it, looking for a reaction from me.

"You got a phone number for Mr. Miller?" I said, ignoring her comment.

"Nope, just an address," and she wheezed like that had been a tough line to get out.

"So that address, can I have it?"

She nodded and handed me a piece of paper in the shape of an orange. It was sticky and smelling of orange juice.

What she gave me was an address in Pompano Beach on Federal Highway. It took me about fifteen minutes to get there. It was in a development of condos protected by a loosely managed gate. The reason I say loosely managed is that the gateman let me through with no difficulty. I told him I was a PI and he let me know that security was a big thing for them at the development. Must have thought I was a company plant checking up on how well they were doing. He raised the bar immediately and gave me a knowing smile.

I decided not to ring Jack Miller's residence. I took the stairs to the sixth floor and knocked on his door. No answer. When there was no response after several knocks and hellos, I decided to use my master key to gain entrance.

The lock slipped open easily and I looked into a great room. There were several rooms off to each side. Closing the door, I went directly to some double glass sliders overlooking a parking area in the center of the high rise to check on the security gate. No one looking my way. The sliders were protected by lime green sheers framed by a valence that matched the couches. Several marble stat-ues of angels and naked cherubs stood on either side. I expected the Godfather to appear at any moment, ask me, *Whaddya want?*

White brocade couches covered with clear plastic faced each other in the center of the living room. There was no television. In-teresting. A magazine on the glass table between the couches, *Island Boating*, was addressed to Mr. John Miller. Bingo. I was there.

The master bedroom on the left had a miniature office: a small ornate, cream-colored desk with claw feet, a designer file cabinet, a computer on the desk, and a fax machine on a small table. Cluttered but efficient. I was looking for anything that would begin to point me in the right direction. The case was beginning to feel like I had entered a one-way street that had a sign, No Outlet. I went through the papers scattered on his desk top: some opened mail, empty en-velopes, bills from the electric company, a phone bill, and several pay stubs from the orange broker. I took the phone bill to the fax machine and made a copy.

I also learned that he owned a black Mazda Miata, touring mod-el, insurance payment overdue. I noted the license number and headed for the door. Unfortunately someone was also trying to get in as I was leaving. I ducked into a half bath near the front entrance and heard a woman talking to someone and telling him that he was going to be all right, that all he needed to do was lie down and get some rest. The man groaned and said he was going to throw up.

With my stomach in my throat, I peered through the crack be-tween the inside edge of the door itself and the frame and saw them head for the other side of the apartment. There was a bedroom there. As they disappeared inside, I stepped out cautiously from my hiding place and slipped through the still open door.

As I started down the hall, someone behind me called out, "Are you looking for someone?" I turned around to see a dark haired young woman, about thirty-five, standing in the doorway I had just left. She had a puzzled look on her face.

"You weren't in our apartment, were you?" she asked suspiciously.

I couldn't decide whether to confess or not. But decided not to. *Never confess to anything,* a judge friend of mine once told me. *Ninety percent of all convictions are the result of a confession,* he had said.

"I was just—"

"I know you're probably a private dick hired by that bitch to check on Jack to see if he's sleeping around. Yeah, well give her this for me," she said giving me her middle finger.

"Who's that?" came a voice from behind the doorway.

Then a head appeared around the door and stared in my direction. I was about twenty feet away, but could see his face distinctly— sharp features, ash blond hair lying over to one side, unshaven and a nose that was laid over like it had been crushed in a boxing match.

"You Jack Miller?" I asked.

"Who wants to know?"

"My name's Cooper. I'm a detective investigating the death of your oldest son, Ethan."

Jack Miller looked at the woman briefly and then back at me. She didn't seem to oppose so he shrugged and waved me in. It wasn't as though it were the first time I had seen the apartment, but I let on as though it was.

"Here, let me take the plastic off the couch," the dark-haired woman said as she pulled the covering off one of the brocade couches. "Sorry about the hallway. My name's Lola."

"Cooper," I said. "No problem. I understand your concern. I'm not here to bother you with divorce stuff just to find out more about Ethan's death. You knew he was killed?" I said.

"Yeah. Hanna left a message," he said.

"He is your natural son, right?"

"Yep." He turned so that his nose angled away from me. I wanted to reach over and straighten it out.

"The police haven't talked to you yet?"

"No. Why, am I a suspect?"

"Your wife claims that Ethan was supposed to be with you this weekend. What happened?"

"I forgot," he said. "Son's dead and it's my fault. I know. Don't have to say it. I got drunk and never woke up 'til the morning."

I stared at him for a few moments, watching his eyes. For a man whose son was just killed, he didn't seem broken up.

Jack Miller's eyes were blank. "I mean, I got nothing against her and my kids. I just never see them. She don't want me around," like don't blame me. I'm the victim.

"You don't seem too broken up by your son's death. Actually you don't seem to give a shit about what happened to him." Tell it like it is. See what happens.

"Who the hell are you to come in here, tell me what I am or not," his face turning scarlet. "Get the hell out of here," he yelled, rising from his seat. I didn't move.

"So you said you drank too much on Friday night. Where were you?"

He stopped himself midway between me—I hadn't gotten up—and where he had been sitting.

"Where was I?" red blotches all over his neck and face. "What? You think I killed my own kid? Where was I, Lola. Tell this jerk where I was that night."

"He was here. All night."

"All night?"

"All night."

"Drinking?"

"Yeah, drinking."

"While your son was being murdered?" I was furious and rose from my seat.

Jack started for me. He was about five feet ten, and about a hundred and seventy five pounds, big arms. I'm about six foot three and a hundred and ninety. No contest. I was going to kill him. He hesitated. Good thing for him.

"Look, the police are going to ask you the same questions and more when they find you. I'm just asking them first. You better have some good answers for them," I warned him. "They're going to be a lot tougher than me. Believe it."

He backed off and looked at me thoughtfully, but still mad.

"Okay. But I'm done talking. You wanna talk, you talk to my lawyer," as in *Kiss my ass.*

I doubted he had a lawyer. But I nodded anyway.

"You'll need one," I said as I moved toward the door. "And I'm going tell the police where you are," my back toward him as I entered the hallway. I looked around to see his reaction. He was staring at me, his mouth partly open as if to say something.

I nodded and shot him with my index finger.

CHAPTER 18

Trujillo

I called DeFelice as I left Powerline Road and headed for the Florida Turnpike, the fastest route to south Miami, especially during rush hour. It was almost 6:00 p.m. Everybody's leaving the city in a hurry. Driving I-95 at this time of day, you need to qualify for the Indianapolis 500. Either that or be crazy. I opted for paying a toll and driving in relative isolation. There must be a lot of people short of money at that time of day since there was no line at the toll gates. I grabbed my ticket, phoned DeFelice, and steered the Volvo with my knees through the on-ramp to the Turnpike.

No answer. So I left a message, "If you want to talk to Jack Miller, Tony, I got an address for you. Give me a call." Short and sweet.

I wanted to get to the center before it closed for the day—see if I could catch any of the volunteers. I think I already said that the center is on the southernmost end of Oceanside, at the western edge, near the Everglades. I mention this again because Oceanside is tucked in between Shark Valley, a vast prairie of grass and gently flowing water to the north, and the Everglades to the west and the south. To the east is the Atlantic Ocean. While I can enter Oceanside from the east by exiting the Turnpike at Homestead, I usually choose the northern, scenic route, exiting the Pike at US 41 and heading south on the 997. It gives me a chance to skirt the edges of Shark Valley, peer over the endless tract of marsh and wildlife and look for alligators. Like I said before, I don't like them. I'm actually afraid of them. But I'm intrigued as well and search them out. Crazy, I know.

It was dark when I pulled into the center. The lights were on in the church and in the student center as well. So I headed for the center.

Some students were sitting around one of the circular tables in the main hall of the building and listening to Father Trujillo who was leaning over the table, focused on one of the students. He looked up as I closed the door and came toward me.

"Hola, Detective Cooper," he said. "Good to see you again. Come to get saved?" He grinned at me as he held out a hand.

"Uh huh. It's been years since my last confession. You hearing tonight?"

He smiled.

"We talked about some volunteers. I hoped I might be able to talk with some of them tonight. They here?"

"Sure. These students are all volunteers," he said, pointing toward table he had just left. "Come on over. I'll introduce you."

The students had been watching us the whole time and they continued to when we walked toward them. They were all young, maybe twenty to twenty five years old at most. Three men, three women. I sat down next to a Hispanic guy who moved over to make room. Father Trujillo told them briefly about what I was doing.

I showed them the pictures of Ethan and Tamara.

"Do any of you recognize either of these two kids?"

They passed the pictures around, each one shaking his head. No, none of them had ever seen either one of the kids around the center.

I pressed them again about Ethan. "Nobody saw this boy here?" I said again, and I looked for hesitation. Nothing. This was beginning to get strange. I looked over at Father Trujillo. He just shrugged.

"His name is Ethan," I said. "He was murdered several days ago. His body was found not too far from here. His mother told me he worked here as a volunteer." Nothing.

"I never seen him, mister," said a young Hispanic kid from across the table.

"Uh huh," I said. "You heard about the killings, right?" looking around the table. "I mean they happened near here."

"Yeah, man," the same kid said. "Lots of gangs here. Drugs. They use kids all the time as runners. Sometimes the runner gets killed. The way it goes." He shrugged, like that's life on the streets, man. Short and sweet. Dead at fourteen.

"How about you?" I asked, looking at the kid sitting next to me. He tensed.

"I don't know nothin', man. Bangers don' like people messin' with their business, askin' questions. Makes them nervous."

"Uh, huh. What's your name?"

He hesitated, looked at Father Trujillo, and didn't answer.

"Jaime, tell the man what you know," Trujillo said.

"I don' know nothin', Padre."

"Jaime used to be a gang banger. Doesn't want anything to do with them now," Trujillo said.

"You want to know something, man, you should talk to the guys from the sem. They know things. They work with kids in the neighborhood all the time," Jaime said.

"The sem?" I said.

"Seminary," Trujillo said.

"Anyone in particular?"

"I'd say Gunner." He anticipated my question. "Eogan is his real name. Eogan Clery. You won't be able to miss him. Big guy."

"Why Gunner?"

"Seen a basketball player that likes to shoot?"

"Likes to be the big shot."

"Exactly. They'll be here Thursday. You best be here early—before they head out into the neighborhoods."

"To the hood. In their collars and seminary clothes," I said.

Trujillo smiled. "They'll wear their street clothes."

"Be in disguise."

He smiled and shook his head, walking away. "Be here Thursday," he said without turning around.

CHAPTER 19

The Gangs

Monday Night, October 18

It was late by the time I got hold of Tony. I had stopped at my house, fed Sammy and had a glass of wine—in my hammock, near the dock, not too far from where Herman hangs out. Herman is my pet alligator. Only thing—he doesn't know he's a pet. He's somewhere between thirty five and forty years old, according to a neighbor who has lived in the Swamp longer than that alligator. And he's about twelve feet long. A guess. I never actually measured him.

I called Tony's again. He answered after five rings.

"Hey, Tony. Cooper here. You sleeping?"

"Hell yeah. It's still dark out. What time is it? Jesus!"

I looked at my watch. Yeah, 9:30, big as life, staring me in the face.

"It's night, Tony. Not morning."

Silence on the other end. "Damn. Must have been those beers. Been a long day." A pause. "So whaddya need?"

I waited a moment while his head cleared. "I need some information about gangs in south Dade County. By the way, how's your shoulder?" feeling the pain in my own as I pulled the phone away from my ear and put it on speaker.

"Yeah. Still hurts. Damn kids. Shoulda run those bastards in."

"Tell me about it. They disappeared into the Hole before backup got there. That place is a rat-infested piece of shit," I said. "Some day I'm going in there and dig those bastards out." I paused for a moment, cooling down. "Right now I need some names. I could use your help."

"About the shooting?"

"No. Hannah Miller hired me to follow up on her son's murder."

"Hannah?"

"Yeah. Left you a message. You get it?"

"I got it. So?"

"You on her case?"

"You know I am."

"I'm thinking his murder might be gang related."

He was quiet. "Just because you were working that case with me when you was on the job, don't mean you are now. You're a private dick, Coop. Not a cop. And," he paused, "I don't want you messing around in it now." He let up for a moment. "Hey, you're the guy that quit! Remember?" Still pissed with me.

There was a long silence while Tony tried to get his mojo back. He finally did. "Okay, just so we unnerstand each other—it's my case, not yours. This is a god-damned homicide investigation, not some penny-ante case. Got that?"

I said I did.

"Keep me informed, okay!" An order. Not a request.

"I left you a message to the effect that I had taken her on as a client."

"Don't listen to my messages. Anyways, you need some help, you got it—seein' as you and me was partners, formerly." Back to the old DeFelice.

"There's a new woman cop...what's her name?" He thought for a moment. "She works the gang detail."

"Yeah. I remember. She came on when I left."

"Uh huh. Nice Catholic girl, Coop. You'd like her. Came over from North Miami. Name's Louise Delgado. Carryin' some history though. She came here as a kid from Colombia. Her father was a cop there, killed in a drug war. Anyways, she knows about gangs—you know, bein' from Colombia."

"Sounds great. You got a number?"

He gave it to me. "And why don't you wait 'till the sun rises before you call her," he said. "Good manners."

I spent the rest of the evening sipping at my Columbia Crest and catching Hannah Miller up on what I had done so far. Which wasn't much. I then went inside to my office—which is my kitchen table—sat down at the computer, and typed out what I had so far. I made a spreadsheet:

Suspects: Jack Miller (not likely),

Gangbangers (probably),

Serial killer (maybe),

Aliens from outer space (best guess).

It didn't look promising. I shut down the computer and said goodnight to Sammy who followed me into the bedroom and found a comfortable spot on my bed. I had to shove him over to make room.

CHAPTER 20

A New Client

Tuesday Morning, October 19

I called Louise Delgado early to make sure I caught her before she headed to work. No answer. So I left a message to call me back and continued catching up on my bills and paper work. Life must go on.

It was late afternoon and the sun was burning into the tar and oil the county had recently poured over the dirt road that fronts my house when my cell played out Pachelbel's Canon. I chose that tune because it was reflective and calming. It was DeFelice. There goes the reflective and calming.

"Guess what, guy," he began, "I got some bad news." My heart skipped a dozen beats.

"We've got a missing kid."

I let out a silent sigh. Not Maxie.

"I got a job for you. The kid's twelve years old, been gone now for about eight hours. Apparently he takes the city bus home from school—it's a private school in North Miami—and gets off at a shopping strip where one of the parents meets him. Thing is, he never showed."

All the feelings I had when I first heard about Maxie came back. I waited for more.

"Father teaches criminal justice at the community college. He knows the system and wants someone working on finding his son—full time. So he asked if I knew the name of a private dick. I gave him yours."

I didn't know whether to thank him or not. This was almost too close to home. I didn't say anything.

"I know what you're thinking, Coop. Believe me, this will be good for you. Focus on somebody else's kid instead than your own."

I still didn't say anything.

"You need to think about it, I understand. But lemme know."

I couldn't seem to clear my mind on this one.

"I don't know." I was about to say I'll call you back when I thought what the hell, time to get off the...So instead I said, "Okay. What's the contact info on the family?" my chest tightening. Another missing kid to worry about. But I finally thanked him after I shook off the thoughts of my son.

"You got it, bud." He paused as if to make sure really I meant it. Then, "Okay, a little more background: The parents live in Coral Gables. We caught the case 'cause the kid disappeared in Miami. Moved here from Worcester, Mass last year. Wanted to get away from the cold—and the crime," he added. "Go figure." After a pause he continued. "They got one kid, Eddie—who is now missing." He was quiet for a moment. "Sucks, doesn't it?"

"Yeah," I said. "It sucks."

He gave me their address and phone number. "They're expecting your call," he said. "And not at 6:30 in the morning, okay!"

It was 5:15 in the p.m. My body said it was later. I punched in the number Tony had given me.

"Yes?" A woman's voice, small and uncertain.

"It's Cooper," I said. "Detective DeFelice said he had given you my name and that you would be expecting a call from me. Is that right?"

"Oh," she said, as though suddenly coming back to reality. The missing child thing. It takes the life out of you. "Yes," she said quickly. "My husband and I are anxious to talk with you. Can you come to our house or do we need to meet at your office?" sounding like she was out of breath.

"I'll come to your house. What's a good time?"

"Oh, the sooner the better," she said.

"How about tonight?" I said.

"Tonight? Yes, please. As soon as you can. We'll get our son settled down…" She stopped and realized what she had said. "Seven-thirty, okay?"

CHAPTER 21

Eddie

Tuesday Evening, October 19

Coral Gables, Florida is one of the nicer places to live in the Miami area, bounded on the north by the city of Miami, on the east by the ocean and on the south by South Miami. I took the 997 north to the Tamiami Trail, Route 41, and that took me straight to Coral Gables which is just a mile south of 41 just before you hit the city limits of Miami. I could have taken U.S. Highway 1, but I prefer the scenic route as I said earlier. The gators would have missed me if I had done that. I was at the Dougherty's home by 7:40. Ten minutes late.

Their house was an old two-story Florida adobe shaded by date palms, hung with fronds that had long since died, now just waiting to fall to the ground. The grass was growing wild, the landscaping, what there was of it, untouched. It reminded me of *Wittgenstein's Garden*, an analogy that the philosopher, Wittgenstein, used to question the existence of God. A believer would look at a garden and see the hand of someone tending it: upturned earth here, a tomato plant growing over there, while the nonbeliever would see only the weeds and no caretaker. I wondered how the Doughertys saw their garden.

I reached for the bell as the door opened. A man stood there, no emotion at all—bags under both eyes, dark hair falling over his brow, about six foot two, and straight as an arrow. Must be the husband. He looked like he hadn't slept in days, though it had just been hours.

"Detective Cooper?"

"Yes."

"Good to meet you. Ned Dougherty," he said, extending a hand. "Come on in."

I followed him into the entry as he called for his wife.

"I thought your name—"

"Was Michael. Still is," he added. "People just call me Ned. Been like that since I was a kid."

The entry was cluttered: shoes scattered near a closet to the left of the door; several umbrellas leaning against the wall; a tree-rack near by with a variety of hats hanging on it; a bicycle parked at the far end of the hall, near the door to the kitchen; a baseball bat, and some equipment for a catcher—glove, shin guards, all strewn across the floor, like a boy had just come home and dumped his stuff.

"Pardon the mess, Detective Cooper," said the wife. "It's mostly all Eddie's." Then, "I'm Catherine Dougherty" and she held out her hand.

"Cooper is fine," I said. "And I don't notice messes. I'm a bachelor. To me your place looks fine." She nodded. Like she was grateful.

Then, "We're happy you came so quickly," she said, glancing over at her husband.

"Please," Ned said, and pointed to a sectional that surrounded a large screen TV. It was all situated in a sunken living room. Catherine asked if I wanted something to drink. I said no thanks.

I took a seat on the couch facing Ned and Catherine. "I understand that you want to hire a private investigator to look into your son's disappearance."

"That's right," Ned said quickly. "I'm in law enforcement, and no disrespect to our fellows in the service, they are busy, and quite frankly I don't think they will devote the kind of time I feel is necessary to find our son." Determined.

I hesitated for a moment. "As you already know, the local police and maybe the FBI will be working this case and I'll have to be careful I don't trip over any of their feet," and I studied Ned as I spoke.

"Absolutely, understand that. I wouldn't expect anything else." He paused, focusing all of his attention on me. "Are you willing to work with us? Detective DeFelice gives you high marks," he added quickly.

I thought for a moment then nodded. "Okay. Absolutely."

"Great," he said, letting out a breath as though the whole world was lifted from his shoulders. And they both settled into the couch and waited for me to say something.

"Okay. Then let's get started," I said. "Detective DeFelice filled me in on some of the details of your son's disappearance. But I would appreciate it if you could go over them one more time for me." I looked at both of them. They were silent for a few moments. Then Ned began.

"Every day Eddie rides one of the county school buses home and gets off at the mall. It's only two blocks from our house." He pointed as though I could see it. "The school is private," he explained, "but it contracts with the county to pick up our kids. One of us always meets him at an ice cream store in front of the mall where the bus stops. He's only twelve, so..."

"Almost a teenager," I said.

"He turned twelve on October 12th. He's growing up quickly, still small for his age." Ned hesitated as if contemplating the consequences of what he was saying, then took a deep breath and continued. Catherine was gripping the arm of the couch like it was about to escape.

"He never got off the bus. I was there and he never got off," he repeated, as if to make sure I knew that what he was saying was true. "I asked the bus driver where he was and the driver said he hadn't seen him get on the bus to begin with. Must be still at school, he said. I called the school and the principal said that Eddie wasn't there. He said he would check with the assistant principal. But the AP hadn't seen him either. So I drove to the school to meet with admin. When I got there the principal called the school security guard into his office. He hadn't seen Eddie either. *Good kid*, he told me. And I said, *Doesn't anyone watch these kids get on the bus?*

"The principal said he is out there everyday, but that there are two hundred and fifty four kids in the middle school. *So I do the best I can to check they all get on a bus*, he told me. The teacher remembered releasing the kids for the buses and Eddie was one of the first to leave. *Saw him go into the parking lot*, she told me. We moved to Coral Gables so we could be safe, and this is what we get?" throwing up his hands.

I nodded.

"So now what do we do? I just can't sit around while the police sit on their…Sorry, no offense."

"No offense taken."

Then I asked them to fill me in as much as they could about their family life, friends, enemies, in short about anything at all that might give me a clue about Eddie's disappearance. Ned told me he was in law enforcement at one time. He had been a cop for a number of years in Boston, taught at a community college there. He knew how the system works: The longer a person is missing, the less chance for a good outcome.

We sat in the living room for a few minutes after they had talked themselves out and stared at the fireplace. It was electric with fake logs that burned with a dull red glow. A nice touch for the Christmas holidays still a few months away. But maybe not this year.

I asked to see his room. His bedroom was upstairs. Twelve-year-old kid stuff there: posters covering most of the walls, a partially built navy attack helicopter on the dresser, a Captain America comic book on his bed.

"He loves Captain America," Ned said. I nodded.

"Nothing here that I can see," I said, looking back at Ned and Catherine who were looking over my shoulder as I rummaged— feeling guilty—through Eddie's dresser.

I shrugged and headed for the door. "Let me know if you see something that might give us an idea of who took him, okay?"

"Absolutely," Ned said.

He was walking me to the front door when he stopped, "Your fee."

I had forgotten.

"All in good time," I said. Some businessman, huh?

Ned asked me to wait and disappeared into a cluttered room just off the entry hall on the left. He left the door open as he wrestled with papers strewn across a desk. Then he disappeared again behind the partially open door. He emerged shortly after with an envelope in his hand.

"I made it out to Cooper Investigations, that all right?" he said.

"That's fine," I said. *I've got to get better with money,* I thought, if I want to survive.

"Cooper, that your first name?"

"Yes. First and last. My dad loved James Fennimore Cooper— and so voila: Cooper. First and last."

He didn't laugh. He just smiled. But there was worry in his eyes. I couldn't think of anything to say to ease his pain. They were both at the door as I pulled away.

CHAPTER 22

The Dad

Tuesday Evening, October 19

I left the Dougherty's house with the autumn moon rising. It cast shadows over the street, outlining the palms and lamp posts that line it. I headed south on Dixie Highway toward the University of Miami and Coconut Grove, looking for a café along the way where I could pick up a sandwich. But no such luck—until I got to Coconut Grove. There the streets were busy—the Grove never closes. There was no place to park except for valet so I pulled into an empty space in front of a busy shop and gave my keys to a kid. I told him not to drive it. He looked at me like I was crazy. "I mean it," I said. I've seen them do it—valets—take a nice car for a spin. Not that my Volvo was that nice.

So I ordered a cappuccino—decaf—and a bagel and thought about my next steps. I hadn't figured it out by the time I was ready to leave. So I did the next best thing—visit my buddy, Tony DeFelice. Thank him for the new client. He lives nearby. On the way I would stop and pick up a six-pack of Guinness. His favorite.

He lives alone in a neighborhood located between Coral Gables and Coconut Grove, a residential area not far from the University of Miami. I took the 953 south and headed for his place, only about fifteen minutes away. His house is in an area where there is a lot of student housing, so the neighborhood is a mix of residential homes and rundown frat houses. There was parking on the street and lights on in the house. The doorbell played out a tune from *The Sopranos* which convinced the door to open. A bent, grey haired man stood in front of me and asked if he could help me. *And it's pretty late,* he added. I'm thinking I had the wrong house.

"Who is it, Dad?" came a voice from another room. DeFelice.

"I dunno. Some young man." Then he turned back to me. "Who are you?"

I told him I was a friend of his son's and could I see him?

"He's not my son," he said and stepped back from the door.

DeFelice stuck his head around a wall on my left and stared at me. "What're you doin' here this time a night?" I showed him my six-pack.

"Hey, my kind of beer. Thanks, bud," and he waved me in. His dad was already shuffling through a room on my right, a dining room overstuffed with furniture.

"This is Coop, a friend of mine," he called out to his dad who had now disappeared.

"I ain't your dad!" called out the old guy from somewhere in the back of the house.

DeFelice looked at me, shrugged, and motioned me in.

"The old guy's cracked."

We headed for the living room. It smelled like a hospital bed. We settled in, DeFelice in an Archie Bunker kind of overstuffed chair and me on a couch. DeFelice's chair had a bird's eye view of the television

"Your dad died," I said. "Who's this?"

"My father-in-law. My ex left town and deserted the poor old guy. I figured I owed him. Always treated me like his own son. He's getting senile now—in case you can't tell."

"You never told me Edna left town and you never mentioned you were having to take care of her dad."

"Lotta things I ain't told you, Cooper. You oughta know me by now."

DeFelice is a tough Italian cop. Gruff exterior but soft on the inside. His wife decided to ditch him. You know, cop's hours and that kind of thing. She wanted a normal life. After twenty-seven years you would think that she would have figured out how cops live. I always wondered what triggered her leaving. DeFelice was devastated by the divorce. She didn't seem to give a damn. And now she left town and left her father. Didn't give a damn about him either, it seemed.

"So, how long has this been going on—I mean taking care of the old guy?"

"Bout a month or so. The Evil One took off about a month and a half ago and never told me. Left her father in the apartment she was renting to make do on his own. Only reason I found out was I called over there and old Stan answered the phone. Said Edna was gone. I said gone? Where? The store? No, he said, just gone.

"I mean how could somebody do that? Just leave her father alone to take care of himself. What a shitty thing to do. Helluva shitty thing to do," shaking his head the whole time.

"So," he said, "enough about me. What the hell you doin' here to-night?" Then he remembered the Guinness and grabbed two bottles, handing one to me.

"I wanted to share a few moments of—how can I describe it?—quiet joy with my former—and favorite—partner."

"Shut the hell up, Cooper. You're the guy deserted me. Hey, we were partners for five years. And not even a warning. So shut the hell up and drink your beer."

So we sat in silence for a few minutes and drank.

"Rodriquez have a problem with my taking on Miller as a client?" I said, breaking the silence.

"No. LT don't care. Hey, what he don't know can't hurt him anyway, right?" and he tipped his bottle at me. It was his third in almost as many minutes. I nodded.

"So what's happening? What did Ned Dougherty and his wife have to say?"

"They didn't have anything new to say. I hate to think of what happened to their boy. Kids..." and I was going to say *are worth a lot on the market these days*, but I thought of Maxie and didn't.

"Yeah. Crazy world," and he meditated on that for a moment. "I figure the FBI are gonna stick their nose in one of these days. Bastards." Then, "You just stay out of trouble," he said, "and keep me in the loop!" like we were still partners. "And don't do nothing to piss off Rodriguez or we're both fucked."

"No problems," and I finished off the last of my beer and got up to leave.

"Good. Just remember," and he was slurring his words, "if my job goes down the toilet, you're taken care of both me and my dad in there, kapish?"

"I ain't your dad," came a voice from down the hall.

It was after 10:30 when I left DeFelice. I was under the limit so I felt okay driving and decided to stop by the student center since I would be passing it on the way home. See how the padre was doing.

I got to the center at 10:45. Father Trujillo was already locking up when I pulled into the parking lot. He was at my car before I had a chance to open the door.

"We've got a problem, Cooper. The seminarians don't want to meet with you."

"Why's that, Father?"

"The rector. He told them not to talk with you."

"That's interesting. I'm not a cop and they're not suspects, I just have a few questions."

"I understand," he said, pulling back from my window. "They're going to be here tomorrow. Nobody can stop you from dropping by."

"Would I be getting you into trouble?"

"No. No more than I'm already in," shrugging it off.

So I headed home, wondering why Murphy was so damn worried.

Another clue to add to my spreadsheet.

CHAPTER 23

Louise Delgado

Late Tuesday Evening, October 19

I called Louise Delgado on the way—it was after 11:00.

"Yeah?" she said.

She sounded annoyed.

I told her who I was. "I think DeFelice talked to you about me."

"That's right. He did. But he never said you'd call in the middle of the night." Uh oh.

"'So you and Tony were partners in South District?"

"That's right. He said you were the one to talk to about gangs. That's why I'm calling." I paused. "Is this a good time?"

"Well, it's late—"

"Right. I didn't mean tonight. How about sometime tomorrow? Maybe get some coffee? I won't take much of your time."

"Sure, no problem. You know Ronnie's Deli in Oceanside at the corner of—?"

"Absolutely. What time?" I said.

"Nine?"

"Sounds good. Nine in the morning, right?"

"Yeah, of course. Morning."

"Great," I said. "I'll buy."

CHAPTER 24

Ronnie's Deli

Wednesday Morning, October 20

Ronnie's is a typical Jewish Deli with old-fashioned metal tables, Formica tops, and shiny metal chairs—the kind you would expect to find in a 50's diner—and a jukebox off in a corner. Jars of kosher pickles, pickled beets and sauerkraut on each table. You could fill up on those alone. I ate some pickles and waited for Delgado.

"Cooper?" came a voice from across the room.

I looked up and saw a dark haired woman signaling me from a corner table, a coffee cup in her hand.

I joined her.

"You recognized me?" I said as I sat down.

"I Googled you," she said.

She looked young, maybe in her late twenties, well-defined features, the kind you see in a model's face. She saw me looking at her and smiled.

"So, Cooper, tell me what's going on," she said.

I nodded. "Why don't we eat first, then we can talk. How much time have you got?"

"A couple of hours. No problems," she said as she picked up the menu.

"Thing I hate about this place, too many choices. So I usually order the Special. It has everything and no decisions," she said smiling. "Why don't you try it."

So I ordered the Special for us both: bagel—I ordered cinnamon/raisin, she ordered the Everything; two eggs over hard for me, poached for her; rye toast; orange juice and coffee. Oh yeah and some grits. She had hash browns instead of the grits.

"Jeez, Cooper. Decaf? That's not even coffee and at 9:00 in the morning?"

I smiled and didn't answer. She doesn't want to know what happens when I drink regular, even in the morning.

I told her about the Dougherty kid and about the killings. She already knew about them. Asked me why I was working the cases since I was no longer on the job. I told her the Miller case was mine before I left the Department and that I promised the mother I would still look into it. She listened and nodded.

"Why do you want to know about gangs?"

"Besides the fact that a gangbanger shot Tony and me, I'm thinking that the killing of the two kids—and maybe the kidnapping—might be gang-related."

"I see," she said, playing with her napkin. Then she started to fill me in on her work with gangs in the Miami and Oceanside area, about how this was the last job she wanted, about how her mom got her out of Colombia to get away from the gangs, and *What do you know, I got the same thing here,* she said.

"Right." I paused. "Colombia. I heard about your father."

"I can't talk about it," she said and fooled with her napkin again, folding it in half then folding it again. She was pretty. Her nose small and slightly turned up.

"Excuse me. I'll be right back," she said, getting up and heading for the restroom. She was wearing a tight, ecru dress, mid-thigh length. A man at a booth across from me noticed her as she swung her hips toward the back of the restaurant. He turned back around and saw me watching him. He looked down quickly, turning slightly to see if his wife noticed. She was busy with her cell phone.

When she got back, the waitress was there with our orders, four plates balanced on two arms. She refilled our coffees and asked if there was anything else we needed.

"Jelly," I said.

"You got it," she said and looked at Louise. She shook her head.

"Okay, how can I help?" said Louise as she began to dig into her Special, dipping her bagel into the eggs. She was thin, about five foot eleven. I wondered how she kept the weight off.

"Yoga," she said as she ate. Must have ESP.

"Yoga?" I said.

"Yoga and Leonard Cohen."

I hadn't heard that name in years. "So you must know 'Hallelujah,'" I said.

"My favorite. He's my muse. I listen to him every morning when I do my exercises and meditation. He's so cool!" and her face lit up when she said it. Seventy plus years old and cool! I hoped that was in my future.

"Okay. Tell you what we can do. I've got a couple of bangers who owe me. I'll talk with them, see what I can set up. But remember, you're not on the job anymore. I don't want to lose my badge because of some screw-up. Okay?" Just like DeFelice.

"I got it," I said. I felt like adding that I was on-the-job when she was in school, but I didn't.

"When I Googled you, Coop, I saw that you used to be college prof. How did you wind up in law enforcement?"

I didn't tell her about my son. Maybe she already knew. I thought of the Dean coming to my class. I thought about the dead boy in the cemetery. I thought of how easily he could have been my son. I thought about the girl's body in the Oceanside cemetery, and now the missing Dougherty kid. Missing is bad. But dead is unthinkable. I knew every painful thought the Doughertys were experiencing, every terror that crowded their thoughts, the ironic moments when they looked out into the sunny streets of paradise and realized that somewhere out there their son might be in the hands of some maniac who might be inflicting every sort of unimaginable horror on him. So I knew why I quit.

She must have sensed my pain—or it showed on my face. "Hey, sorry if I spoke outa turn, Cooper," looking at me hopefully as she said it.

"No problem," I said and paused for a moment. "You must not know about my son."

She looked puzzled. "No."

I filled her in—briefly. She stopped me short, "Sorry, you don't need to—"

"Thanks, I won't. But that's the reason I quit my teaching job. I wanted to spend my time looking for my son. And Tony told me about a kidnapping ring in Miami—it was a lead, okay?—Didn't work out. But I was here so I went to the Police Academy and got a patrol job with Miami PD—a good way to look for my kid, right? I did that for a year, then I took the exam for detective, and worked homicide another five. So—same issue again—I wanted to spend more time looking my son, not working cases. So here I am, a PI, still working cases—but at least they're my own, and I can look for my son whenever I want, see?" looking over at her and shrugging. "So that's my story—short version."

Louise nodded. "You didn't need to—"

"I know. But I get it off my chest. Thanks for listening."

"You're not eating," she said.

I held up my hands and stared at my food. "You're right," then took a chunk out of the bagel. "Maybe I'll get a doggie bag."

She smiled. "Tell you what. I'll head into headquarters, see what's on my plate, and call you later, okay? We can strategize. In the meantime eat your breakfast," she admonished.

CHAPTER 25

Eogan

Early Wednesday Afternoon, October 20

It was a few minutes after twelve when I left the deli and headed for the student center. The university was only twenty minutes away and the center was a short walk from the main entrance. The parking lot for the center is the same one used for the church. A few cars were scattered in the lot, just two by the building itself—a black Jeep Patriot and an old '69 Volkswagen bus. I parked next to the bus, figuring that's what the seminarians drove.

I spotted Eogan as soon as I came through the door of the center. A guy with hair that was a cross between the color of beach sand and a washed out red, was bending over listening to a kid who was at least a foot shorter, a kid whose cargo pants hung down so far that his shorts were the only thing that kept him from being buck naked. The tall guy looked up at me briefly then went back to listening. I walked over and waited until he quit listening.

"Can I help you?" he said. Polite.

"Eogan Clery?" I said.

"Yeah." He brightened. "Where'd you hear that name?"

"Father Trujillo."

He smiled. "Nobody's called me that for years—except my ma, and she died a few years ago." He paused. "How can I help you?" turning to the kid next to him and nodding that he needed some time. I watched the kid walk away, amazed that his pants stayed up. Eogan noticed. "Crazy, huh?"

I introduced myself.

"Cooper," he said, like he heard it before. "Murphy told us not to talk to you," watching me thoughtfully.

"The rector?" I said.

"That's right." He paused. "And here you are. So what are we not supposed to talk about?" almost whispering now.

I told him about the two cases I was working: Eddie Dougherty and Ethan Miller. I told him about the girl also. "The one found in a cemetery," I said, "killed not far from here—"

"Yeah, yeah," he said, cutting me off. "The Cemetery Murders," he mused, probably picturing the headlines in the *Herald*. "What does that have to do with me?"

"Nothing," I said, wondering about this guy who wasn't supposed to talk to me. "Hopefully," I added, watching his reaction.

"I hope not too." Then, "Hey, let's get out of here. I know a good bar where we can have some privacy," he said quietly, as though it was a big secret. "Besides, I could use a cold one." He noticed my surprise. "We do drink," he said, smiling.

It was an Irish pub near the university, walking distance from the student center. We settled in a dark corner not too far from the bar. A waitress, probably a college student, was at our table before we had a chance to talk, told us her name was Kayla, and asked what we were having. Eogan ordered a pint of whatever draft they had that was dark. I ordered a glass of Kendall Jackson—the house wine. She brought the drinks and asked if we wanted anything else. I said *no*. So we just sat for a few minutes and drank, looking around at nothing in particular.

Eogan broke the silence. "I like my work with these kids. They live on the street, you know. They get into gangs to make easy money. They got no family—most of them. Gang becomes the family." He studied his liter of beer, took a long drink, and then continued. "The local gangbangers are not happy with us. They see us as interfering," he said.

"We?"

"Three other guys from the sem. We work together." He paused and looked at me for a few moments. "Cooper your first name?" lifting his pint toward me, using it like a pointer.

"That's right," I said.

"So we're making some people nervous with our work, are we?"

"Uh huh. Like the rector?" I said.

"He's nervous about you," he said, taking a long pull from his Guinness. He leaned back, drank the rest of the pint in one swallow, held up two fingers to the waitress, then looked over at me waiting for me to say something. I was staring at the empty pint. He smiled. "No women in this gig, so I drink," he said, smiling.

So I filled him in about the Doughertys and their son, about Hannah Brown and her dead son, Ethan, and about Tamara. He nodded. I pulled out the pictures of Ethan and Tamara, placing them on the table and shoving them toward him.

"So?" he said.

"Do you recognize the boy?"

He picked up Ethan's picture, looked at it carefully and set it down. "No," he said, leaning back, taking another pull on his drink.

"You're sure?" I said. "He worked at the center—according to his Mom."

"I don't recognize him. Maybe one of the other guys might." He paused. "But then again, maybe his ma lied," still leaning back. He was playing me.

We drank some more and stared through the silence. I heard "Hallelujah" coming from somewhere outside—maybe one of the dorms. "Do you remember that song?" I said, picking up my wine, swirling the liquid, and watching it catch the sides of the glass.

"Leonard Cohen, 1984," he said. "Jeff Buckley's version, number eight in Ireland in 2006, 2007. Over two hundred cover bands have done that song in the last decade."

I stared at him as he drank the last of his fifth—or was it his sixth?—pint. He slammed his hand on the table, rose, steady as a rock, said goodbye, and headed for the exit. His large frame filled the doorway completely, then he disappeared into the street.

I called Louise Delgado.

CHAPTER 26

Gangland

Late Wednesday Afternoon, October 20

"I told you I had a couple contacts, Cooper. No problem. Why don't you come down to the South District station, pick me up. I'll be there in about a half hour. See what happens. Okay?"

The South District is just a few miles from the city of Oceanside. Miami PD is big on community policing. So the Chief has divided the city into three districts: the Patrol North District, the Patrol Central District, and the Patrol South District. The South District includes Flagami—a portmanteau of two areas: Flagler (a street in Miami) and Tamiami (the Tamiami Trail)—Coral Way, Coconut Grove, and Little Havana. It's the largest of the police districts, diverse economically and socially. Coconut Grove is probably the most famous: home of Vizcaya, the Ritz Carlton hotel, a bunch of nightspots and up-scale, funky restaurants. The Grove is the signature of Miami and all that is famous about it, as much as Little Havana is its heart. I had a feeling we were heading for Little Havana.

I didn't have to park at the South District Headquarters. Delgado was waiting for me at the curb. She was wearing navy pants; an open-neck, white blouse, open just to the point of no return; a navy jacket thrown over her arm; no jewelry. She had a Glock on her hip. She threw the jacket into the back seat and got in.

She was pointing almost as soon as she climbed in. "Straight ahead and hang a right. We're headed for—"

"Little Havana," I said.

"Not quite. Oceanside. See if you can figure out who we're going to see."

"The Colombian connection," I said. I wanted to say, "Whom, not who…" but stopped myself. Old teacher habits.

"Two teens, both still in school. But they're bangers so they're dangerous."

"Tell me about it," I said, like I wouldn't know that.

We passed stores with bars on windows and row houses with bricks missing and windows blown out. Kids played in the streets like it was a soccer field so I had to slow down to keep from hitting them. They gave us looks, like *What the hell you doing here?* Being in a Volvo didn't help. A fire hydrant was pouring out a swimming pool for kids in their underwear. No cops in sight to enforce the drought regs. Maybe we should stop and enforce or maybe that's the street cop's job. After all, if we do that, what do the cops do to keep busy? The kids laughed at us and kicked water as we passed.

"So where we going?" I said, feeling for my .38.

"School grounds. They're getting out about now."

"*Bangers Go to School.* Sounds like a good teen book."

She laughed. "Go figure. But, you know how it works. They're kids. And kids go to school. Only difference here is they run the school. Other than that, they're on the street—no parents probably, maybe a home, maybe not, maybe brothers and sisters, maybe not, so they need protection. And the gang is their protection—until it's not—and they pay the price—dead at sixteen," and Louise seemed lost in her thoughts, thinking about the streets, maybe, "and the reason they pay the price is because they extracted the same price to get into the gang—you know you gotta kill someone to get in—the boss will just point to a bystander, anyone, tell the recruit, go over and shoot the guy in the head, right now. Bang, that's it," and she aimed with her finger and shot someone on the street, "or at least diss another gangbanger— but that's a death sentence, cause the homeboy has to avenge the diss and kill the guy or hurt him so bad he might as well be dead," and she shook her head as she talked, "and all they want to do is to get home alive." She turned to me, "You're not that far away from the job to forget, Coop." And then she slipped back into her cop *persona*—tough—yet almost delicate— her face I mean—but she had that outer layer of toughness that cops have to have—that's the *persona* I'm talking about. We all have one. In normal life we act like everyone else. When we get around other cops, we slip into our cop *persona*. It's a protection.

"I never dealt with gangs. My bad guys were adults." And I thought about my own neighborhood back in Cleveland. There you worried about the mob.

"You carryin'?" she asked as I looked for a place to pull over.

"Uh huh," and I checked under my jacket—second nature. I use a shoulder holster when I carry the .38. It's small and fits comfortably under a jacket—the Glock's a bigger gun. Easier to carry on the hip.

It was closing in on 5:00 p.m. as we came to an old red brick school building surrounded by a high cyclone fence. I drove through a gate in the fence that was hanging on its hinges and wide open. You could drive a school bus through it. Great protection for the school children. The blacktop playground inside the gate was broken and heaving, a few kids hanging out on the front steps of the main building at the other end of the parking lot, several leaning against the fence, all of them watching us come through the gate. I wondered if my car would still be there when we got back. I parked in a space in front of the building that was actually level.

"Anyone want to earn a coupla bucks?" I said to the guys watching us from the steps. They all looked like either junior high kids or high school. I couldn't tell.

One kid got up and held out his hand. "When I get back and my car is still here and undamaged, okay." It was not a question. He nodded.

"They're over there, Coop," Louise said, pointing to two guys across the blacktop on our left. They were sitting on the steps of one of those buildings that populate many of Florida's school grounds—double-wide temporary classrooms—temporary meaning forever since they never get replaced with a real building.

So we headed their way, the distinct odor of weed catching my nose as we neared them. Louise had pulled on her jacket when we left the car—it covered the Glock she was carrying on her hip.

"Did you check your gun?" she whispered as we crossed the lot.

"Uh huh," I said, resisting the urge to check again.

As we got closer, I noticed a tattoo on the arm of the guy on the right: PIRU. He was short and thin. His face was decorated with acne.

"Bloods," Delgado said, as if reading my mind. "That's Juan," nodding toward the guy with the tattoo. "The other one's Casto."

They both got up and took a step toward us. Casto was taller than Juan, though tall was relative. I could've looked down on both of them. I stared at Juan as he approached. Something clicked in my primitive mind. Where had I seen him before? I continued to stare—and he noticed.

Casto held up a hand blocking our approach. We were about ten feet away. I saw a gun in his belt. The principal must have missed it.

"So what're we talking about?" he said, staring into Delgado's eyes.

I stepped away from Louise thinking it was better to have some distance between us. Just in case.

Delgado spoke to them in Spanish, the shadows of late afternoon creeping over her face as she talked, like in a late night, black and white movie where the sound has been cut off and all you see is the silhouette of a mouth moving. She pointed at me several times as she talked, Juan looking at me, like maybe he was beginning to think back also.

I was intrigued with how his tattoo moved, weaving and rippling with the movement of his arm, like a snake working its way up and down. I wondered if the artist planned that effect. There was a crossed out "C" below the PIRU. The C would be the Crips, a rival gang that started with the Bloods in LA and moved east, all the way to paradise. Miami, Florida. The cross-out would be a diss.

"So why do you think we might know something, cop lady?" said Casto, finally breaking into English.

"Cause you know what happens down here." She paused as she pulled out the pictures of Ethan and Tamara from her back pocket. "These two kids were killed near here," and she watched both Casto and Juan as they looked at the pictures. "You know anything about what happened?"

I didn't say anything about Eddie Dougherty. I didn't trust them. He was still out there somewhere. Hopefully still alive.

"No," said, Casto, looking over at Juan. "You?"

"No," Juan said. Just like that. *No*, not even glancing at the photos. Then, "So what you want from us, Delgado?"

"So what I want from you is what you know," and her hands were on her hips like she didn't believe them.

"Hey, we don't know nothin' about those kids," said Juan. "Maybe you oughta look somewheres else for this one. Whyn't you talk with the padre and his homeboys at the center—maybe they know somethin'."

"What homeboys?" said Louise.

"I don't know. Any of his fanboys." Then, "Talk to Hector." He paused, noticing me staring. "What're you lookin' at?" Then he turned to Louise. "Who's this dude?" nodding at me.

"I'm the guy who's looking for these two kids," I said, saving

Louise the trouble. "So...let's see. You don't know anything, but the guys working at the center might." I paused. "Why would you say that?" And just then I realized why I recognized him.

Casto jumped in. "We done here."

CHAPTER 27

Dinner Date

Wednesday Evening, October 20

We were done there all right. And Louise wasn't happy with me.

"What the hell was that all about, Cooper?" she said as we climbed back into my car. Casto and Juan were still hanging out on the steps of the double-wide, smoking. "I mean—between you and Juan. You guys dating?"

"I think he's the guy who shot me," I said.

"Shot you?"

"That's right. Remember the kid who was killed on Northeast 36th a couple of weeks ago? Near Little Haiti."

She thought for a moment. Then, "You were the cop?" she said.

"Right again," I said.

I was pulling away from the school and back onto the main road that led out of the Hole. Ironic, I thought. A school right in the middle of this jungle. I wondered what kids learned there and I watched the building disappear in the rearview mirror. Probably nothing much. The whole district had been taken over by the State of Florida several years ago. The gangs have taken it over from the State.

"So, that was you and DeFelice," Louise continued, looking over at me like someone new. "And then you quit the Department and now here you are a private dick.

"Can we think of a better word?" I said.

"How about public dick?"

I glanced over. She was smiling. "Uh huh. Why don't we find a place to eat."

The sun was sinking fast in the west over the Everglades as we hit the 826 south. Louise lived in South Miami, near the University, just off Sunset Road. I told her I would drop her off after we grabbed a bite to eat.

"So is this a date, Coop?"

Silence.

"If it is, you're gonna' pay. And hey, you owe me," she continued.

"Uh huh. There's a nice place not far from here on Sunset. Italian okay?"

"Love it."

"Of course. Mediterranean influence."

"How do you figure? Colombia isn't anywhere near the Mediterranean."

"Spain is."

"There you go. General bias. My family never came from Spain."

"Maybe at one time."

"Yeah. Maybe. But at one time, Cooper, you came from the Garden—that make you Mediterranean?"

"Good point. Talking about garden, the name of the restaurant is Sicilian Gardens. It's coming up at the next exit. Do you know it?"

"Since I'm not Mediterranean, no."

The lights in the restaurant were low, casting the room in a patchwork of shadows and soft light. Roman statues lined the entranceway to the dining area and a few more were scattered around the edges of the room. Someone had draped a hot pink boa around one of the statues—nice touch. Large angels hovered overhead in a domed ceiling. I could picture the Godfather, played by Marlon Brando, cane in hand and family behind him, slipping a twenty to the maître d'.

The restaurant wasn't busy. The maître d' seated us at a corner table. It was dark there—the conversations around us quiet, other tables ten feet or so away. At one table a man was talking loud enough to be heard to a girl young enough to be his daughter.

"He's a general," the maître d' whispered. "Comes in all the time," he continued reverently.

"Hmmm," I said—quietly.

"That's his daughter," he said, putting my mind at ease.

"Thank God," I said.

He gave me a puzzled look and headed back to the front of the restaurant. A young waitress took his place almost immediately.

"So have you decided?" she asked. Almost pushy. I looked around at a few empty tables and decided she didn't need to hurry us.

"Give us a few minutes," I said. "Do you have a wine list?" And she gave us the few minutes and grabbed a wine list from an empty table near the general. He looked our way. I nodded.

I asked Louise what she drank. She said wine. I suggested a California pinot noir from the Greenwood Ridge Vineyards. She said that was fine, smiling at me like she was studying my behavior.

"What?" I said, smiling back but not knowing what I was smiling at.

"This is pretty nice," she said, looking around and then coming back to me. "Thanks," she said. "You didn't need to do all this." I waived her off, kind of wondering about why I was doing it.

A waiter dressed in black pants, a black jacket and white shirt with a black bolo tie and matching black hair took our wine order. He was back in less than two minutes of uninterrupted silence in which Louise and I looked around the restaurant pretending that we were interested in studying the place.

The waitress showed up as soon as the wine steward was finished pouring and took our orders: spaghetti and meatballs for me—about all I ever order in an Italian restaurant—and linguini with white clam sauce for Louise. She looked at me over her wine glass and studied my face.

"What?" I said.

"Trying to figure you out, Cooper," she said. "A college prof, leaving his job, coming down here, becoming a cop and now a private dick."

"Investigator," I corrected. "Dick is a little strong."

She smiled, nodding. "Yeah, good thing it's not your name."

"Lucky me," I said, smiling back. "So you've asked me a couple of times about myself, how about you? You haven't told me anything about yourself."

"Nothing to tell, Coop," she said.

"How about your family?"

She looked at me for a moment then away, staring into the distance, and then started talking, not looking at me but at that place that was far away, and she told me about how she was born in a small village outside Cartagena, how the family moved into the city when her father was promoted to a ranking officer in the Policia Nacional de Colombia. "The CNP," she said. "He was the boss in Cartagena," going on to explain that it was one of the six metropolitan command centers, one in each of Colombia's six major cities. "In the 1990s," she continued, "the National Police were being called up on charges of corruption." She went on to explain that as a result the National Police lost the trust of the general population, and how, since the mission of the CNP was to protect the common welfare of the nation, some of the leaders of the National Police, including her father, tried to clean up the department and get rid of the guys who were in the pocket of the drug cartels.

When she was ten years old, she continued, her father was gunned down outside their apartment in the central city. She had watched the scene from a window where she always waited for him to come home each day. And as soon his car would pull up in front of the apartment, she would run out and he would grab her and they would both laugh as he carried her up the stairs to their apartment. Only on that fateful day, as his driver was dropping him off and before she could get through the door, two men got out of a passing car and shot her father. He was on the sidewalk—at the bottom of the steps to their apartment.

"I will never get that image out of my mind now," she said, looking directly at me. She paused. "And then my mother sent me to my aunt's house in Miami. And that's the last time I have been back to Colombia," and she brushed some hair away from her face. Her eyes were red.

"And your mother?" I said.

"She visits me here. She says she never wants me to see our old apartment again—ever." She hesitated. "And frankly—I don't think I could handle it, Cooper."

We were quiet for a few minutes. Then I took her hand. "Thanks," I said. "Thanks for today. And thanks for sharing your story. I know it was hard."

She smiled. "Thanks for listening. But we're not done with those bozos. Let's go back and try it again, okay?"

I nodded and squeezed her hand a little tighter. "Okay."

I dropped off Louise around 9:00 p.m. and called Trujillo. No answer. It was late so I headed home down the 997 that runs through the Everglades at the northern end and along the Great Swamp as it heads south toward Oceanside. It was my favorite place to live because of its proximity to the River of Grass, and also because in that great swamp reside the objects of my greatest fears, those primeval creatures who live among us as we push further and further into their home.

They've been around for several hundred million years and lived through the extinction of many thousands of other animals. The difference is that today, we are the main threat to their survival. Yet, I fear them. The alligator is a hunter by instinct and a killer without equal. An alligator's brain is so small that it cannot process good and evil. As someone once said, there is no such thing as a nice alligator.

So, you might ask, why do I allow a twelve-foot alligator to live in my back yard? Simple. Keep your enemies close. Watching Herman grow over the years has helped me understand the behavior of the alligator. And so when I drive the roads that run by the swamps, I look for eyes that protrude just above the water, for a nose that rises just in front of those eyes. When the gator lurks like that, it is in its hunting mode, looking for easy prey. And that should be a warning to the smart person walking near.

So, why am I dwelling on the gator? Because I saw in Juan's eyes that same look. He lurks, waiting for the easy prey. I would have to go back and visit him again. He is a hunter. And he tried to kill me once.

CHAPTER 28

Night Terrors

Late Wednesday Evening, October 20

I pulled into my house on Everglades Road at 10:45 p.m. I had two messages. One from Ned Dougherty, wanting to know if anything new had happened. One from my former wife urging me to give her a call as soon as I can. Has something she wants to tell me. She does that. About every two months she calls, says she has something important to tell me. So I looked at the clock and thought about it as I poured myself a drink. I called her at 11:30.

No answer, so I left a message: "Hey, Jillie. Got your message. Give me a call."

She's going crazy, just like me. Sometimes the pressure of living with uncertainty is too much. Better to have answers than nothing. What did Eric Berne say in *Games People Play*? Life is uncertain and people don't like that.

The night closed in quickly as the drink took effect. Shadows turned into dreams.

I was hauling a crippled boy on my back. It wasn't hard at first. Then he grew too heavy and I let him slide to the ground. But I fell asleep and when I woke he wasn't there. And I panicked, looking for him everywhere but I was searching the swamp and there were no sounds except for the noise of my sloshing and I worried about the gators I knew were there. Then I heard him calling in the distance, through the mangroves that stood in my way, through the marsh grass that grabbed at me and cut like a razor, through the muck that pulled at my feet, and I hurried, but his voice was still just as far away, and I was breathing hard trying to fight through the mangroves, and I couldn't even feel my feet any more to pull them out of the mud..." and then I woke.

I had fallen asleep in a chair in the living room, my glass of wine turned over on the carpet. I stared at the stain for a few moments, trying to figure if it was a dream or if it really happened. It happens all the time. Doesn't it? You have a dream and then carry the remnants of that dream around with you for the rest of the day, feeling the reality of it. And that's how my dreams usually go—only they are usually about Maxie, and I carry them around with me all day. And this one was probably about him also.

And the reality was it was only 5:30 a.m. and I wasn't tired any longer. So I got up, made coffee, and carried it into my office—after I cleaned up the wine spill on the living room carpet, that is.

I sat at a table that I had confiscated from my outdoor lounge set, pulled out an 8" x 11½" pad and began to write.

Two clients:

One with a missing son

One whose son was murdered

Possible suspects:

Father Trujillo (not likely)

Juan and Casto or other gangbangers (likely suspects)

The father, Jack Miller (maybe)

The rector (not likely)

Eogan (not likely)

Hannah (not likely)

Ned and Catherine Dougherty (not likely)

While I had never seriously considered the priest and Eogan, their reactions to Ethan's picture made me suspicious. Either they knew something more than they admitted or Hannah Miller was lying. I couldn't buy Hannah as a liar. So...

Leads come from talking to people. And that's what I had been doing. But in the end, what I needed was a confession. Ninety percent of all crimes are solved by a confession, not by the discovery of some elusive clue. Nobody volunteers a confession. So perhaps I could torture some suspects. Break them down like in a James Cagney movie. Somebody like Eogan. So I headed for the student center. It was Thursday. The day the four sems were scheduled to be at the center. It was 6:00 a.m. Time enough to catch an early mass, beat up some people, and then go to confession.

CHAPTER 29

Hector

Thursday Morning, October 21

I pulled into the center at 7:35 a.m. after stopping for a glazed donut and another cup of coffee at Dunkin Donuts. Lights were on in the church, a few cars scattered in the parking lot. I headed for the front door and entered. The padre was at the altar celebrating mass. I took a seat in the back. Three young men in black suits sat up in front. Eogan was standing at the altar, facing the congregation, and handing cruets to Trujillo who took each one and poured some of the contents into a glass chalice. In front of the Sanctuary and to the right of the altar, a young girl with hair down to her waist was strumming a twelve-string guitar while three others sang a hymn set to the tune of "Michael Row the Boat Ashore". Woodstock.

Father Trujillo looked my way and smiled. I sat back and waited for the end of the ceremony.

"Cooper," said Eogan, stepping down from the altar when the service was over and walking toward me. He wasn't smiling. "Long time, eh?"

"Eogan," I said, wondering if everyone called him that.

"Gunner," he said, as though reading my mind. "Everybody calls me Gunner."

"Gunner?"

"Easier than Eogan."

"No question," I said. Then we stared at each other for an uncomfortable few moments.

"So what's up?" he said, finally.

"Maybe I could meet with the other volunteers from the seminary and tell you all at once."

Gunner rubbed his chin, looked over at the three black suits who had been watching us since our conversation had begun and waived them over. They came, one after the other. A tall guy in front, thin, and a face that looked like it had seen hard times. The next guy was short and stocky, like a gofer for a big shot. The third black suit was average height, sandy hair. He had that all-American look with the features of a teenager, a soft face and no sign of a beard. All three lined up with Gunner.

"So this is Hector Ramirez," Gunner began, indicating the tall, thin suit to his left, with the face that looked like it wanted a fight. "And this is Joe Pacholewski," he continued, motioning to the short man to Hector's left. "And this is Justin Crane," he said. Justin was standing just behind Hector, and almost out of sight. He looked around the tall man and nodded. The silent All-American.

"So what is it you want to share?" Gunner said. "We're all here." He was challenging me and I didn't like it.

I showed them the pictures of Ethan Miller and Tamara Thompson. They passed them around—Gunner didn't look at them.

"Do you recognize either one of these two kids?" I said. Each one shook his head.

"That's peculiar," I said. "The boy, Ethan Miller, whose body was found in a cemetery near here, was said to have worked at the center. And yet, none of you have seen him." I was getting irritated and puzzled. "Now either the mother was lying or someone here is," I said, looking at each one of them.

Crane and Pacholewski shifted nervously on their feet.

"Do you know Juan?" I said, pausing to look at each person.

Everybody shrugged and made a face like *Not me.*

"Who is Juan?" said Gunner, looking perturbed.

"He's the guy who said I should talk to you guys about these two kids."

Gunner looked confused. The others showed no affect.

"Juan said you should ask us?" said Hector.

"That's right. I mean why would he say it if he didn't mean it?"

"What the hell, Cooper? You relying on what a gangbanger tells you about a murder case? Give me a break," Hector said.

"I didn't say Juan was a gangbanger, Hector. You said that. How did you know what he is if you don't know him?" Gotcha. "Actually he said to ask *you*," and I held his eyes for a few moments. "Like he knew you," I added.

Hector thought about that for a moment then, "Okay, I've heard of him. But that's about it. What I can do is tell you we don't know those two kids. Never saw them before. And they never worked here— that's it. Period." He paused and looked around at the other three.

I stared at him like I didn't believe his bullshit story. And we continued to stare at each other until Gunner spoke up.

"Look. I want to help." He looked around at the others. "We all want to help you find the killers of these poor kids." Hector didn't look like he gave a damn. "There's a guy in the West End. Name's Frankie D'Amico. He knows everything that goes on in Oceanside. You check with him. Tell him I sent you. He owns a restaurant on Sunset. Frankie's Place. Maybe he can help."

Pacholewski and Crane nodded. Ramirez stared at me. I didn't like him at all. Maybe we would have a fight. Maybe I would bring Richie with me. For back-up.

CHAPTER 30

The Italians

The West End in Oceanside is Florida's version of Boston's North End, largely Italian, with some Russians and Albanians thrown in. No Blacks or Hispanics there. About one square mile of real estate with lots of restaurants and bakeries. It could be a popular tourist place if tourists ever heard of it. It's there mostly for the local Italian population in the greater Miami metropolitan area and for anyone who wanted to be Italian, including me. I always wondered what it would be like to be connected. One of my friends once asked me, *Hey Coop, ever thought about bein' a lawyer? Could use a good one.* I was thinking of the Godfather and Robert Duval, the Irishman who played his consigliore. I must have looked uncertain. *Think about it* (pronounced tink), he had said.

I thought about it this afternoon as I drove west on Midnight Drive, past University Hospital, the seminary, and over to the West End. To get to the West End from the center, you have to skirt the easternmost bounds of the Everglades, along Midnight Drive, an east/west road that swings sharply north on its western leg toward Shark Valley. The West End is just south of Shark Valley and butts up against the edges of South Miami. It's a little like an Italian Coconut Grove, the honky-tonk part being all Italian with lots of fruit and vegetable stands in the streets, people calling out, *Hey, Buddy, ya gotta look at these tomatoes I got here. Come on over, you check it out.* Or *I gotta a deal for you, you're not gonna wanta pass up.*

They weren't talking to me, they were talking to the poor guys on the street. I was driving, safe for the time being. But I took a chance, pulled over, paid a kid five bucks to watch my car, and asked a vendor for directions to Frankie's Place.

"Over there" (pronounced 'dere'), he said, pointing to a red brick building that had apartments above it, with an old fashioned, neon sign that read __AN_IE'S PL_C_. I hoped the food was better prepared than the storefront because I was planning on eating there. The dining room looked like the place where Louise and I had eaten, same statues, same kinds of paintings. Must be they used the same decorators. Either that or someone runs the statues and oils back and forth every day.

"So, welcome to Frankie's, sir. Have you been here before?" asked a waiter in black and white. I shook my head. He led me to a table away from the bar. I was the only one there. It was a fancy place with white tablecloths and servers dressed to the nines. I could smell the olive oil and garlic. The odor permeated the very walls.

"And what kind of drink will the gentleman be having today?" he said.

I asked what his house wine was. He said Chianti. I said fine and was Frankie here today?

He said he would check with the maître d'. "And who should I say wants to talk with him?" he said, straining to be polite.

"What's your name?" I said.

"Marius," he said.

"Thanks, Marius. Tell your boss that I'm a detective," using my best smile.

Marius came back with my glass of wine and a short, fat man with a big wart on the side his nose. I guessed he was Frankie.

"So welcome to Frankie's," he said as he held out his hand and leaned over the table so I could smell his breath. It almost knocked me off my chair.

"What's the problem, detective?"

So I told him about Gunner and about the cases I was working on, starting with Ethan Miller and ending with the Dougherty kid. He knew all about them and listened attentively.

"You with Miami PD?" he said.

"I'm a private detective, Frankie," I said.

Frankie pulled up a chair next to me and got in my face.

"And what's your name, Mister Private Detective?" he said. Downright impolite.

"Cooper," I said, taking a sip of the Chianti. It was a good wine.

"Listen here, Cooper—can I call you Coop?" he said, leaning in closer so I could smell his body odor. "You got a lotta fuckin' nerve to come in here and ask questions in my place. And Gunner's got a big mouth. Gonna get him in trouble one of these days. Only thing you got goin' for you is that yous my guest here at Frankie's Place. But once you leave here, that's a different story."

I held up my hands. "So what's the problem, Frankie?" I said. "When somebody threatens me, I figure they have something to hide."

"Fuck you, Cooper and get the fuck outta my place," he said, rising up, spit flying out of his mouth. "And tell Gunner to stay the fuck outta my business! Marius, throw this fuck outta here," he yelled at the waiter. "You wanna talk to someone, Cooper, talk to the priest. He knows more'n I would ever know. Now get the hell outta here."

I didn't need an escort. I knew when I wasn't wanted. The air smelled cleaner in the streets, the trash in the gutters less noticeable, the people hawking food less irritating.

Gaslights were slowly coming to life along the street, creating shadows where there were none before, the largest ones settling in my mind as I tried to figure out what I had walked into. Evil has a way of disguising itself in the most seductive ways. After all, wasn't Ted Bundy an attractive guy? I looked for my car, hoping that some local, baby-faced kid whom I paid a fin to watch it didn't key it and run off with my money. The kid was still there when I showed up.

"Everything okay, mister?" he asked. I nodded and gave him another five. He stared at it. "Thanks," he said, stuffed the bill in his pocket and took off.

"No problem, kid," I said to his back. Big talk. I felt like Bogart in a gangster movie and climbed into my Volvo with the heated seats. In Miami no less.

I took Midnight Drive north to Terrace where it intersects Sunrise to check out some office space DeFelice told me about. He wants to see me successful now that I'm out of work. It was late when I got there, shadows falling across the street. The building was a two-story adobe, with offices on two floors. I figured I could get a second floor, $300/$350 a month. Get by until I could afford the big rents on Miami Beach. Kidding. It looked promising.

I headed home while I was still awake and pulled into my drive. A night-light comes on automatically when anything moves in the front. I have a similar light in the back. The only kind of movement that happens back there is from the big gator that set up housekeeping in the bayou. I've told you about him. Herman. Usually gators move at night. From swamp to swamp. From lake to lake. So you have to be careful when you walk at night—near lakes, or ponds, or the Everglades. Except Herman is too old to go anywhere these days. He just hangs out in my backyard. Still, I like to be in after dark. Bad things happen in the dark.

The darkening for me lately happens within my own dreams where nightmares play havoc with my sleep. About Maxie. About where he might be. And...well, it is so difficult for me to sleep when I think of him. If only...

I called my friend in Cleveland, Richie Marino, for some help. It was almost 1:00 a.m. Late. But Richie doesn't sleep.

CHAPTER 31

Richie

Thursday Night, October 21

It only took one ring for Richie to answer. "Hey Cooper, what's up."

"You got caller ID, Richie?"

"I ain't no mind reader, Coop. Wanna know who the hell's calling me. What the hell you need this time of night?"

"Need some help, Richie. Maybe you should bring your ball bat."

Richie solved most problems with an oak baseball bat that he got from one of the Cleveland Indians who had a car loan that had gone into arrears. Problem was the loan officer was a collection man for the local mob, your local savings and loan organization in the Italian part of town known as Murray Hill.

"So whose legs I gotta break, Coop?"

So I told Richie about Frankie D'Amico, about the kidnapping and the killings. Asked him what he knew about D'Amico, if he was trouble. Richie said he would check on Frankie. Get back to me tomorrow.

The nights go slowly when you can't sleep. The Everglades are in my backyard. I swear I can hear the sounds of the great swamp as I lie there in the silence of the early morning. What drives me crazy is looking at the clock and seeing 2:30 a.m., then drifting into a dream and coming out of it and seeing only fifteen minutes ticked off. The dreams that come these days creep up on me. They don't seem like dreams, more like memories of earlier days with Jillie and Maxie, and when I wake, I wonder if I was really dreaming or just lying in bed, remembering. I don't seem to know anymore.

So it was tonight. But it was a long night. They've all been long nights since...that time. And no one ever talks about it—with me—they probably do when I'm not around. It's my problem. Not theirs. So... It's like when you get a cancer, and—well, it's all hush-hush when you're around. It's been seven years now. A lot of silence around me. A lot of nobody wanting to talk about it. Hush-hush.

My phone rang out its tune. In the dark the red numbers on the clock read 4:00 a.m. I knew who it was but I couldn't move myself to answer it.

CHAPTER 32

Blackberries

We would—Jillie and I—take Maxie into the woods on a summer's late morning, the sun warm on the road and the trees, dust rising from the road, and look for the rich, full, fruit of the blackberry bushes, the berries protected by sharp needles that poke unprotected fingers until they bleed and run red and mix with the juice of the blackberries—and Jillie would make a bucket for Maxie out of a used tomato juice can with a string looped through two holes poked in both sides so he could carry it around his neck and Maxie would run ahead so he could be the first to pick the berries then run back to us, his hands covered purple and red from the berries and the poking of the briars, his bucket partially full and he would show us and we would laugh as he showed us because his lips were purple and we would say Maxie, you're not supposed to eat all the blackberries, *and we told him that he shouldn't eat them because there would be plenty of time to do that when we get back home where we would wash them and put them into a bowl and pour milk over them and then, and only then, would we eat them, and he would say,* But I would never eat the blackberries, *unaware of the evidence on his face and on his hands, and I would never tell him he had been found out and honestly I don't know if even today he would think he was—but...*

And I would chase those thoughts from my mind when I would drift back to those times, because the things I wanted to remember were the sun and its softness on the woods and its warmth on our bodies and the smell of the woods, and the sounds in the woods, and the running of Maxie, and the happiness that we shared together on those trips into the countryside—in central, rural Ohio, and...

But that was then, and now is now.

CHAPTER 33

The Stiletto

Friday Morning, October 22

I called DeFelice at 7:00 a.m. and asked him to meet me at a deli near the university in Oceanside. My treat.

"No problem, Coop," he said. DeFelice has a good appetite in the morning.

When I got there, a lot of college kids already filled the place. But DeFelice had nailed down two good seats near the window. He was already drinking coffee and munching on some pastries.

They've got good breakfasts at the University Deli. Two eggs, rye toast, orange juice, hash browns or grits, and coffee or tea. All for $3.95. What does DeFelice order? Steak and eggs, orange juice, toast, and hash browns. That's on top of the pastry that he's already polished off—before I got there. Me, I get a cup of decaf and a cinnamon-raisin bagel—butter and jelly. DeFelice calls it a chicken-shit breakfast. One without coffee even, because "Decaf ain't coffee, Cooper. What the hell, get a life. Eat some real food already."

"Got a call from the monsignor about you messing with his boys," he continued, eyeing me over his cup of coffee. "Better back off. Also got a call from guy by the name of Frankie. Says you're bothering him. Rodriquez, asking me what the hell you into. Tell you the truth, I wonder too," setting his cup on the table. Then, "Heard you were questioning some gangbangers in Oceanside. Whaddya think you're doin'? You ain't a cop no more. You quit, remember?" Reminding me again. He was still pissed—or hurt.

"Besides, you're messin' with some bad people, bud." He paused then looked up at me—he had been squeezing some catsup onto his steak. "Anybody got your back?"

I shrugged and filled him in on my latest adventures and my take on the meetings with Juan and with Frankie. I told him about Richie and said he was going to check on Frankie. DeFelice nodded as he took another piece of steak and dipped it into the eggs and catsup. I looked away.

"What'sa matter?" he said.

"You've got to be kidding," I said. "Those three things don't go together."

"Says you. You oughta try it."

Then I filled him in my meeting with Gunner and Hector and the other two holy boys.

"And what's up with Murphy?" I said.

He shrugged. "Be respectful. The guy's a monsignor." He pushed another forkful of steak and eggs into his mouth. His breakfast would last me a whole day. "But to answer your question: I don't think anything's up with him. Christ, he's just protecting the future padres from assholes like you, Cooper." He paused. "When was the last time you been to church?"

I shook my head. "You gotta be kidding. I ask a simple question. You give me the same lecture *you* just got—yesterday."

He ignored that. "So Coop, whaddya want from me you can't get from Delgado?"

"Hey, you and I go back a long way," I said. "Remember we were partners? What's it been, a week? You and me and Richie, we grew up together, remember?" DeFelice nodded, interrupting his breakfast again. "So Richie's getting some information on Frankie, maybe you can give him some help. Give him a call, okay?"

"Christ, Cooper, I never said I wouldn't help. But I gotta tell you Rodriguez ain't happy that you're messin' in his cases—you bein' retired and all. But, okay, I'll do some digging. Louise can check out the gangbangers. You realize, though, we can both collect some shit handing off information to you, I mean you not being on the job no more."

I nodded and said thanks.

He got up, sighed like he was taking on the world for me, shook his head, and looked back once more as he headed for the door. "Thanks for the breakfast, sport," he said, and disappeared.

I got a call from Richie as I was getting up to pay the tab. I love Pachelbel's Canon on my cell. It brings peace into my life.

"Hey, Coop. Got something," he said.

"Yeah?"

"Seems like Frankie is muscle down there for a small time guy who thinks he's big shit, controls most of the business in Oceanside. Name's Jimmy D'Augustino. Young guy. Lives in the Italian neigh-

borhood on the West End. Jimmy works for Big Al Marrazzo. He's
the man. But I wouldn't talk to neither of them. I got a contact there,
Mr. Morelli. Old guy, maybe eighty or so. He knows everything that
goes on around there. I unnerstand you can find him in the neighborhood sitting on a bench most evenings in the park near City
Hall. Go talk to him. But don't do nothin' to antagonize him. That
cane he has with him—that ain't just any cane. It's got a long sticker
in it." He paused. "Hey, you need some help, just gimme the word.
I'll be there in a second," he said.

I thanked Richie, and headed for the West End. My cell rang
again. This time it was Ned Dougherty.

"Hi Detective Cooper. Ned Dougherty here," sounding like he
was in a total depression.

"How are you doing?" I said.

"Not so good," he said. "I can't teach, I can't eat, and I can't sleep.
Same with my wife. Have you got anything yet?" he said, anxiety
riding every word.

"I'm working on it. Any phone calls?" I asked.

"No, nothing. The Coral Gables Police say they're going to hand
the case over to the FBI." He stopped for a moment. Breathing hard.
"I've got to do something, Cooper. I know you don't want me getting in your way. But—"

"Just stay with your wife. She needs your support. And let me
know if you get any calls—immediately, okay?" I waited for a few
moments. He was quiet. "I know how difficult this is for you," (I
wanted to tell him about my own son but didn't) "but you've gotta

trust me on this, you're more valuable letting me do the looking. You just keep your eyes and ears open. Let me know if anyone contacts you." And I waited.

"Ned?"

"I'm here."

"I'm heading out to talk to someone now. I'll let you know if I learn anything. Matter of fact, I'll call you tomorrow—one way or the other," figuring he needed some contact to stay calm.

"Thanks." Another pause. "By the way I know about your son," like he was reading my mind.

He let that sink in. It took me a few moments to get over what he had just said. All those worries and nightmares back again. .

"Mmmmm," I said. "Okay," and ended the call. But I wasn't okay.

CHAPTER 34

The Park

There he was, Morelli, at least it looked like it might be him. An old guy, sitting on a park bench, a cane between his legs, leaning back on the bench like he was thinking of something and staring at the sky. I had parked on the street and was maybe fifty feet from him when he said, "You can stop right there. What's your name?" still staring at the sky. It was an order. You know, like *Who the fuck are you?* I saw him fingering the cane like it was a favored thing.

"Cooper, Mr. Morelli. Richie Marino says he knows you. Says maybe you might be able to help me out."

He looked at me without dropping his head from the view overhead. Like he was studying the night sky.

"Richie Marino, huh. So you're a friend of Richie's?" More like a statement than a question.

"Sure. We go back. Cleveland."

"Cleveland, huh? That river still on fire?"

The Cuyahoga hadn't been on fire for years. But it's what people remember about the city.

"Come over here, Cooper, and sit down." He pointed to the open seat next to him—near his cane. I studied it, looking for the blade.

"You got another name besides Cooper?"

"No, just Cooper. First and last." He looked at me.

I shrugged. "It is what it is."

"Fuck do I care, Cooper. Your name's your name. Now tell me what you want," fingering the cane.

I told him about my visit with Frankie. I waited while he fooled with his cane. He saw me staring at it.

"Don't worry, kid. This thing's just a needle. I stick it into some wise kid tries to take advantage of an old man. Nobody ever sees it. Cause if you see it, I used it. Get it?" He waited for a reaction. I nodded. What else?

"Lemme give Richie a call, Cooper. You come back tomorrow. We'll talk," and he went back to his sky.

CHAPTER 35

The Muscle

I made it back to my home office around noon and noticed my door was open. I have a side entrance to the office—which is really a third bedroom that I converted. In fact though, I usually work at my kitchen table. I had the side door installed so a client doesn't have to enter through my living room and survey the crap that's lying around. I'm a bachelor. I would move all this once I rented the space in downtown Oceanside.

"Come on in, Cooper," a voice called out from inside.

Two guys, one sitting behind my desk, the other leaning against a wall near the door to the living room. They were both fat. I wonder if they considered Weight Watchers. I was sorry my .38 was in my desk drawer and not in my hand. Then I noticed it was already in the hand of the guy sitting at my desk.

"This yours, Cooper?" he said. "Looks like something your mommy gave you. Protect you from the bad guys—guys like us." He was grinning as he said it, like he had just told a great joke. Nobody laughed.

The big guy leaning on the wall motioned to a chair, indicating I should sit down.

I didn't move. "Who the hell are you?" looking at both of them.

"Tough guy ain't he, Shorty," said desk man. 'Shorty' was about six feet two.

"Yeah, real tough," said Shorty, not leaning anymore.

I looked around for a weapon. All I saw were office supplies: a paper-weight, pencil sharpener, some pens—I could poke them in the eye maybe.

"Got a message for you, Cooper. Stay the shit out of stuff that ain't none of your business. Unnerstand?" said the man behind the desk still holding my gun.

I shrugged. "Get the hell out of my office."

Shorty pulled himself off the wall and stuck his face in mine. "Only one time we gonna come here, Cooper. And that time's over. We come again and the man behind the desk's gonna kill you with your own gun."

I kicked him in the groin as he said *gun*. Shorty screamed, both hands on his groin, and fell back against the wall he had been leaning on. I heard a gunshot explode behind me and something like a bee sting my arm as I turned to the man behind the desk who was no longer behind the desk but standing and staring beyond me, my gun limp in his hand, and...

"Fuck you do, Tony, shoot me?" and I looked back at Shorty who was staring at his chest, his white shirt now mostly red and he grabbed for the spot where the bullet had penetrated, trying to stop what was now a flow of blood.

"What am I gonna do? I gotta get to a hospital!"

I hit the emergency number on my cell and yelled for Tony to get some towels from the kitchen. Shorty was leaning against the wall, his face now white. He looked up at me disbelieving. I told him he would be okay. Tony came back with a handful of towels. Together we took off Shorty's jacket. The bullet had ripped into the upper left side of his chest, away from the heart—I hoped.

I heard sirens in the distance.

I called DeFelice as soon as they left. He was at my house in twenty minutes with Louise Delgado.

"Jesus, Coop, what happened here?" said DeFelice as he looked around the room, chairs turned over and the desk on its side. "This your gun, sport?" said DeFelice as he picked up my .38 with a pencil. It was lying next to the overturned desk.

"Yeah, it's mine," I said. I had forgotten all about the gun. I was glad it wasn't in Tony's pocket.

"Gotta hang on to your hardware, bud," DeFelice said. I really didn't need reminding right now.

There was fresh blood on the floor. DeFelice knelt down and studied it. "Yours?" looking up at me.

I looked at where he was staring. I was wearing my prized bomber leather jacket. Two hundred dollars plus. My left arm was bleeding. That does it for that jacket, I thought. Blood was dripping off my sleeve to the floor. I pulled it off. The bullet had cut a nice groove in my left arm, the jagged edges of the wound red and purple. So I ripped off my shirtsleeve and took a closer look. I finally felt the pain. The shock of a gunshot wound takes time to wear off. I watched the video of a cop, who had been shot multiple times, chase his assailant, catch him, and then pass out, never realizing he had been hit.

Delgado went to the bathroom and found bandages in a medicine kit that I keep under the sink. She did a good job of cleaning the gash, first soaking it with peroxide, and then sealing it with a large gauze pad and plenty of adhesive tape. "Let's get you to a doc," DeFelice said.

Delgado was already through the door and headed for the unmarked Taurus. "We'll talk on the way," DeFelice said, as he helped me into the back of the car.

I got patched up at University Hospital, the doc wanting to know what happened, DeFelice saying *No problem, Doc, police business— should see the other guys.* It made some of the pain go away. Still hurt like hell.

Afterwards we wound up at a 24-hour diner on A1, the Ocean Highway, in Oceanside. It looked like a silver camper trailer, one of the shiny metal types that cost five hundred thousand—or more. The waitresses looked like truck stop women, tough, quick, and no nonsense.

"Whaddya have, gentlemen?" asked a waitress who said her name was Lola. Delgado gave her a look.

"Sorry," she said, catching the look. "I just thought—"

"That all cops are guys."

The waitress shrugged.

I ordered the full Sunset Diner Special: grits, pancakes, two eggs over hard, toast and decaf. I didn't know what I was worried about staying up for. What else can happen after getting beaten up and shot? Delgado ordered the fruit plate and yogurt, DeFelice, The Works. It's called that. The Works. Let your imagination roam and you have the idea.

"So, Coop, tell me what's goin' on here. This is crazy stuff. And, by the way, I gotta keep your piece—on account of it was used in the commission of a felony."

"You've already got it," I said, "seeing as you seized the weapon at the scene."

He ignored me. "So tell me what happened there, hot shot."

"I figure Frankie sent the two goons." I paused. "Thing is, they will probably be back."

DeFelice nodded. "Okay. But we gotta let Oceanside PD know. This ain't my jurisdiction—as you know, partner." He hesitated, shaking his head. "In the meantime, like I told you before, you're stirring up a lot of shit," pausing like he was thinking about it. Then, "If you need help, just call for Christ's sake."

Just then my cell rang. I got up when I saw it was Richie.

"Gotta call from Morelli. Said you'd been to see him. I gave you a hunnert percent endorsement. He said tell you to stop by when you're in the neighborhood again. Said you're scared shitless of his cane. Is that right?"

"Uh huh. Shaking in my boots. By the way, I think I got a visit from some of Frankie's boys today." I told him what happened.

"I'm on my way," he said. "Need some of that Florida sun," and he hung up. That's Richie. Call him, he's here.

I closed the cell and sat back down. DeFelice and Louise looked curiously at me.

"That Richie?" said DeFelice.

"Yeah, how'd you know?"

"How's he doin' these days?"

DeFelice, Richie, and I grew up together on the near east side of Cleveland in red brick, row houses that stood guard over Euclid Avenue, a street that runs from downtown Cleveland to the eastern suburbs. The story was if there was a red light in your way through our neighborhood, you should run it. Stopping at a light was an invitation to be robbed. So nobody stopped for red in East Cleveland, including me.

"Richie's doing well," I said. "He's running a sports bar in South Euclid, a legit business. Partners with your old friend and mine, Danny Barrett, the crazy Irishman."

"No shit. Danny boy's out of prison then. Good for him. A real fuck-up that kid. Glad you ain't running with his crew no more. So what's he doin'?"

"He's coming down for some sun. Said it's too cold up there. Looking forward to hooking up with us."

Delgado was watching our conversation like it was something out of a boy's-night-out movie, shaking her head and barely suppressing an *I don't believe you guys look.*

She jumped in.

"So Coop, let's set up a meet with Juan again, push him a little harder, see what shakes out."

I nodded. "Good idea. You gonna call him?"

"Maybe. Maybe not. I'll let you know. Maybe we'll surprise him. Bring a gift."

It was early evening when I left DeFelice and Delgado and headed back to the West End. I followed Sawgrass Road west toward the Everglades and Shark Valley. You can almost see downtown Miami from there, the glow of the bank towers, indigo and scarlet, burning a hole the size of an inverted volcano into the night sky. If you take the time, you can catch its aroma in the autumn air: summer breaking up, a fresh breeze blowing the salt air in from the ocean. There is one last month of hurricane season and then the storm weary natives can rest, at least until the beginning of another season.

Long lines of thirty-foot palms guard both sides of the street all the way to Midnight Drive, the last residential street before the Everglades. It runs north and south along the perimeter of the Everglades. It's where I live. Sawgrass dead-ends at Midnight Pass. So I make a left and head south toward the West End where Morelli should be waiting. As you enter the Village, Midnight Pass becomes Main and is lined with old fashioned gas lamps that flicker over the streets like candles and throwing about as much light. But the stores had their night-lights on and those helped cut into the darkness. Nobody was out and I wondered why Morelli would be. But as I approached the park, I saw him, seated alone on the same bench where I had seen him before. I pulled over and parked under one of the gas lamps.

Morelli didn't move as I approached. He was resting his hands on the top of his cane that rested between his knees.

"Cooper, good to see you. Sit down here," motioning to a spot next to him on the bench.

Morelli kept his eyes forward—staring into the darkness, as though he were talking to someone in the distance. "I only got two things to say to you. One, about Frankie. He was no good as a kid," and he paused as though thinking about that, then, "and he ain't no better as a man. If you're gonna talk with him, you should take Richie with you," still staring into the darkness. "It's too bad about those kids. But I don't think Frankie had anything to do with them. Second, if anybody knows anything about the Hole, it's the priest. He might be afraid to talk to you, because it's dangerous to open your mouth around here. You talk, you might lose your tongue—or your life," he added. Then he turned my way—a warning in his eyes. "Have to be careful, Cooper," nodding his head like the Oracle of Delphi.

"One last thing (he pronounced 'th' like a 't'—as in 'wit' and 'ting'), the Hispanics (he really said 'spics'), they're taking over from the goombahs. So Frankie and his bosses are in a war with them. You might be wise to look to the bangers for this thing," and now he was focused on my eyes—to see if I understood. I nodded that I did.

"Now you get outta here," he said, pointing his cane at my car, waving it up and down like that's where I should head and soon.

Conversation over. Then he went back to contemplating the sky as though I was never there.

I thanked him but might as well have been thanking the park bench. The student center is only fifteen minutes south on Midnight Drive as the road heads east back toward the ocean and away from the darkness of the Everglades.

CHAPTER 36

Deny, Deny, Deny

Later That Evening

"So Cooper, what can I do to help," asked the padre, fingering the buttons on his cassock. He seemed nervous.

"What I'm asking, Father, is why somebody like Morelli would tell me I should ask *you* about a missing kid? Simple question."

The priest shook his head. "Morelli? Man's getting senile. Used to attend mass here—every day. But he stopped once the Hispanic kids began to come. 'Can't stand those spics,' he would say—maybe forgetting I was one of them."

"Morelli says you know what happens in the neighborhood. And that includes what might have happened to a couple of kids who were murdered not too far from here—and one of them who supposedly worked as a volunteer at the center—and whom you say you didn't know. I'm wanting to believe you but you're making it hard, Father."

Trujillo looked away for a few moments, screwing up his brow like a man deep in thought. "I do remember Ethan," he said, staring into the sky. Maybe he's related to Morelli.

"Why didn't you tell me before?"

"I'm sorry. I should have" and he looked down, avoiding my eyes.

I didn't say anything. Better to let the silence force him to talk.

"Yes, Ethan was volunteering at the center. He was very diligent. I was horrified when I heard the news of his death..."

"Killing," I corrected. He nodded.

"Killing," he continued. "I was going to call the police and give them what information I had about Ethan, about his work here when..."

"Somebody called you," I said. He didn't have to nod. I could see it in his face.

"Somebody called me..."

"Yes?" I prompted as he hesitated. "Let me guess—" I started.

"The rector of the seminary," he finished.

"Murphy? What the hell...?" I caught myself.

"He got me assigned here."

"Is he your boss?"

"No. But he's a monsignor and the head of the diocesan seminary, so he has the ear of the bishop—and will probably be in line to succeed him."

"I don't believe it. You didn't call the police because the rector told you not to."

Trujillo didn't look at me. He didn't say anything.

After a short silence that must have seemed to him like an hour, I said, "Why would he do that—ask you not to call the police about Ethan?" My God, I thought. What the hell was going on?

He looked up. "Murphy said that the publicity would be bad for the center. A young kid, underage, volunteering at the student center, getting killed only a mile or so away from here. He said it might raise questions about the work we were doing here—an investigation—headlines in the newspaper..."

"And it might jeopardize his chances for becoming the next bishop."

"Yeah. I guess so," and he was wiping his hands on his cassock like they were unclean—not saying they weren't.

"You realize you've been withholding information that could easily be tied to the murder of these two kids!" I was furious—thinking back on of my own son's case.

Trujillo stammered through a few more attempts to explain what he had done but finally..."I'm so sorry." Then he hesitated. "What are you going to do?"

"I am going to tell the police, of course." I paused. "And I'm going to have a sit-down with the rector. Is there anything else you're not telling me?"

He hesitated, fooling with the buttons on the sleeve of his cassock.

"I hear there's a prostitution ring operating in the area."

"What area?"

"I don't know exactly. In the area—just a rumor. I was thinking—"

"That Ethan might have been a victim of—"

"I was just thinking. Maybe."

"Any idea who might be running it?"

"Maybe the local gangs."

"Or Frankie?"

"I doubt it."

"Gunner and Hector know about it. Maybe you should talk with them." He paused. "Maybe Joe and Justin also. They're trying to keep the street kids safe."

"Joe and Justin?"

"Pacholewski and Crane." He looked at me. Nervous. "You're going to tell the rector?"

"My intention is to visit him."

He shook his head. "He won't be happy."

"So don't tell him about our conversation," I warned. He nodded.

I would make it a point to visit Murphy tomorrow. On the way back to my house I tried Richie. No answer.

CHAPTER 37

Richie

Home was a half hour away. I took Midnight Pass west toward the Everglades where it dead-ends and then heads north. I passed the dimly lighted streets that feed into Midnight Pass and wondered why anyone would live in such a dark and remote place—I figure that says something about me. I like people around me, like Richie, and DeFelice, and Louise—but on nights like this, I like the loneliness of where I live.

I noticed a light on in the front room as I turned onto my road. I never leave lights on when I leave. Saves electricity. So I stared at the window wondering. And I pulled over to the other side of the road. I reached into my glove compartment for my gun and realized that DeFelice had taken it. I had some bear spray so I grabbed it and headed across the front lawn. The screen door on the porch swung open and a voice came from a dark figure, back-lit against the interior lights of the house.

"Cooper? Don't fucking shoot me, you idiot. I had a long flight and I'm beat!"

"Richie! What the hell you doing here? You scared the shit out of me. Get out here where I can see you," I said.

A big, muscular man, built like a tall fireplug with long arms, came across the porch to greet me. "Coop!" he said. "Put away that mace or whatever you got in your hand. It's homecoming! By the way, you had visitors earlier. Told them you weren't home. Coupla big guys. I figure same guys you met the other night. Kind your mother said to watch out for. But Richie is here to help you, my man. Be happy! Come and see what Uncle Richie brought!" finally taking a breath.

He led the way back over the porch—like he owned the place— through the living room and into the kitchen. He pointed at the counter: pepperoni, several tubs of olives, a hunk of cheese—Asiago—fresh parmesan, sausage in a small cooler, a long roll of Genoa salami, and homegrown tomatoes.

"How did you get all this on the plane, Richie?" I said.

"Don't ask," he said and winked. "Uncle Richie has his ways."

I was happy to see him. I remembered the time when I was walking home from school—ninth grade—on the near east side of Cleveland—when I got jumped by five guys. They beat me up pretty badly. I came home—blood running from my nose and my shirt almost off my back. Richie just happened to be there—he was a junior—waiting on the front porch. When he saw my face, he went into the house, grabbed a ball bat and went out the door. I followed him with one of my own. We chased them all the way back to their neighborhood, Richie screaming, "You come back here, I'll break your goddamn legs!" They never came back. So Richie never had to do it. But he was known for his bat. And that's why they never came back.

"I'll grab us a couple of beers so you can fill me in about what's goin' on." He went to the fridge, took out four Sam Adams and opened two. "And don't worry, we're gonna take care of things (pronounced 'tings')," motioning with his arm like it was a done deal.

Richie sat in the Lazy Boy recliner—his favorite—kicked the footstool so the chair would lean back, took a long swig from the bottle and tipped it to me. "So tell me what's happening."

I filled him in on Frankie, the two goons who visited me, on the gangbangers, on Trujillo, on the prostitution ring and the possibility that the killings of Ethan Miller and Tamara might somehow be connected to Frankie, or to Juan and Casto or maybe even to the center.

"So you think maybe the kids got caught in a prostitution thing?"

"Maybe. There are some seminarians working at the center. My guess—they know something. They're just not talking."

"So, since Frankie has done what he did, we gotta pay him a visit first. Set things right with him." He paused. "Otherwise..."

"Yeah, I know. Need to back down the bullies. Bring your bat?"

"Sure thing. It's packed in my duffel bag. By the way, you got any protection?"

"Police took my .38. I've got my Glock."

"Kid's gun, Coop. You need to grow up, get adult toys."

"Come on," and he headed for the guest bedroom where he usually stays when he comes. "Like to stay there," he said once, "cause I can keep an eye on that friggin' pet gator you keep in your back yard."

There was a large, long airline bag lying across the bed. Richie unzipped it and began rummaging through it like a man looking for gifts he brought home for the kids. He produced two handguns that looked new. One a Browning HP JMP 50th that holds thirteen rounds of 9mm shells. It's a beautiful piece with ivory grips and a polished blue metal finish. I could see the Browning signature on the left slide with a gold scroll background. A real gem. He handed it to me with a smile broader than my door.

"Whaddya think, Coop?"

I told him it was beautiful and how in the hell did he get it on the plane.

"Got my ways, Cooper. Don't ask."

He then handed me the other, a Glock 19 9mm with fixed night sights. A more sophisticated model than mine. It holds fifteen rounds with a double action. This gun is a smaller version of the Glock 17, making it especially useful as a concealed weapon. The black finish gives it a more menacing look than the Browning.

"Pick either one, Coop. They can both do the job. I'll take the one you don't."

I picked the Glock since I'm a simpler guy than Richie. I knew he liked the Browning.

"Okay, we got the toys, lets talk about how we play with them. Frankie is connected with the Miami mob. Small potatoes, Cooper, but he thinks he's a big shit. Word is he ain't real popular with The Man down here. Got a big mouth, can't keep it shut. But we got permission to shut it for him. So tomorrow we're gonna give Frankie a visit. See if we can't get him to be more cooperative."

Richie and I talked into the night; talked about the old neighborhood, about how DeFelice organized us, how we fought our way home everyday, how Madman Sonny Gorzkiewicz would sit on his porch swing, waiting for us to pass by, calling out insults until one day he was waiting in the street for us, with ten or fifteen guys or more, and waded in on us. Only Richie wasn't there that day, just me and DeFelice and a friend, Charles, just fourteen years old, but big for his age. We were beat up when we got home, cuts on our arms and legs and bruises where they landed punches. A little while later Charlie's sister came in the door, crying, dress torn, and furious. She said Sonny and his guys had chased her and her friends, calling them names and talking about how we were all pussies.

I saw red and called Richie. He was over in ten minutes with his Louisville Slugger. Charles and I each had a bat. We were out the door before his sister could stop us, but she had a smile on her face anyway. Sonny's house was on a hill in Cleveland Heights overlook-ing Euclid Avenue. He was sitting on his porch when he spied us. When he saw Richie, he panicked and took off down the steps and away from his house. I screamed at him, "Yeah, you run Sonny. And you keep runnin'!"

He never looked back, never bothered us again. I could picture my bat descending on Sonny's head, splitting it open. He must have read my thoughts.

CHAPTER 38

Frankie's Place

Saturday Morning, October 23

In the morning Richie made espresso. The real stuff this time. No decaf and no skim milk. And the aroma of the beans was in the air. We sat and talked about the day. Richie was all business now, no funny comments, no wasted time.

"Got your piece, Cooper?"

I nodded.

I noticed Richie also had a ball bat with him, a sawed off version. He must have sneaked it in his bag as well.

"Ok, Coop, let's go see this goombah."

We pulled up to Frankie's place at 10:25 a.m. The front door was open, so we walked in. No sign of anyone around until a voice called out from the darkness.

"We're closed!"

This time I noticed the pictures of famous movie stars lining the walls, signatures and all. Frankie Sinatra: "Best wishes, Frankie!" And Dino De Laurentis: "Great food! The best outside of the North End!" And, "Frankie, you're the best," from someone I never heard of.

"Hey, I said were closed. You deaf?" the voice called out again. This time a guy appeared with it, a bouncer type, big shoulders, his face still hidden in the shadows.

Richie had the bat concealed behind his back. "No, bozo, we ain't deaf, but maybe yous blind, seein' as we're standin' right here!"

"Fuckin' matter with you guys. Get the fuck outta here!" he said. He had walked over and was getting in our face.

Richie pulled the bat out and hit the guy in his fat stomach, doubled him over and then hit him over the back, putting him on the floor. Even face down I recognized the 'bozo'. Tony, the guy from my office who had taken over my desk and gun. The big man groaned and tried to roll over. When he finally did, he looked carefully up at Richie to see if it was safe to get up.

"What did I do?" he said. Then he saw me. "You...!" a cross between a question and an exclamation.

"That's right," I said. "Surprise."

"Where's Frankie?" said Richie.

"Fuck do I know. He ain't here. Who're you?"

"Friend of the family, bozo. Who're you?" Said Richie.

"That's Tony," I said. "One of Frankie's boys."

"Tony," said Richie. "Tony The Mouth? I remember you from the old neighborhood. How long you been down here?"

Old home week!

"Come on, Richie," I said, "let's get on with it, okay."

Richie looked hurt. For that matter 'The Mouth' looked hurt as well.

"So, Tony, where's Frankie?" I asked.

"He don't come in till 10:00—or so." He looked at the clock, then at me looking at the clock.

"It's 10:35, Tony," I said. And as I said it Frankie came through the front door.

"What the fuck. You back here again, Cooper. Thought I told you to stay outta here." Then he saw Richie.

"So who's this clown?" he said.

"A friend of mine from Cleveland," I said.

"This is Richie Marino from Cleveland," said Tony, jumping in. "He's okay. From the old neighborhood," he added.

"I don't know from no 'old neighborhood,'" said Frankie, screwing up his face. "I just wanna know who the fuck you guys think you are comin' in here again after I told this douchebag to stay out," pointing at me.

I looked at Richie. Tony looked at Richie. Then Frankie looked at Richie.

"What?" Frankie said, raising his hands, palms up.

Richie held Frankie in his stare for a few moments.

"Cleveland Johnny had a little talk with Mr. D'Augustino about you, Frankie. We, meaning me and Mr. D'Augustino, heard you gave my friend Cooper some trouble. I'm here to offer him protection," pulling the bat out from behind his back and letting it drop to his side.

"Hey, what's a matta witch you. I got no beef with Cooper. Just didn't know who he was. You say he's good, that's fine with me."

Richie held the bat like it was his best friend, stared at Frankie and moved his head up and down like he was waiting for something.

"So...what?" Frankie said, like he didn't know anything.

"So why did your send your goons after me, Frankie?" I said.

"Thought you was some punk workin' with Gunner. How'd I know who the hell you was!" said Frankie, looking for approval from Richie, but getting none.

"Yeah, so now you know," said Richie. "Whyn't you tell us what you're so nervous about. Got somethin' to hide?"

"Gunner and Hector are a coupla jerkoffs, sticking their noses where they don't belong. That's my problem," Frankie said.

"Hey, we're talkin' about future padres here! Let's be respectful," said Richie.

"Okay, but you gotta tell those guys, future padres, whatever the hell they are, stay the hell outta my business."

"So what's your business, Frankie?" I asked.

"I got a nice, respectful family restaurant here. We do a good business. Don't need no kids poking their heads in here giving me trouble."

"So, Frankie, I am still trying to figure out why you're in trouble here. What ain't you telling us?" says Richie, spinning the bat in his hands. "I think you got something goin' here you're not telling us about. Does Big Al know what you're into?"

Big Al Marrazzo is the crime boss in the South Miami/Oceanside area and controls most everything that goes on there. When Big Al walks into a room, you can smell the sauce just like it's coming off the stove, hot and served with garlic bread, cheese and all. When he speaks no one says anything. To do so would risk his anger which can end badly for the subject of his wrath, and that would be Frankie or anybody else who screws up.

The look on Frankie's face told me he was picturing Big Al even as we spoke. Pure terror. I figured there's got to be a connection between what Frankie is doing and the gang-bangers—some rivalry—fighting for the same territory maybe. Frankie is the muscle for Jimmy D'Augustino, a small time hood who works Oceanside. Big Al lets him alone mostly because Jimmy married Big Al's daughter. Supposedly Frankie hates Jimmy because *he's a weasel and chicken shit coward who messes around in sleazy stuff* (his words), not the regular mob business, namely, protection, gambling, prostitution, and drugs. I figured maybe the gangs are beginning to challenge the mob action and they don't like it. But I couldn't figure where the padre and the seminarians fit in.

We left Frankie wondering about what's next. So we headed for the Sicilian Gardens on Sunset and University where Louise Delgado and I had dinner just a few nights ago.

Time was slipping by quickly. The word is, if you can't find someone in the first forty eight hours, the chances of success diminish rapidly each hour after that. It had been four days now and no clear leads about Eddie Dougherty, and no real clue about Ethan Miller's killer. Not good.

CHAPTER 39

Sicilian Gardens

Saturday Noon, October 23

The Gardens are usually busy on Saturdays, especially on the first Saturdays of the month when Catholic families attend Saint Anthony's Church for the Five First Saturday's devotion, and then come to the Gardens afterward for a late breakfast or lunch. Frankie always opened up early on Saturdays, even though he didn't usually serve lunch—or breakfast.

This wasn't one of those Saturdays, but it was busy anyway. Maybe a funeral or a wedding at the church. So the tables at the Gardens were full. Kids hanging onto their parents, complaining that they're hungry, mothers telling them, *Hey, you should be happy considering all of the starving kids in the world.* Back in my day, it was always about the starving children in China. I was straining to hear where the hungry kids were today. Maybe right here in the United States in some of our own neighborhoods.

We waited for the host to see us. Finally, "You gotta wait—just a short time—maybe twenty, thirty minutes, tops," the man at the front said.

"Hey, Richie," said a voice behind me. "What are you doin' here!" DeFelice appeared behind us, pushing me aside to grab Richie in a bear hug. It's hard to paint a picture of what took place. Two big Italians hugging each other in a crowded restaurant like they hadn't seen each other in thirty years, which is the way it was actually. DeFelice banging Richie on the back like he's a long lost brother, Richie pounding him back just as hard. People stared at the two like they were watching *Godfather 2*. I stared too. Then I saw Louise, standing behind DeFelice.

"Louise," I said, "what are you doing here?" sounding like DeFelice did a minute ago and wondering what she really was doing here with DeFelice. And she noticed the look in my eyes as I said it.

"What? You jealous, Coop?" She paused, looking at me sidewise and smiling. DeFelice and Richie were still visiting the old days. "Tony and me were just recounting the business of the day. The FBI is looking into the missing Dougherty kid and also the other two murders—they're thinking maybe some connection. Rodriquez figures they'll take over the investigation. By the way, Mrs. Miller said give her a call. Hasn't heard from you in a couple of days."

"That's strange. Wonder why she didn't call *me?*" I said.

"She called to see what progress we had made. Said she hadn't heard any news from you as yet. Just a heads-up."

"Thanks. I'll call her." I wished I had some news to give.

So we finally got seated—the four of us—and we talked through a good portion of the afternoon, with kids' voices raised in the background and waiters dressed in black pants and crisp white shirts hurrying to meet the needs of the hungry families all on their way to heaven once they finished their novenas; DeFelice wondering if I had any more information about the Miller kid—my response, *No.* Then, did I had any more information about the young girl? *Ditto,* I said, wondering if he had any more questions for me that I couldn't answer. He looked at me like I was falling down on the job. I already knew that. Here was a young divorced woman with three kids, one now dead, a family who lost a daughter, another family whose son is missing, and what did I have to show for it? Nada. Not one damn thing. So I looked at Louise and she was staring at me while DeFelice talked. We both smiled like we knew there was no end to Tony's talking and that the only thing that would come of it was that I would get more and more frustrated, so I said,

"Hey, Tony, I don't have anything, you don't have anything, nobody has anything. It's a sum zero game, okay."

And Tony nodded and Richie nodded and we slipped back into a discussion of the neighborhood again, and Richie was filling us in on how everybody was doing, how the old stores were getting renovated, how Murray Hill was a tourist place now (Richie owns a walk-up there where he takes care of his ma), how the place was really looking up, *A pretty cool place now, guys! Place has got some class!* Meaning the near East Side. Like we were supposed to believe that. I mean, come on! This is Cleveland we're talking about.

"So all I know is we have to talk to some people again (meaning Juan, Frankie, maybe Jimmy D'Augustino, and the padre). Somewhere in there is the answer. I can just feel it." I was trying to talk over the noise in the restaurant, Richie and DeFelice interrupting their conversation and turning to me and nodding, like *Sure, bud.* But Louise was listening. And she looked sad.

"Not to worry, Coop. It'll come together. I'm sure of it. It always does."

And I smiled. She was trying.

CHAPTER 40

Dead End

But I didn't believe it. There was only one thing I knew for certain and that's about dead end roads. And that's where I felt I was. And I knew there is only one way out of a dead end road—and that's the same way you came in.

After lunch I cornered Louise while Tony and Richie continued to reminisce about old times. We talked about going back and visiting Casto and Juan once again. And then I would corner Gunner and talk to him and Hector Luis Ramirez, and, yeah, the rector...

But I was getting weary of how long the cases were dragging out. It felt like I had started the investigation years ago though it had only been weeks. But cases go like that. The crime happens, you get assigned, then suddenly it starts to go cold. A couple of days go by and you forget how fast the time flies; meantime the bad guys are getting further and further away. It's kind of like the dreams I've been having this past year, about getting lost in a strange place where the roads look familiar but always wind up in the same place, facing the same dreary hills, and the same houses scattered along the roadway, and there's a dead end sign posted there—in case I didn't know it—and my only escape is to wake up, except in this dream I'm already awake, and that's the nightmare of it all—being in a dream where I can't wake up, with nothing but the road that leads to nowhere once again spreading before me.

The sun was high when we left the Gardens. Its heat, though gentler in the autumn, reminding us we're in Florida. I never needed much reminding of that, especially in the summer. But falls in Florida are mild by comparison, the Atlantic breezes already bringing in the cooler air that comes with the winter months.

Louise went on her way with the promise to meet me tomorrow at the deli and *We'll pay a surprise visit to Casto and Juan again.* Today was my time to meet with Gunner and Hector and press them some more about the disappearance of Eddie Dougherty, about the murders of Ethan and Tamara (they gotta know something), and about Frankie. I mean, why did Gunner give me his name? My goal, shake the tree a little, see what falls.

I had said goodbye for the time to Richie. He was busy with DeFelice still talking about the old days, you know, when things were better: times when kids could play in the street and parents not worry about them; times when you could walk to the dime store and buy candy for a penny and not worry about some pervert picking you up; times when you walked to the neighborhood pool and swam until dark, nobody worrying about where you were; times when every road led to an adventure and to hills beyond which were hidden treasures.

But today there's a bad guy on the way home from every pool, on the other side of every hill, and near every dime store. Today, parents can't even let their kids deliver the paper without shadowing them.

Today, there is danger in every lonely place, in every alleyway, and even in the busy shopping centers and in the school grounds, and at bus stops. Take Eddie for example.

But that's the way it is, I guess. Times have changed.

It was two o'clock by the time I reached the student center. Inside the hall it looked like preparations for a Halloween party were under way: pumpkins, plastic and real; crepe paper, black and burnt orange; skeletons scattered around the center, hanging from the ceiling and walls; and spider webs—they looked so real I wanted to knock them down.

I saw four black suits mixing with the students. I walked over to Crane. He was short, dark hair, and friendly looking. That's why I started with him. He looked up. Nervous. Like I was holding a gun to his head.

"Are you going to get in trouble if we talk?" and I noticed Hector and Gunner watching us.

"No," he said, quickly, stealing a look at Hector. "What do you want to talk about?"

"Ethan Miller and what you knew about him. It seems like everyone around here never heard about the kid. And yet—"

"Cooper," came a voice from behind me. "What's up?" Hector circled around me and put an arm around Crane. It was a move to either console him or to shut him up. I figured the latter.

Hector looked more like a gangbanger than a guy studying to be a priest. A thin, hollow face, mean eyes, and an Adam's apple that looked too big for his neck.

"So what do you need, Cooper?"

I watched him for a few moments. Then, "I'm trying to figure out why no one here knows Ethan Miller. Yet..." and I paused while Hector stared at me, "he worked here. Don't you find that strange?"

"I don't find that strange, but I find your questions strange," and he shifted from foot to foot as he talked. Nervous energy.

"Those kids, Ethan and Tamara..." I paused, "were they being used as prostitutes?"

"What the...?" and he caught himself.

Pacholewski had just walked over and, as he caught our conversation, stopped short and hung back.

"Joe," I said. "Did you want to say something?"

He shook his head and looked nervously at Hector and Gunner.

"We're busy. And I think we're done here," said Gunner, taking Pacholewski and Crane by the arm and pulling them back to the tables of students who had now turned toward us, staring.

CHAPTER 41

Murphy

The seminary is only three miles or so from the student center. You get there by driving streets lined with palms and the transplanted live oaks that overhang the lawns of southern estates. I called Hannah Miller on the way and got her voice mail. I left a message that I was making some progress (a lie) and would fill her in on the weekend (truth). I watched the afternoon shadows trail the trees as the five o'clock sun settled in the west over the Everglades. The seminary is situated across the street from Saint Augustine University, one of the oldest Catholic universities in the nation. The seminary campus is composed of a number of adobe-like structures with red tile roofs. Grassy courtyards separate the buildings. A walkway leads to the main entrance of the administration building. It's flanked by two stone pillars with a sign in large metal letters arcing overhead and resting on the two monolithic structures: *Ama Deum et age quod tibi placet.* "If you love God, you can do whatever you want." I considered the implications of those words as I found a spot to park on the street.

The neighborhood looked safe. No need to pay a kid a fiver to guard my car. I stared at the two massive wooden doors that fronted

the main building. They looked ominous. Maybe that was deliber-
ate. Keep the evil spirits away. So I didn't lock my car. What holy boy
is going to steal an old Volvo?

I stood briefly in front of the doors studying the design carved
into the dark, rich-looking wood. Probably oak. It was an intricate
design. A wreath of swirling faces, wings jutting out behind them,
crowded the tops of both doors. In the center of the door on the
right was a weathered brass knocker that was larger than my head. I
pulled it and let it fall. It struck a metal plate beneath it with a dull
thud. No one responded. So I grasped the heavy metal handle and
heaved the door open.

I was facing an open hall that must have been twenty feet wide
and a football field long. It was lit only by the dying sun that shone
through windows hung high up on the walls on either side of the
entryway and creating the feel of entering a medieval church. Far
down the hall there were two more double doors. They were cur-
tained and out of them music emanated, soft and monotonous, like
an eastern chant. Men's voices—barely audible—riding on the odor
of incense. Everyone was in chapel it seemed.

I took that as an invitation to explore. I opened the door to the
rector's office and was standing in a large ante-room, facing a dark
mahogany desk with two decorative lamps resting on either side.
They gave off only a modicum of light. The secretary was not there.
I hesitated for a moment, listening to the chant drifting from the
chapel, and then figured, *What the hell. Breaking and entering only*

applied if you had to break something to enter. I was breaking nothing, so I circled behind the secretary's desk and tried the door to the rector's office. It was open.

I paused for a moment and looked at my hands. No gloves. But really, who would be looking for fingerprints? And besides, it takes forever to track down prints—if you ever do. Except mine, of course. They're on file everywhere.

I'm sure you've seen movies where a private detective entered someone's office illegally and began to search—and you were sure he was going to get caught. I had the same feeling as I made my way around the office.

First, I went to his files looking for information on Hector and Gunner. I found nothing. Probably in HR. I opened his desk, a large heavy, old piece of furniture constructed of a rich cherry. It matched the wood paneling that overlaid the walls. The light that filtered through the metal-framed glass windows lining the wall behind the desk gave the wood a deeper shade of red than it really had.

I had the sensation that someone was peering over my shoulder as I dug through drawers. So I turned to the window behind me to see if someone was hanging from a scaffolding, spying on me. I stayed carefully behind one of the drapes and pulled it back just far enough to get a good look outside. What I saw was a ball field. It served as a centerpiece for several stone buildings surrounding the field and forming a classic college quadrangle. I searched the windows in the closest building to see if anyone was watching. I thought

I saw a drape rustle in one of them and then fall back into place. So I hurried back to my rummaging.

In a side drawer, hidden under envelopes and some letterhead paper, I found a picture of a young boy, maybe eleven, maybe twelve. I stuck the picture in my coat pocket.

I found nothing else and headed straight for the door, opened it slowly, and after checking, stepped out into the hallway.

"What are you doing here, Mr. Cooper?" came a voice behind me from the direction of the chapel. The rector. I wasn't sure just what he had seen, so I said I was looking for him and did he have a few minutes.

"Did I see you coming from my office?"

I assured him he had not and asked again if he had a few minutes to spare. He stared at me for a moment, debating whether he should press his question further, and then continued.

"I suppose I have a few minutes. But that's all, Mister Cooper."

He stressed the 'Mister'. No Detective Cooper here. No civil tone. I was being called down to the office by the principal.

He motioned me back through the door I had just passed through moments before, then through the door behind his secretary's desk and back into his inner chamber. He walked over to his desk and stood behind it, studying me, suspicion still riding in his eyes. He didn't invite me to sit. When he had settled in his chair, he folded his hands on the glass surface. The richness of the cherry shone through.

"Well?" he said. "What can I do for you?"

I told him about my visit with Frankie DiCarlo. "You know him, right?"

"Yes. And...?"

I told him what Frankie said about Hector and Gunner: that they should stay out of his business.

"So what business are they in?"

If he felt something, he didn't show it. Then he cleared his throat. "These are good boys, volunteering at the student center, and have chosen to help young boys in the neighborhoods get away from gang life, boys that are poor. So the seminarians bring them to the center where they can get some sustenance and some support." He paused, drumming his fingers against the glass desktop. "Now this is the last time I will talk with you about them. After all, they will be ordained as priests less than eight months from now."

I nodded. "Fair enough. I won't bother you again. But, I will..."

"Talk to the boys again," he finished.

I nodded.

"I'm just giving you fair warning—"

"Uh huh," I said, cutting him off at the warning. I was tired of threats.

When I left he was still seated behind his desk, the very one I had just searched. He never attempted to rise to shake hands or even to say goodbye. I'm sure he wanted to say, *Don't let the door hit you in the back,* but he didn't. He thought it though, I'm sure.

It was late afternoon when I climbed into my car again. My seat was warm. I checked the dash. The seat warmer icon was lit. I turned it off. The palms and oaks seemed taller now, leaving shadows behind them as the sun drooped ever so slowly into the horizon. It was cooler. The average temperature in southeast Florida in October is about seventy-five degrees in the day and sixty-five at night. Just right for All Hallows' Eve. And it felt like Halloween today, though it was still a week away. But I was out tricking and treating, getting no treats and looking to pull some tricks.

I watched the ghosts of the evening make headway into the day as the shadows from the oaks and palms grew even longer, turning from a light shade of gray, as the sun fell lower in the sky, to charcoal. Soon even these shadows would be swallowed up in the darkness. Just like my investigation that was gradually falling into the abyss of unsolved cases. It bothered me that I had so little to report either to Hannah or to Ned other than I have been hard at work.

And then there's Maxie—and Jillie—and my failure to help either one. Maxie who was still out there—dead or alive? Who knows? The only memories I have of my son these days are from my nightmares. And those have become more frequent lately.

CHAPTER 42

Where's Crane?

Same Day: Evening

My cell rang. "Cooper." I was almost at my house.

I looked at the clock on my dashboard. It was after 10:00.

"Gunner, here."

"Yeah?" There was trouble in his voice.

"I've been looking for Crane all afternoon. And I can't find him. Has he contacted you?"

"No. Why should he call me?" How strange, I thought. "He probably just took off for a few hours. I'm sure he'll be back."

"Not Crane. He's not that kind of guy. He doesn't go anywhere without one of us...I don't know." He was quiet for a moment.

"Somebody threaten you?" Just a hunch.

Silence on the other end.

Then, after a few seconds, "No. No problems. Just thought I would check in with you." I could hear him take a few breaths. He was working on relaxing.

"Thanks," he said and ended the call.

I stared at my cell for a few moments then put it down as I approached my home.

I put the call out of my mind. I would feed Sammy, pour myself a cold glass of wine—Columbia Crest H3 Chardonnay 2013, the best in my book at least for wines under sixteen dollars—and catch up on some quiet time in my hammock—the one that hangs near my dock, the one that swings not too far from where Herman, the gator, relaxes in the evening.

CHAPTER 43

Shark Valley

Saturday Evening, October 23

Solving a crime is a tedious affair. It begins in darkness, the path lit only by the clues that you find at the crime scene. Usually all you find there are some names, maybe find some evidence, like fingerprints which usually take weeks—maybe months—to track down. It begins at the scene, however. You get the victim's name, the names of the people the victim knew, like friends and family, and that starts the process going. Then bits and pieces begin to appear on your imaginary screen, like fragments of a puzzle embedded on the surface of your mind. Kind of like the stones on a climbing wall. You begin to ascend and each stone gives you a foothold that helps you climb higher. And you can only hope that at the top of this mountain you will have a better view of where you are and where you should go. I wasn't anywhere near the top—yet.

When I got back to my home on Shark Valley Road, I saw DeFelice's unmarked parked in front and a light in my living room. I knew Richie must have let him in since he would have the key. They were all there (that would be DeFelice, Richie, and Louise) in my kitchen drinking beer, DeFelice smoking a cigar, Louise waving the smoke away from her face and just about to complain.

"Come on in, Coop," said DeFelice. "Join us."

"Gee," I replied, "Thanks. Why don't you just make yourselves at home, have some beer, enjoy your cigar—stink up my whole house while you're at it."

"Hey, easy. We're guests here," said DeFelice, leader of the troublemakers.

I heard what they were talking about from the porch: *His cases ain't goin' nowheres* (DeFelice). *He's hitten' the wall (DeFelice). Happens.* Fact is, he was right. Hannah Miller and the Doughertys must be antsy about my lack of progress.

DeFelice had shut up when I came through the door. Then, "Hey the Fibbies are gonna touch base with you about the kidnapping. They wanna help." He was embarrassed.

"Uh huh. Like the IRS," I said.

I could save him the trouble and tell him: Nada! Zilch! Nil! Zero! I grabbed a beer and joined them.

"Not to worry, we'll talk to Casto and Juan again," said Louise, jumping in.

Louise works Oceanside as well as the South Miami PD region. Oceanside doesn't have the resources to cover special details like gangs, so Miami PD provides the personnel. Since she's a junior detective, DeFelice acts as lead in cases where he partners with her. If Casto or Juan were involved with the missing kid, it would be DeFelice and Delgado's case. Oceanside would be coordinating since the gangbangers were in their jurisdiction.

"I'll set up a meet for tomorrow," she continued. "Pick me up at the same place, the South Miami District Office, and we'll head over to Oceanside from there." She looked over at me. "Okay?"

I nodded and took a long drink from my beer. All that thinking about that glass of wine, out the window.

We talked late into the night. I finally hit the bed at 3:00 a.m. Everybody was still up, Richie and DeFelice gabbing on about the old days.

"Remember how we scared the shit out of Sonny?" Richie said to DeFelice, both of them laughing. Just a couple of old guys from the neighborhood.

Delgado must have left shortly after I turned in. I heard her goodbyes and then the screen door slam. I never heard DeFelice leave. I was long gone by then, dreaming of marshes and alligators and being chased all over the damn place by those primitive devils. And then of course, there were those never ceasing nightmares...

CHAPTER 44

The Meet

Sunday Morning, October 24

I got to the District Office by 9:00 a.m. and Delgado was waiting on the steps in jeans and a leather jacket. She looked good in the jeans; I knew how the boy gangbangers would react.

We talked as we drove, Delgado asking what was the latest. I filled her in on Gunner's call about Crane.

"That's strange," she said, and pondered that for a while. "Why'd he call you?"

"Good question. I don't know. Maybe they're in trouble."

"Uh huh. Maybe." She paused.

"What's Hector's last name?" she said.

"Why?"

"Just wondering."

"Ramirez," I said.

"Hmmm," she said.

"Hmmm?" I said.

"Ever since Juan mentioned his name as someone who might know about the kids, I've been wondering."

We were getting close to the Hole. Buildings were beaten up like old soldiers. Windows were splintered, plywood covered storefronts, bars blocked doorways, and cyclone fences surrounded houses. Mostly the fences were useless, large portions missing. If there was a gate it was hanging on one hinge. I shook my head.

"What?" she said, glancing over.

"We live in a different world. And—"

"We don't have any idea of how the other half lives."

"The other seventy five percent," I corrected.

"Right."

"So, why are you asking about Hector?" I continued.

She didn't answer right away. Then after a few moments:

"There was a Hector Ramirez—he would be about thirty-five now—who lived in Cartagena. His father was on the police force. A city cop."

I nodded.

"Hector followed in his father's footsteps and joined the force. The National Police not the city. My father was investigating Hector for corruption. Word was he was being paid off by local gangs and was cut in on the take from prostitution and drugs."

"Hmmm. But what are the chances?" I said to myself as much as to Louise. I studied the streets and the garbage that lay there and thought what a growing ground for drugs and selling sex.

"So maybe we get Interpol to check on Hector?" I said.

" I could do that. I've got a contact who can access the records quickly—kind of quickly," correcting herself. "You know how we define 'quick' in Law Enforcement?"

"No, tell me how we define 'quick' in Law Enforcement, Louise."

"You get the info while you're still alive," and she laughed. She looked over at me. I didn't react.

"You've got no sense of humor," she said, poking me in the ribs and shaking her head.

"Because that's a terrible joke," I said.

"How did you get a contact in Interpol?" I said, ignoring the ribbing.

"My father was killed in an Interpol investigation," she said, quietly.

We drove in silence past deserted, red brick apartment buildings and broken fire hydrants and black garbage bags and garbage that wasn't in a bag.

Finally, "So I need to send them something: DNA, fingerprints, photo. Who knows? Maybe you'll get a break in your case."

I nodded.

"A cigarette would work, right?"

"That would do it."

"If my Hector is the guy from Colombia, how in the hell would he have gotten into the U.S.?"

"Illegally, of course. The best way would be through the Everglades."

And I thought of Everglades City. A great place to land. Remote. Lots of water. Surrounded by the Ten Thousand Islands, where everybody is hiding from someone.

Everglades City Population 402

That's the sign that welcomes you to the town. The images of summers I spent there as a kid ran through my mind: the lighthouse at the entrance to the town, the playground in the city center, the little store with the sign—You're in Skunk Ape Territory—the Smallwood Store, and the waters of Chokoloskee Bay stretching into the Everglades and beyond through the Ten Thousand Islands.

It's not easy to forget a town so many criminals have called home, a town whose bay has welcomed pirates, smugglers, and drug runners. And the people who live there... they are good keepers of secrets. They could teach a priest the meaning of the Seal of Confession.

I needed to call Huxter Crow, an old friend who lives in Everglades City.

"Cooper, you still with me?" said Louise.

I turned. She was studying me like I had an illness.

I nodded. "Um. I'm here."

We got to the meeting place at 10:00 a.m. No activity in the schoolyard. A few cars parked helter-skelter on the asphalt, their windows and headlights smashed. No heads bobbing in the classroom windows. It was Sunday. Peaceful. And no sign of Juan or Casto.

"Hey lady," came a voice from outside the fence. A young Hispanic was motioning us from a park across the street. "Come on over here."

We left the same way we came in, through a hole in the cyclone fence. I wondered who this fence was supposed to keep out. The park where the kid waited for us was a mix of green and brown. All weeds. I had to walk carefully around the trash: empty coke bottles, feces—human or animal, I couldn't tell—McDonald's carry-out trays and a lot of other garbage and crap. An empty hull of an old bus sat on rusted wheels near the open doors of s storage barn. A cheap cavern of tin that at one time probably stored the buses for the school kids.

From there the neighborhood deteriorated even further. We passed abandoned apartment buildings, red brick with the mortar crumbling. Probably nice living in another era. Now just a smelly, decaying slum with blown out windows and doors hanging on hinges or missing entirely. Not a great place to spend an evening after a hard day at school.

I had strapped on my shoulder holster before I left home. I patted my Glock to make sure it was still there. Louise pulled her Glock, ejected the magazine, checked the load, slammed it back in place, and chambered a cartridge. The noise was sharp and loud in the empty space causing our leader to turn around and shake his head.

"Don' do that!" he yelled, his voice subdued but angry. "You make everybody nervous."

We were approaching a ten-story brick building on our left, the first in a row of multi-story red-brick structures that that lined the street on both sides as far as I could see. More deserted than a graveyard at midnight. The kid who was still about a hundred yards ahead stopped in front of the first building and turned around, arms folded and waiting.

When we got closer, he waved. "This way, police lady, don' worry, nobody gonna bite here," he said. "They inside. But you gotta leave your bang-bangs with me. Juan don' want no guns in his house, you got that?"

No way was I going there without a gun. I shoved past him and climbed the steps. Five. I counted them. Louise was right behind me.

"Whatcha doin', man?" the kid asked. "You can't go in there 'less you give me your guns. I tole you Juan don' want no guns in here. This is his house," and he grabbed at me as I got to the top of the stairs.

I swung around at him, jerked my arm away and bumped into Louise. "Easy," she said. Then, "Back off asshole," to the kid.

"Hey, your funeral gringo," and he stepped aside and gestured toward the open door. There was no door in the doorway, just an empty space leading into darkness and the stench of rotting food and urine and feces. So I entered the hallway clutching my nose and reaching for my Glock.

"Jesus," said Louise. "A real hell-hole," and she looked around at the garbage that littered the hallway and then at the stairs that led to the second floor.

"Where's Juan?" I said to the kid. He was still standing on the stoop outside the entry.

He pointed up the stairs. "Second floor, last room on the right. Good luck, homeboy."

"You're going to take us to him," I said, pushing him toward the stairs and up.

They say it's the ones you don't hear that you have to worry about. But I heard it, noises all around me, like rain pounding on the walls, but I realized it wasn't rain because...and then I was stumbling on stairs and the stairs were hard, concrete, and I tried to get my footing, but the walls were exploding around me, blowing white powder like flour tossed around in a kitchen and choking me, and I felt stings on my arms and legs, like bee stings, but my arms were bleeding, and then the kid fell into me and now we were both tumbling down the stairs and into Louise and she tumbled with us, and I wanted to apologize to her—for my stupidity—but the hall was spinning out of control and I sank into a whirlpool of darkness, and I heard the muffled cries of Louise and the kid, but I could do nothing about it.

CHAPTER 45

Dying

Monday, October 25

I remembered dying once. Only I didn't know I was dying. The only way I knew was because a priest visited me in the hospital said he had given me the Last Rites. I asked him why. He said because you were dying, informing me like I must have known it. I told him I had no idea and was he sure? The priest smiled at my question and simply said that I was a very lucky man and that the Sacraments had probably brought me back to life. It was then that I realized that dying wasn't so bad after all.

I thought of how Shakespeare described death as *knitting up the raveled sleeve of care,* of Raymond Chandler's, *The Big Sleep,* and of John D. MacDonald's, *Slam the Big Door.* Only I never heard any door slamming; I only felt the *Big Sleep* of Chandler.

I slowly rose from it to the angry voice of DeFelice and the concerned face of Richie. DeFelice's words made no sense, like the ramblings of a drunk, only he wasn't and I felt like I was.

"What the hell, Cooper, whaddya think you was doin', going in there like some kinda cowboy, risking your life—and Delgado's?" he added. I felt the guilt.

Then his face and words faded out, like a bad connection on a cell phone. *Then I saw Richie reaching for me and I drifted off again… or died…*

∽

Tuesday Night, October 26

It must have been hours later when I awoke again—or maybe days. It was dark outside with only the whirr of machines and blinking lights flashing in the darkness. I felt strapped down with hoses and bandages, but couldn't see anything. I called out for the nurse.

"Yes?" came a voice in the darkness? Then a shadow appeared in the doorway. "Mr. Cooper, I'm glad you're awake. I was worried about you," and she smoothed my sheets and straightened the pillows. "But you're doing better now, I see."

"How long have I been in here?"

"A little over two days. You were shot up pretty bad."

"But I'm alive, right?" I said, making sure I wasn't dreaming—or dead.

It felt strange to have lived in a semi-conscious state for days while the world went on. I was as good as dead during that time.

"I know you have a lot of questions, Mr. Cooper, but you're going to have to wait until tomorrow. The doctor will be in early," said my young caretaker, looking like a high school kid. She smiled at me.

"How's Ms. Delgado?" I asked.

"She's on the same floor and doing fine. She got shot up pretty badly too."

I asked about the kid. She said he died. Dead before he got to the ER. "Sorry about that," she said.

I said he wasn't any friend of mine.

"Nobody else came in with us?" I asked.

"No," she said.

But then again I never got a shot off, never even got my gun out of my holster. Looks like it was a one-way fight where the other guy came out clean. Couldn't say, "You should see the other guy!"

In the middle of the night, it came to me: who the gangbanger was. I thought back over the shoot-out in the alley, the baby-face kid I saw there, the one I figured was the new gangbanger, the one who shot little Darly. I was sure now that it was him. And so he got what he deserved after all. But I wouldn't tell Darly's mother. Nothing to be gained by that. Just raise old nightmares.

The pain came mostly when I moved and when I did I felt like I had lost my arms and legs. The medication helped me sleep. The pretty blonde nurse said that the doctor had taken three bullets from my body: two from my legs—one in each—and one from my right shoulder. I could feel the shoulder wound especially. I couldn't raise my arm at all and when I tried, it hurt like hell. My legs felt like someone had taken a sledgehammer to them. Another shell had grazed my neck and there was a ridge there to prove it. Other than that, I was alive. *Lucky to be alive*, the nurse told me. A lot of bullets flew around in that hall; amazing that one hadn't killed me. I wondered about Louise. And then my mind went blank again and my eyes were staring into pitch blankness—like a horse with blinders. Only I wasn't racing to any finish line.

CHAPTER 46

Visitors

Wednesday Morning, October 27

My room was full of visitors when I awoke. They were standing around me like statues at a casket viewing and I was the body on display. The faces didn't come clear right away. I was looking through pain, hearing only remnants of conversations, names tossed around like waves in a storm, whispers that I couldn't make out, nodding heads and bodies drifting in and out of view. A few words came through. Someone had died. A voice I didn't recognize was speaking. Was it Delgado? I struggled to raise myself up but couldn't. Someone put a hand on my shoulder and told me to rest. I fell back and tried to make out the face. It looked like DeFelice. He told me not to worry; it wasn't Delgado that had died. She was fine. He said it was Crane who was dead. I strained to focus. Crane?

An Oceanside cop had found him early in the morning in a car on College Street—near the seminary, one shot, middle of the head, like he was executed. No clues, nothing. Just another dead body piled up with the others. The voices kept murmuring. I think they were talking about me, but I couldn't tell.

In my dreams, that I experience fitfully during the day and at night, I am surrounded by voices, mostly those of clients who had died or who were still missing: of Hannah Brown whose eyes looked hopefully into mine for answers where there were none; of Michael Dougherty who searched my face for the same determination that he had to find his son before it grew too late; of Jillie who blamed me for our son's disappearance—and I could see it in her eyes— and I heard them at night—the voices—while I struggled to sleep and then, when I finally did sleep, I heard them in dreams, no, in nightmares, when sleep should have been a respite but was instead a prolongation of the hell that burned into my days.

I am convinced that the dead whose killers have never been found, haunt the lives of detectives like me, and together we roam empty streets lined with homes that are deserted and dark, some boarded up, others with windows peering out on the world through vacant eyes, revealing nothing that is hidden within. But the dead are drawn to them and they motion for me to follow—to search for clues that I know I will never find. And yet they hope—and I do also—that I will find something and that what I find will finally bring an end to their ordeal. And to mine.

CHAPTER 47

Crane is dead

Wednesday Afternoon, Oct. 27

"So Justin Crane is dead?" I asked in one of my lucid moments.

DeFelice nodded. I was feeling better, almost well enough to check out of the hospital. I had visited Delgado's room earlier in the morning. She was recovering. She took two bullets: one in the leg, another in her left buttocks. She was sleeping on her side when I saw her, protecting her bottom I supposed. The nurse told me she would be staying for a few more days.

"Crane is dead and the seminarians are scared shitless. Murphy wants to see you," DeFelice told me.

"You saw him?" I said.

"The rector?"

"No, Crane." I said. "How was he killed?"

"Already told you, bud. I guess you was in a coma." He paused, then, "Single shot to the head."

"Any ideas?"

"Looks like a professional hit."

"What does Richie think?"

"Same thing. Thinks a pro did it."

"Hmmm. Anything else?"

"Too clean for a gang killing." He paused. "Think we better talk to Frankie."

CHAPTER 48

The Uninvited

Thursday, October 28

It was early Thursday morning when Richie came to pick me up at Oceanside Memorial Hospital. Whenever I hear the word memorial, I think of someone who's dead. I wondered who was being memorialized. I was just glad it wasn't my name on the building. Cooper Memorial Hospital. I have to admit though, it does have a ring to it.

I still had dents in my shoulder where the bullet hit and exited the other side. Shells were from a .22. A bigger gun would have taken half of my shoulder with it. Two Oceanside cops stopped by my room and told me there must have been several shooters with all the bullet holes in me and in Delgado and in the kid and in the walls. They also said there was no sign of the gangbangers. Casto and Juan had disappeared, apparently, into the Hole. And nothing in the building except for garbage.

Freaking stinkhole, he had said. *So much debris around nobody's gonna find any clues, Cooper.*

We'll get the assholes, the fat cop told me, belly sticking out so far it almost pushed me out of bed.

So that was their big visit with me in the hospital. The fat guy telling me how he was going to get the assholes. His partner, a candidate for a Weight Watcher's Poster Boy, just nodding. *We'll pay those assholes back for shooting one of our own* (Louise), *for shooting up a private dick* (that one I didn't believe). He was cocky, like a big-shot homicide detective. I was glad when they finally left.

I talked with Richie about what the Oceanside cops said about the shoot-out, or should I say about the one-way battle at the OK Corral. Said I wasn't too confident about their investigation. Said we might need to do some investigating on our own.

"Fucking cops," was all Richie would say.

"Fucking cops? That's all you're going to say?"

"Hey, what else is there to say? Fucking cops. Says it all."

As we pulled into my house I noticed DeFelice's unmarked Taurus in the driveway.

So it was the three of us sitting around my kitchen table, drinking beer and eating fried salami sandwiches, something that Richie had prepared for my homecoming. I wondered when he would start cooking the red sauce.

Richie had taken off his silk jacket and laid it carefully across the dining room table. His white shirt, crisply ironed and starched, sported gold cufflinks. He pulled his tie loose, unclipped his cufflinks and rolled up his sleeves. DeFelice was still jacketed but looked like he had slept in it all night.

I was like the walking dead, my shoulder burning like it caught fire, my leg not as much. But the drink that Richie made helped ease the pain—dirty martini, lots of Grey Goose, huge green olives filled with blue cheese, chilled and shaken. So the conversation went on with me more as an observer than a participant. The sounds of their voices filled the spaces around me like ghosts whispering about their past.

"Christ, Coop," Richie said. "Whyn't you hit the sack. You look like shit. I'll keep this dago company," nodding at DeFelice.

I nodded and limped my way to the bedroom and the softness of the mattress. I must have fallen asleep because the murmurs stopped and all I heard was the sound of my own snoring, a sound that woke me up around 1:00 a.m. That wasn't the only sound I heard. I looked quickly from the alarm on my dresser to the clock on the TV converter. They both confirmed the time. I must have slept through the entire day and most of the evening. But in the dim light of the clocks I confirmed something else. There was somebody in my room. Whoever it was moved quickly and was on me before I could get off the bed. I felt a fire roar through my shoulder as I struggled with the man. His fingers worked like a vice against my throat and I knew he was cutting off the blood to my brain because the darkness of the night was turning inward and I felt myself begin to sink into black hole and so I swung blindly—hoping to contact something—and I heard a lamp crash to the floor...

And then, suddenly, my attacker's hands were gone from my throat, and his body lurched upward as if struck by a massive blow and then was heaved off me as if by some violent force. And when I finally shook off the black void that had taken over my brain, I saw a light and realized it wasn't the light at the end of the tunnel reported by people who have died and come back but rather the overhead light in my bedroom and a big man was lying on the floor and over him was Richie, a baseball bat hanging from his left hand and sweat pouring from his face and soaking his white shirt. He was breathing hard, like he was about to have a heart attack.

"Who's this idiot?" he asked pointing his bat at the body on the floor. A big man. Jet black hair, brown skin. Probably Hispanic. "And what the hell's wrong with him. Didn't he know I was here?" sounding insulted.

"He must have seen DeFelice leave and didn't figure anyone else was here, I'm guessing," I said.

The Oceanside police came within ten minutes of Richie's call. Must have been the persuasiveness of his tone that got them here so fast. It was our fat friend again with his skinny partner. This time they introduced themselves as Detectives Sandy Neumann and Randall Flagg. Flagg was the skinny guy. His face was a thing to behold—his skin pitted with acne overlaying the pits.

In the meantime the guy that jumped me was staring at the detectives and resting his bulk against the wall.

"So," said Neumann, "what happened here?" like he was going to take care of everything because he was so damned cool.

"I don't know," I said. "Somebody delivering a message." I had a good idea who it was.

"Hmmm…" said the fat man and turned to look at the heap leaning against the wall.

"Take that son of a bitch down to the station and lock him up —after you read him his rights—in Spanish," he said to his partner. "Find out what the hell he was doing here." He paused and turned back to me. "You talk to him, Cooper?"

"Do I look like I talked to him?" I said, pointing at my shoulder that was still bleeding.

"Better take care of that," he said. Then, "Maybe your new friends from the Hole are unhappy with you."

I nodded.

"I know you're a hot-shot ex-homicide cop from Miami, Cooper. But that don't mean shit to me. My take—you're a wise-ass private dick who's nothin' but trouble." Then he motioned to Flagg. "Let's get out of here." He paused and turned to me. "Maybe next time that son of a bitch will finish the job."

Richie grunted. Neumann turned his way, a question on his brow. Then he noticed the bat in Richie's hand and decided to let it go.

It was 3:00 a.m. when Flagg and Neumann finally left. Richie cut the ceiling light and I fell back into bed again, the burning pain in my shoulder failing to keep out the shadows of sleep. The next voice I heard was Gunner's, Richie holding the phone to my ear and lip-synching that the guy is panicked.

"You heard about Justin, Cooper?" He didn't wait for me to answer. "He's dead! Now I'm supposed go down to the morgue and confirm that it's him."

He said all that like he was on speed. I told him to slow down so I could get the whole story. He said, *Sure, sorry.*

"You have any idea why anybody would want to kill Justin?"

"No idea."

"None?"

"No." Silence.

Since the conversation was going nowhere, I suggested he come over to my place. Tell me everything.

"I'll put on the coffee," I said.

"Thanks. I'll be there—in one hour," he said.

"Alone," I said.

"Alone," he said.

CHAPTER 49

Get to the Bottom of It

Friday Morning, October 29

"So what's this 'alone' business, Cooper?" asked Gunner, peering over his coffee. "And what happened to you?" he added quickly, staring at my shoulder brace.

"I ran into some gangbangers," I said. "Maybe your friends?"

He stared at me. "No friends of mine. What are you talking about?"

"Maybe you can tell me." I paused. "I talk to two gangbangers about the killings of Ethan Miller and Tamara Thompson. What do they say? They tell me, talk to you guys. You tell me to talk to Frankie. I talk to Frankie. He tells me you're messing in his business. I talk to Trujillo, he says talk to you. Let me ask you this. How many people do I have to talk to before I figure you are somehow involved?"

Gunner didn't answer right away. He shrugged and leaned back in his chair—it's Richie's favorite—a Lazy Boy—so it caught Gunner off guard when the back gave away under his weight and he was staring at the ceiling.

While I had him on the couch, so to speak, I asked one final question,

"Who killed Crane?"

"Yeah," said Richie, suddenly emerging from the bedroom. "Who killed Crane?"

"Who's this?" said Gunner, staring at Richie who was now sitting down on the couch next to me. "I thought we were alone?"

"We are alone," said Richie, winking at me.

"Say hello to Richie," I said. "Believe me, you will need him."

Gunner looked stunned, then confused, then he shook his head. "Okay, okay," he said. "So...you want me to tell you who killed Crane?"

Gunner picked up his coffee, stirred it with his index finger, then dried it on a napkin. "I have no idea," he said, not looking up at first, then deciding to make eye contact.

"Why don't I believe you?" I said.

"Yeah," said Richie. "Why don't we believe you?"

Gunner sat back in his chair again—being careful not to tip it all the way back—and stared at me like he was deciding what to do.

"I asked you why you wanted me here alone," he said. "So why?"

"Because I don't trust Hector. I don't trust you either. But I trust him less."

He thought about that. Then, "We would like you to find out who killed Justin," he said. "That's why I'm here," and he looked from me to Richie as he said it.

"Why not the police?" I said.

"The police?" He paused. "Because we thought we might need some protection."

"Who's we?"

"Murphy, Joe, Hector and me," Crane's name conspicuously absent. "We can pay you," he added.

I told him I would consider it, but only after I had a chance to talk with the others. He agreed and said he would arrange for us all to meet later in the afternoon. I said I would look forward to it.

CHAPTER 50

The Meeting

Friday Afternoon, 3:00 p.m.

We met in the rector's office. I had brought Richie with me. Murphy had pulled six ornate straight back chairs into a semi-circle with him at one open end and me and Richie at the other. Hector sat next to Richie, Pacholewski and Gunner near the rector. Murphy was wearing his monsignor robes, black cassock with scarlet piping around the cuffs and hems. The blood red drapes, hanging over the windows behind his desk and flanking the two dark oak doors that served as the entrance to his office, matched his outfit. A four-foot gold cross with a figure of Christ hanging on it was suspended over a mantle. Christ was looking right at me. I felt guilty about something. I guess that was the idea.

"…and that is what we would like you to do, Mr. Cooper," Murphy concluded, leaning into the circle so he was directly facing me.

I stared at him, trying to figure out how to explain I hadn't heard him. I decided I wouldn't.

"So, Cooper, what about it?"

"A few questions," I said.

He nodded.

I turned to Hector who was leaning forward in his chair. "Who do you think killed Crane?"

He just shrugged, his long fingertips playing against each other rhythmically. "If I knew that, we wouldn't have asked you," he said, trying hard to be polite. The trouble with guys that try hard to be polite is that they can't carry it off. It would be better if they didn't try at all.

The rector, who was watching quietly, got up and walked slowly to the doorway where a long scarlet cord with a gold tassel hung and pulled it hard. A bell rang in the distance, then shortly—almost like a scene in a medieval play—a nun in black, her face framed in a white starched cotton cloth that looked unbelievably uncomfortable, appeared.

She might have said, "You rang?" but all she said was, "Yes, Monsignor."

"Sister, would you please bring our guests some tea and cookies."

I couldn't believe he said cookies. I mean, who eats cookies? Scones and bagels and biscuits—okay. But cookies?

"Water," said Hector.

"Water?" said the rector.

"I don't drink tea," Hector said. I wondered who was in charge here.

"So Cooper," Murphy said, turning his full attention to me now, "we need your help. Frankly, we are all…," and he looked around at the others, "afraid of what might happen next. In short, we would like to hire you to find Justin's killer. At the same time I would like you to offer us some form of protection from whomever it is that is threatening us."

"Is someone threatening you?"

"Enough of this crap," said Hector. "We don't need this guy. We can take care of this ourselves."

Richie cleared his throat. Hector looked over at him, then quickly back into the center of the room. For the first time I thought I detected uncertainty.

"Now, Hector," Murphy said, "we need Detective Cooper. And personally, I don't feel safe with a killer lurking about in the shadows." Then, as though that issue was settled, he continued, "Cooper, what can you do for us?"

"What makes you think the police can't help you?" I said.

"Frankly, we need protection as much as we need an investigation. But you could do both. I have enough money to take care of your fees and expenses—for weeks if necessary—as long as it takes to find the killer," he added quickly.

"Okay," I said. "But I can't be your bodyguard full time and investigate a murder." I paused. Murphy waited. "But I have someone who can help," I said, putting my hand on Richie's shoulder.

"Sounds great," said Joe Pacholewski quickly. "I don't know who in the h..." and he paused as Murphy cleared his throat, "heck is trying to kill us...but, uh...this is great," he finished, looking over at the monsignor for approval.

Murphy ignored him as though he were an after thought.

"So...please introduce your friend and tell us what he'll be doing?" Murphy said.

"I would like you to meet Richard Marino. Everybody calls him

Richie." I paused as the three sems and Murphy focused on Richie who was now looking uncomfortable.

Richie cleared his throat and shifted in his chair. Everybody was staring at him. I continued. "Richie is someone I would trust my life to—and I have. Besides, he's the best bodyguard in the country because nobody—and I mean, nobody— would fool with him."

There was silence in the room as Murphy and his boys studied Richie. Even Hector was quiet.

"I'm sure this gentleman will be fine—if you say so, Mr. Cooper. So let's consider it done," and he didn't look around for approval. "Just let me know your fee."

So I told him my fee. He nodded.

"Okay, so we're protecting you all and I'm looking for a killer," I said, looking around at each person. "One *caveat*," I continued, "don't tell the cops that. We can't be perceived as interfering with a police investigation."

I paused, waiting for a question. There wasn't one, so I continued.

"Then let's get started. I have a few questions." I turned to Hector. "Tell me about Juan and Casto," I said.

He looked surprised and glanced at Gunner. Gunner shrugged and nodded an okay.

I didn't have Delgado's report from Interpol but I thought I would take a chance. "You and Casto came from the same home town in Colombia, right?"

For the first time since I had met him, Hector looked unsure about what to say. I pressed on hoping it wasn't leading to one of those dead end roads.

"Cartagena is Officer Delgado's hometown by the way," I continued. He didn't respond to that either.

"Who's Officer Delgado?" said Hector. Sarcasm in his voice.

"Miami Homicide," I said. "She's helping me with the Miller killing."

He nodded. Indifferent.

"Something's not right here," I said, pressing on. "Ethan Miller—none of you ever saw him, right? A kid who worked as a volunteer at the center, and you never saw him?"

I looked around at two nervous faces and one blank one, Hector's.

"And you want me to believe that?" I said.

"Yeah, we want you to believe that. And I think we're done here," Hector said as he crushed his cigarette and rose to leave.

Richie, who was sitting next to him, grabbed him firmly by the arm and pulled him back down into his chair. I saw Hector struggle against Richie's grip without calling attention to it—but he was overmatched and gave it up.

"Stick around," I heard Richie say under his breath. Then he released Hector's arm. "Remember, I'm you're new bodyguard," he whispered, loud enough for all of us to hear. We all watched the two of them without saying anything.

Murphy, who had left his desk during the exchange came back with an envelope.

"This should cover your fee for a few days." He paused and glared at Hector who was still fuming in his seat. "You have to pardon him. He was raised in a depraved environment."

I nodded, took the check, and thanked him.

"So, Mr. Marino," the rector said, turning to Richie. "I can have a room set up for you here in the seminary. A faculty room, if that's okay."

"No thanks," said Richie. "I'm good. I got my own place."

"But how will you protect us if you're not here."

"Don't worry. I'll be here. You just won't see me."

"But—"

"And the bad guys won't see me either. Don't you worry," and he winked at me as we headed for the door.

I leaned over and picked up Hector's cigarette on the way out.

"I hope you know what you're doing!" Murphy called from behind us.

I waved on the way out the door. "Trust me. You're in good hands."

I dropped off Richie at my house so he could pick up his car and then headed to the hospital to visit Louise Delgado.

CHAPTER 51

The Hospital

I was at the hospital at 7:30 p.m. I took the stairs because it was after visiting hours. Louise was watching a rerun of a Miami/Clemson game. She looked pleased to see me and motioned to a chair near her bed.

She said, "So what've you got in that bag?"

"Chicken soup from Max's Deli. Fixes everything."

She smiled and reached for it.

"How am I going to eat it?" and she opened the bag. "Wow," she said, pulling out the carton. "There's two in here."

"Uh huh. One for you and one for me. Spoons and napkins in the bag." I paused as she laid the dinner on a table near her.

"Been a long time since someone brought me take-out. This a date?"

I smiled.

"Sit here," she said and nodded to the spot on the bed she had created by moving over.

"I heard Crane was murdered," she said as she began to spoon the soup to her lips.

"How did you hear that?"

"A little birdie."

"DeFelice?"

"Uh huh," she said. "Bring any crackers?"

I laughed and pulled some out of my pocket.

"So tell me more about Crane. Who do you think killed him?"

"I don't know. Maybe Casto and Juan."

"DeFelice said it looked like a professional hit."

"They could've hired someone. But my guess—they did it."

She nodded and spooned the last bit of soup into her mouth.

"Good soup, Coop."

"Aw. That's terrible."

She smiled. "Don't like my humor?"

I shook my head. Then, "I got a new client."

"Uh huh," and she waited.

"Murphy and his holy boys need protection. And they want me to find Crane's killer."

She whistled. "They give you big bucks up front?"

"They did. Hector didn't like it." I paused for a moment. "And talking about Hector, I picked up something for you when you're all better," and I pulled out the vial I had used to collect Hector's half-smoked cigarette.

"What is that?" she said, leaning in close to get a better look.

"What are you wearing?" I said, catching the odor of her perfume.

"A bathrobe," she said, smiling.

"I mean...You know what I mean," I said, embarrassed.

"Michael Kors. Like it?"

"I do," I said, enjoying the nearness of her. "And by the way," and

I passed her the vial with the cigarette butt, "you've got some DNA and some prints."

"Let's hope it's a good sample," she said, setting the vial carefully on the table.

"I'll give it to DeFelice—since you're temporarily indisposed—he can have the prints lifted. Okay?"

"Yeah. Good idea. Then I'll have my contact run the DNA through his data base." She paused. "Do those guys know you might be investigating them as well?" still staring at the cigarette butt, then looking up.

"Be one of my surprises."

She was beginning to look tired. I took her hand and held it, studying one of the tubes that was running to a bag suspended from a pole at the side of her bed.

"I'm sorry about all this," I said, gesturing at the tubes, the IV bags, the bandages. "I should never have involved you."

"Forget it. It's what I do." She tried to look strong.

"First time you've been shot?"

"Yeah," biting down on her lower lip.

I leaned over, carefully moving an IV out of the way, and put my arms around her. "It's okay," I said. "You'll be out—soon."

Her face was buried in my shoulder. I held her quietly.

"It's depressing to be in here," she continued, lifting her head, dampness forming around her eyes.

"I know," I said and leaned to kiss her on the cheek. She turned her face toward me and I kissed her lips instead and we stayed like that until...well until we didn't...and that was a long, long time. I finally pulled away after a few minutes—maybe longer—and then I got up, still holding her hand.

"Surprised?" she said.

"At least, "I said.

Then that serious look again. "What's up?" she said.

Right now I've got to get a bodyguard."

"For who?" she said.

"For the rector and his holy boys."

"Who're you going to get?"

"Richie."

"Tell him I said, *Hi.*"

"I will," and I leaned over and kissed her again.

CHAPTER 52

Fingerprints

Friday Evening, 8:00 p.m.

I couldn't believe what had happened as I climbed into my Volvo. Louise was a cop, not a girlfriend. What was I thinking? And what about Jillie? I hadn't dated since our divorce. We separated because of what happened to Maxie, not because we didn't love each other. Love had nothing to do with it. Blame was what it was all about. I pulled out my cell still thinking of Louise and the look on her face when I leaned down to kiss her, and called Huck, a friend of mine in Everglades City.

"Hey Huck." I paused. Dead air. "Is this Huck?" I tried again.

Someone answered but I could hardly make out what he was saying.

Then, "Who's this'?" a man answered, like *Who the hell is this?*

"It's Cooper, old buddy. Relax."

"The last time you called the coyotes were howlin' at the Black-berry Moon." That would be mid-summer in Huck's world.

Huxter Crow claims that his great grandfather was Seminole, a survivor of the Indian Wars that ultimately drove his tribe out of south Florida. His great grandmother—he claims—was Miccosukee, a tribe who runs the Miccosukee Resort and Gaming Casino in the western suburbs of Miami.

"So, my friend, who comes and goes with the wind, what brings you to call me on this Friday evening at the end of October when the Falling Leaf Moon is about to rise?" Another lesson in Miccosukee lore.

"I need some information...and maybe a bodyguard," figuring I would need Richie's help with the gangbangers.

"A bodyguard? For you?"

"No, for a client. You interested?"

No response for a moment. Then, "Why don't you come on over and have a sit down. We'll have a beer, get caught up, and watch the moon from my backyard."

"It'll take me about an hour and a half to get there. Make sure that beer's cold."

I called DeFelice—at home, since it was late.

"Okay, what's it this time?" His first words.

I heard someone yelling at him in the background.

"It's some asshole asking for a donation for the Police Athletic Association," he yelled back at the voice. "Dad wants to know who's the asshole calling this time of night," he said when he came back on. "So whaddya need?"

"I need some help with a case."

"What kind of help?"

"Fingerprints."

"Fingerprints? What am I, *CSI Miami*?"

I told him about my visit with Murphy and Hector and the possibility that Hector might be a bad guy from Cartagena who ran a prostitution ring there. "I've got his fingerprints," I said. "And seeing as Louise is hung up in the hospital, I was hoping you could help out."

He was quiet for a few moments. Then, "Okay, drop the damn thing off."

I thanked him.

DeFelice's dad answered the door when I knocked.

"It's late!" he yelled. "If you need police protection you should wait till the morning, young man."

DeFelice showed up behind him. "It's okay, Dad. It's a friend," and smiled, gently laying a hand on the old man. I think it's the first time I had seen him smile in a long while.

DeFelice looked tired, not that it was unusual for him, bags under his eyes and lines running down his cheeks and into the hollows, making him look older than his forty three years. A cop's life is a hard one, especially if you have to take care of a parent—and no wife to help out.

"You wanna come in for a beer?" he said. He was hoping.

I told him I was headed to Huck's place and he said, *Oh. Tell that old hillbilly I said hey* and what was I going to his place for. I explained briefly and then filled him in on Louise's plan to run the prints through Interpol and that's what we needed the prints for and, oh, by the way, maybe he could stop by the hospital and drop in on Delgado.

"Yeah, yeah, sure," he said quickly. Then, "Man, I really blew it with Louise—you know, I'm all caught up with taking care of the old man. But don't worry. I'll get in to see her."

I handed him the vial with the cigarette.

"I suppose these are the prints," he grunted.

"That they are."

"That man still here?" called a voice from inside.

DeFelice shrugged. "The old man's losin' it, Coop." He paused and looked in the direction of the voice. "Least I can do is keep an eye on him," still staring down the hallway. "But he's no trouble," he added quickly, looking back at me and nodding.

I nodded back, patted his arm and headed out. I hated seeing him like this, his energy worn thin, his face showing it. DeFelice hesitated in the doorway, and watched me get into my car. He finally closed it with a wave as I pulled away.

CHAPTER 53

Huxter Crow

I was on Route 41 in twenty minutes and on my way to Everglades City. Old Route 41 that runs between Miami and Naples is a lonely, dark, and forbidding road to travel at night, no lighted rest areas along the way, no gas stations, no restaurants or stores, no tourist stops, no houses anywhere for about fifty miles, just one small diner near the beginning of the highway and a place to rent airboats and explore the waters. There is only the Everglades and it stretches for about fifty miles to the west, and it's completely black. So the trick is not to get stuck out there in the middle of the night, and not enough crazy people drive that highway at night, so if you do get stranded, there is no one to help. And there are thousands of gators in the swamp, and some crocodiles—that's right, crocodiles—and they're protected—but that doesn't help the stranded traveler who might run into one on the highway—late at night—walking across the road—just when you've broken down. And then there are Burmese Pythons, and the water moccasins, and panthers (they're protected also), and coyotes, and maybe even some wolves and wild dogs. In other words it's not a place I like to drive at night. And besides, the gators scare the crap out of me.

I tried not to think of that as I sped along in the deepening dark of the evening. In a little under an hour I came to Route 29, a highway that runs south to Everglades City and eventually to Chokoloskee, a small island at the southern end of the highway and a convenient landing place for pirates, bootleggers and all kinds of criminals.

I turned left—there's a gas station there, one of the few signs of civilization along 41—and headed south past a long stretch of marshland. Palms and marsh grass grow densely along the road, the grass spreading out into the Great Swamp itself like a field of uncut hay along a highway in Iowa farmland. The waters of Chokoloskee Bay opened up on the right and a mile or so ahead I could see the first lights of Everglades City emerge over the water. There's a small stone bridge at the entrance to the town and on the other side of the bridge, a bill-board sized welcoming sign, *Everglades Isle*, and after that an old lighthouse that adjoins a relatively modern motel. It sits just off the bridge to the right and just before downtown Everglades City.

Everglades City is not really a city, it's a small town, five hundred and thirteen people to be exact, as of the 2004 census. I know that because I look up stats on small towns, having grown up in one in southern Ohio—before my family picked up and moved to Cleveland.

I passed one of the city's better motels, one of the few actually, The Everglades City Motel on Collier Avenue (Route 29), a landmark in these parts. Huxter lives in a stilt house just off the water near a popular bar/restaurant, The Oyster House, famous for its stone crabs, when they're in season, and, as the name implies, for its oysters.

I pulled into his drive, little more than sandy ground with some gravel thrown in, and turned off the lights.

"You drive fast, buckaroo," said a voice from the dark. I looked around and Huck was already at my car opening the door.

"Damn, you scared me to death, Huck! Where the hell'd you come from?"

"There's a big gator down there," he said, pointing to the water in the bay directly behind his house. "He's always raisin' a fuss with the stray dogs. I went over to chase him away."

"You're looking forward to the season, aren't you?" I said.

Once every so often the State of Florida declares an open season on gators. Huck has an alligator gun that he keeps polished just for those times.

"Come on in. Let's get ourselves a brew," he said.

I followed Huck under his house and up a set of stairs centered among the pilings that supported its frame. They seemed to lean a little. I wondered if he ever noticed.

Huxter lives among artifacts that characterize his life: an old bow hanging on a wall, a full quiver there also, a dozen or so old shotguns, rifles, handguns, knives with carved handles, a picture of a panther, some gator skins hanging out drying over the back porch rail, and a history of his tribe traced on a wall-sized map in the living room. He's explained that map to me through the smoke of his pipe on countless evenings, while the moon rose over the swamp and the sounds from the Sea of Grass traveled like the whispers of a thousand story tellers as though they were imitating Huck himself and I was just another listener, sitting cross-legged in front of another teller of stories.

In Everglades City Huck is recognized as one of the original crackers, a man whose ancestors staked out their land in the Great Swamp more than a hundred years ago: his great grandfather, a Seminole, and his great grandmother, a Miccosukee, living by their wits, trapping and hunting in the Glades. And Huck bore the signs of that struggle himself: deep-set wrinkles cutting a path down his cheeks and his skin hardened and darkened by decades of working under the sun. Around town there is talk that he's a little mad. But if you get to know him, you will understand that what appears to be madness is really only the outpouring of a philosopher who grew up in the tumult of life in the Everglades in the late 19th and 20th centuries: the scalawags, the pirates, and the drug runners who made the territory the most lawless in the country.

Huxter has never really been one of them. But he had to live among them. He married a young Seminole woman when he was nineteen. She was eighteen. They had one child, a son who died of a lung disease when he was seven. His wife died in childbirth three years later. The girl was stillborn. Huxter vowed never to marry again and he kept his promise, though he has been known to keep the company of women from time to time.

And that's Huxter Crow. Right now he was staring at his map and wanting to tell me his story all over again, but I stopped him.

"A bodyguard. I mentioned I need a bodyguard," I said. It took a moment for him to come back from the map.

"That's right. You did say that, Kemo Sabe. And I understand it's not for you."

"That's correct," I said

So I spent the next ten minutes or so filling him in on the two cases I was working and ending with my meeting with Murphy and his seminarians. "And now, one of them is dead. Bullet to the head. Professional—my guess."

He nodded. "And so...you need your old partner to help out?" More of a statement than a question.

Huck and I have known each other for at least six years, beginning with my time working homicide with Miami PD. He helped track a killer who had fled to the Everglades. Huck wrestled him to the ground and hog-tied him with a whip he used to herd cattle. Man threatened to sue. Huck said *If you do, I'll come a huntin' for you.* The man never did.

"So you want me to bodyguard some sem...itarians?" he said, struggling with the word.

"The rector of the seminary, Monsignor Murphy, and three of his students. They're called seminarians," I added.

"That's a strange word, Cooper. Sounds like they're from a cemetery.

"Anyway, they'll need your help. Are you good with that?"

He contemplated his map while the darkness outside grew deeper. He nodded. "I'll do it. I will keep the evil spirits of the Great Swamp away from them—"

"...and the bad guys that are trying to kill them," I added.

"When do I start?" he said.

"When the sun rises over the Great Swamp—"

"Enough, Kemo Sabe. You disturb the power of nature when you doubt my powers to summon the spirits of my dead ancestors," and he was very serious.

Then he sighed and asked if there was anything more I wanted of him.

"What are you hearing about smuggling down this way?"

"Let's get you a drink first," he said, heading toward the fridge.

"Make mine wine—a dry, if you've got it. Not red," I added. "It'll put me to sleep and you—you won't be fit to drive me home."

"About your question...," he began, handing me my wine then sitting in a high backed cane chair with his back to the bay window.

Lights from a lone boat in the bay flitted in the darkness like stars lost in the vast sky.

"Recently, there has been some activity down here, I'm talkin' down Chokoloskee way. You know the Smallwood General Store and Museum?"

I nodded.

"Well, some go-fast boats been docking illegal over there. Matter of fact, I called the sheriff about it. He told me they probably went up to the gas station, got some donuts and java, and called it a day."

"Go-fast boats?" I said.

"Yeah. Like Baias. Suckers blew the ears out of poor old Mutt over there," pointing at a brown mongrel lying by slide doors that overlooked the water.

"Do you have any idea who owns them?"

"No. But the drivers—they were fancy dressers—maybe Colombian." He paused and shrugged. "Nobody I ever seen before."

"Think they were just getting coffee?" I asked.

"I don't think so. And they sure ain't local."

In Everglades City if your name isn't Brown, or Smallwood, or Hayward, then you're not local.

"Another drink?" he said, moving toward the fridge, which looked more like an old icebox. I nodded.

He grabbed another beer, brought over the bottle of wine, and refilled my glass, an old Mason jelly jar.

So we sat and drank. I nursed my wine since I had a drive ahead, and Huck nursed about a dozen beers, a few over his limit.

"I'll get you pictures of those boats—and the guys that drive them," he added, tipping his bottle at me. "And I'll find out who owns those canoes."

I thanked him and told him I had to go. I don't like driving Old Route 41 late at night.

The gas station on Route 29 was dark when I passed it. I swung right on 41 toward Miami. A deep, dead darkness hung over the highway. As I said there are no lights along that road, just the moon hanging over the swamp like a lantern over foggy London streets.

I hurried along, focusing on the centerline, waiting for the faint glow of approaching headlights. No such luck. I refused to look into the trenches on either side of the road. I knew what I would see there. When you approach Miami from the West, you can see the faintest glow in the southeastern sky. It begins about twenty miles or so from the city and then slowly intensifies as if the sun were rising over it. Only it's 11:15 p.m., hours from the rising sun.

My house was just a short distance away as I approached Midnight Drive. From there I would turn south. Shark Valley would be on my right.

CHAPTER 54

The Sauce

Late Friday Evening, 11:55 p.m.

I smelled the sauce as I was pulling in. It reminded me of late Sunday mornings in Cleveland when I would be at Richie's house and his father was up since three in the morning cooking sauce and meatballs. His father usually had friends over for his weekly Sunday spaghetti meal, friends whose names you would read about in the papers, who were being investigated by the police or under a grand jury indictment. The men would sit in the living room talking business while the women stayed in the kitchen fussing around with plates and gossiping as Richie's dad complained, *Can't you see I'm cookin' here!* Richie and I were allowed to be there if we kept our mouths shut. We did and I learned a lot in that kitchen.

"So Cooper, whatcha you been up to?" called Richie as I came in the door.

I told him I had just been to Huck's.

"Yeah? What did he want?" Richie and Huck fight a lot.

Then, before I could answer, "Let's get you something to eat here, buddy. Sit down," pointing to a chair at the kitchen table. "Try this," putting a small plate of pasta with red sauce and meatballs in front of me. He gave me a napkin. "Put this on. Keep the gravy off your shirt." Then he sprinkled some freshly grated Pecorino cheese over my plate.

I dug into the pasta with a spoon and fork. "Talking about body-guards—how are your charges doing?" I asked.

"I put them to bed nice and cozy. Didn't see no bad guys, so here I am!" and he held up his hands like, Voila! "Gotta get somebody else to do this work though. You and me's got some business to take care of with Frankie and his boys."

"Talked with Huck about helping with that," I said.

"That crazy Indian?" taking off his apron, already stained with the gravy he warned me about. "You gotta be kiddin." He was looking over at me from the stove where he was dishing himself some pasta.

"He'll be fine," I said, ignoring his mood. Like I said, Richie doesn't like Huck. Or pretends he doesn't. I'm figuring the latter. "Meantime, Richie," I added, trying to get his mind off Huck, "let's talk about Frankie."

He nodded. "Damn Indian."

CHAPTER 55

The Man From Cleveland

Saturday Morning, October 30

We both turned in after 3:00 in the a.m. after a long reminiscence about everything under this earth's sun—including Frankie D'Amico and his possible involvement in the killing of the Miller and Thompson kids and the disappearance of the Dougherty boy. None of the clues pointed his way, but somehow, his competition with the gangs for territory and his...I don' know...his nasty temper, made me want to suspect him.

And then someone was shaking me.

"Come on, Cooper. It's 10:00 o'clock," said Richie. "We're gonna visit Frankie." As I tried to clear my head I could still smell the sauce and meatballs and the bread Richie had made.

The drive from my house to Frankie's Place is only about twenty minutes, but in traffic it can be an hour. Except on a Saturday morning, everybody's sleeping in from the long workweek. So there's no early morning traffic, except for the poor guys who pulled weekend duty, or the birds from the Everglades crossing the road. They usually slow the trip since everybody wants to save the wildlife, though I don't think Richie much cared.

Frankie's Place was quiet when we got there. No valet parking this morning. The kid I gave a fiver to watch my car must have stayed out all night. Too early to go to work. I left the car at the curb, unlocked. Seeing a man with a ball bat in the back seat is protection enough.

A muscle man was sitting just inside the door. He barely looked up when we passed him.

"Where's Frankie?" said Richie.

"Inna back," he said, his arms busting out of his suit jacket. "You Richie?"

"You got it," said Richie. Short sentences. Makes it easy for kids to understand.

Frankie and a bulky, bald man came from the back room. "Richie," said the big man with Frankie, holding out his arms like they were best friends.

"Check him," Frankie said to the man at the door.

The big man—the bald one—shook his head. "No need to check nobody. I know dis guy. So, Richie, what's happening?"

Richie shrugged. "Good to see you Big Al," and they hugged— like Italian guys do, pounding each other on the back like they're old friends—which as a matter of fact they were. Frankie stared at them. A new respect in his eyes.

"Come on. Let's find a table," Big Al said, and motioned to the rear of the restaurant where the tables were crowded into a corner far from the front door. Like he might be expecting someone to bust in and let loose. Kill everybody in sight. Two more guys came out of the back room. Sat down at a table on the opposite side of the room, watching Richie and me.

Richie turned to Big Al. "First, I want to thank you for comin' today. I know you's a busy man. But we got a problem here. First off, your boy Frankie here trows my friend Cooper outta his place and then, if that ain't enough, sends his goons over to threaten him— thing is one of them gets shot by his own stupid partner." He paused to let that sink in.

"Then, some guys in a local gang shoot up a cop and my friend Cooper here and the cops don't do nothin' about that.

"Then, we got us a dead semetarian—probly a hit, and on top of that two young kids were killed near here and on top of that we got us a seven-year-old missing kid," said Richie, shaking his head like he was counting up the bodies.

Then he held out his arms, hands turned up. "So Johnny and me is wondering if yous guys had anything to do wit *any* of this?" He paused. "Just for the record. You know what I mean?"

"First off, Richie. You know I love you like a son. But between you and me, Johnny don't have nothin' to do with what we do down here in Florida. Cleveland is Cleveland and Miami is Miami. But since I got a lot of respect for you, tell you what I'm gonna do. First, let me say we got nothin' to do with no missing kids, death of no seminarians. Hell, why we would we want to kill boys who want to be priests—I was an altar boy—Jesus, Richie. And no shootings of no young kids!

"Second, I talked with Johnny before yous got here and I tole him I'm gonna help you with these things." Then he nodded at Frankie. "Frankie here is gonna help you find out what the fuck is going on. You think we want this crap goin' on in our territory? Fuckin' gangs. Forget the cops. Frankie's gonna set up a meeting with some people in the neighborhood, see what we gotta do to get to the bottom of this. Meantime, let's get some fuckin' food over here, Frankie. Richie's gonna waste away here soon, eh, Richie? And, by the way, where's the wood?"

"Out inna car. Just waitin' for one of them spics to fuck with me."

The food was typical Italian: homemade pasta and meatballs, roasted sausage with onions and peppers—homemade—garlic bread, and salad served on the same plates as the pasta. Somehow it all works together. And, of course, a hearty Chianti. By the time we were done eating, the plan was completed. Frankie would go with us back into Oceanside where we had the shoot-out. He would bring along the two guys at the table watching us as shooters. *No screwin' around with them bangers*, he said.

Frankie looked at Richie and asked him if he had enough guns. Richie said yeah and a couple of bats in the trunk.

Big Al said, "We done here?"

"We are and thanks," I said. Richie grunted.

"Okay. Tomorrow," and he dug into the spaghetti and meatballs like he hadn't eaten in weeks.

Richie drove home. We left Frankie's late—the sun had already set and the gas lamps along the streets of the West End were coming to life. I had time to think since neither of us felt like talking.

The way seemed clearer now, traces of light creeping in where it was so dark only days before. Sometimes I think I hear the voices of the dead speak to me—like Ethan Miller's or Tamara Thompson's. I am grateful that I don't hear Maxie's. And I listen to them for clues. But lately they have told me nothing. And sometimes I wonder if those voices aren't of my own making and that I'm simply walking a path created by my own hopes and imaginings and that, in the end, I am only feeding a fire that is burning inside me and consuming all of my energy.

When we got to my house, Richie took the car to the gas station down the road and filled up. I went in and began to prepare. I broke out the cleaning equipment and the guns that Richie had brought. We had fired them at a range earlier in the week and cleaned them. But I figured I would clean them again. Besides it calms me to feel the smooth metal in my hand.

I broke out the Glock19 9mm with night sights. I went outside to my own personal target range that I had set up in the backyard. I had placed a Yule log about three feet in diameter and four feet long on a miniature trestle near a shed. At night the only light to shoot by was a single bulb sticking out of the shed's wall just above its entrance. But that wouldn't be a problem—because of the night sights. I emptied the entire magazine, clustering the shots within the 9 and 10 circles of the target (10 being the bull's eye).

Then I tested the Browning HP JMP 50^t. It's a 9mm gun that holds a baker's dozen. Both the Glock and the Browning have a kick to them when you fire. So part of the trick to hitting the target is keeping the recoil under control. I managed to put six rounds from the Browning within the outer ring of the target at twenty feet. Not bad for night shooting. And no night sights.

"Hey, Cooper, whatcha doin?" called Richie as he stepped out of the Volvo. "Shootin' up the neighborhood."

CHAPTER 56

Halloween

Early Sunday Morning, October 31

The two guys from Frankie's Place knocked on the door at 6:30 a.m. Frankie was in his black limo waiting. "Jesus, guys, we ain't even had breakfast," Richie complained. They nodded and pointed to the limo. "Okay, okay, we'll be right out," he said, standing there in his silk pants and white cotton tee shirt, no shoes. He closed the door, shaking his head. "No rest, Cooper." His stomach was hanging over his pants until he noticed me looking at it and quickly pulled it in. "Gonna start workin' out when I get back to Cleveland."

The morning was cool with a mist hovering over the streets. It cast a shroud around the lamps that light the roads that lead south to Gangland, an area in Oceanside that has no official name. It's a wasteland of deserted houses and abandoned cars that garbage men call the Hole. They never go there to pick up trash because the garbage is in the streets, it's lying in the gutters, it's on the steps leading up to the front doors of the apartment buildings that line the crumbling sidewalks, it's in the hallways where kids in diapers play, it's in the playgrounds where the rusted jungle gyms rest on bent legs, where the swings hang by one chain and the slides don't slide anymore. It's everywhere. It's why they call it the Hole.

We got to Gangland in the early morning, just as the sun was rising. Shadows cast from buildings were long across the streets covering for the moment the filth that lay there. The short man parked the limo down the street from the apartment building where the shooting took place. I wasn't happy about being there again.

We walked down the street, shoulder to shoulder, Richie in a dark blue silk suit, looking like he's a legitimate businessman; the tall man in a black suit, white shirt and red power tie, black shoes polished; the short man with a Burberry raincoat over a suit—it was cold for an October Miami morning—and me in a brown leather jacket and jeans, the Glock stuck in my belt in the back of my jacket and the .38 in my shoulder holster. Richie had the Browning in his belt and a .38 in his holster. The tall man had a machine pistol in his left hand. It was hanging freely at his side. In the open. The short man had a seven shot 12-gauge under his coat. Frankie was carrying, but I couldn't see what.

As we approached the building we spread out, the two men and Frankie followed the alley around to the back of the building, Richie and I stayed in front. There were no sounds from inside. Richie motioned us up the stairs, five in all. I counted them. I took them in two strides and leaned against the outside frame when I reached the top. The front door was still broken and ajar, the windows on both sides of the doorframe, running from top to bottom, were broken as was the transom above.

Richie pushed the door open and looked quickly inside pulling his head back immediately. He motioned that the hall was clear and stepped inside. I remembered the stench. It creeps into your nose and penetrates your lungs, like gas settling over a battlefield. Only there's no mask to pull over your face.

The morning light barely penetrated the hallway, but still I could make out the bodies of rats. They were half eaten by decay—and maggots. There were empty food containers, cups, and paper plates strewn everywhere and covered with dirt that had piled up from what looked like months of living. Busted lights lined the ceiling—a working bulb here and there. And there were torn clothes, filthy and stinking, lying in little piles waiting for a washer that didn't exist. And at the end of the hall, standing in the shadows, was a man, watching, but not moving.

"What the hell" whispered Richie, pulling his Glock. The man didn't move. "Yo," the man called out "Whatcha want?"

"Juan," Richie called back. And we headed down the hall toward him.

The shadow man shook his head and shrugged.

"You got any money?" as we got closer.

Richie looked at me. "You got any money?"

I looked in my wallet. A ten-dollar bill flanked by a bunch of ones. I mean who carries cash? I handed the ten to Richie.

The man looked at the ten. "That's all you got?"

I shrugged.

Richie pulled out a wad of cash in a money clip and handed the man a twenty that quickly disappeared in the man's pocket. He was wearing military style pants and a dirty tee. His arms were skinny and covered with needle marks, patches of black and blue where he had shot up too many times.

"They're up there," the man said, pointing to the stairs and then laying a dirty finger on the side of his face as though considering if he should have asked for more money.

"Hey, what's up?" whispered Frankie as he rounded the corner followed by his two boys. The short guy was breathing like he had climbed stairs. "Had trouble with the damn door. Shorty had to force it," said Frankie, staring at the gangbanger next to me.

"He says Juan's upstairs," I explained.

"Don't you warn him," Frankie said, grabbing the skinny guy behind his neck.

The man nodded and disappeared into a room behind him and closed the door.

"So here's the plan." I paused and pointed down the hall where Richie and I had entered the building. "There's access to the second floor from there. Richie and I will go up that way. How about you and..." I paused looking at the tall man,

"Mikey," Frankie said.

"Take these stairs," pointing up the stairway where the man in shadows had just been standing. Frankie nodded.

"And let..." looking over at Shorty.

"Shorty," said Frankie.

I stared at him. "Shorty? Okay, Shorty, take the fire escape." I had noticed one outside a window in the hallway where Frankie and his boys had just come in.

"Saw it," said Shorty.

"That way we come in from three directions."

Frankie nodded. "Like Custer," he said.

"Yeah, except it didn't work for Custer," I reminded him.

"Question is, how many guys we dealing with here?" said Frankie.

"I don't know. At least two," figuring Juan and Casto. "Probably a few more."

"Okay," said Frankie, "let's go up and find out."

So Frankie and Mikey started up the stairway while Shorty headed for the fire escape. Richie and I headed back down the hall and started up the front stairs. The stairway reeked from the acrid stench of urine. I stepped carefully trying to avoid the human waste scattered in the dirt and trash.

"Jesus," said Richie, shaking his head. "Guys are animals."

At least the steps didn't creak, the reason being there was concrete under the dirt and trash that covered them. A lucky break.

There were two flights in all leading to the second floor. At the first landing we paused, pulled our guns, and climbed the remaining way. At the top of the stairway a metal door hung from a rusted hinge. I was at the doorway first and peeked quickly into a dimly lit hallway. The same stench of human urine from the stairs drove me back, only now it mingled with the smell of decaying meat. Since no one had shot at me the first time, I checked again. There were dead rats on the floor, several of them decaying already; and empty McDonald's bags, food falling out of them, smashed into the floor; and empty beer cans and wine bottles; and needles lying around.

I stepped into the hallway, Richie right behind me. A lone light stuck out of a socket in the middle of the hall. Rooms lined either side. Some had doors, others didn't. And there was another odor: body sweat, like from a men's locker room. And then there was the silence...

"That you, pendejo?" Somebody told. The voice was Juan's. "Whatcha want?"

"We need to talk."

"No problem. Whyn't chu come on down. Third door on the right."

A man stepped into the hall and fired. He missed. Another man came out of the same room behind him and fired also. By that time Richie and I had ducked into an open door. What neither one saw was Frankie who had just entered the hall from behind them. And he and Mikey shot them both. And then the hall was quiet again. That is until Shorty smashed a window at the end of the hall with the butt-end of his Mossberg and climbed through.

Then I heard a baby cry.

CHAPTER 57

Finding Juan

The cry came from across the hall. A door hung loosely by one hinge across the opening to the room, leaving a small triangle of space through which to enter or exit. It was quiet now. I approached the door carefully, staying to one side. It was the same room from where I had heard Juan call out my name.

"Come on out," I said, breaking the silence.

"Chinga usted!" Back at me.

"We just killed two of your boys."

I watched Richie and Frankie clearing the other rooms. Nothing.

"Come on out," I said again. I waited. Then, "Or we're coming in."

I motioned for Shorty. He pumped a shell into his Mosberg, the sound echoing through the hallway.

"Knock down that door," I said.

He did. The 12 Gauge blew the door clear into the room. It fell flat against the floor, dust and the smell of powder from the shotgun filling the space.

"Lemme in there," said Mikey, pushing around the short man into the empty doorway.

And as he said it, he fell back. I don't remember hearing the shot. But I watched Mikey fall to the concrete and grab at this shoulder, blood already spilling over his hand.

I grabbed Shorty's shotgun, pumped a shell into the chamber and fired into the room, the noise exploding into the space.

"Okay, *pendejo*. We comin' out," Juan yelled through dust and smoke.

The first one through the door was a young girl. She was crying and holding a baby—the baby was crying also. Richie pulled them to the side. Then Casto came out, his arm covering his eyes and coughing. After him, two other guys emerged through the smoke. They stopped momentarily and stared at the two bodies sprawled behind us in the hall.

"Qué chingados!" is all Juan said, when he pushed through the two guys in front of him and stopped maybe a foot from me. He surveyed the hall like a defeated man, his shirt and arms splattered with blood. Then he turned and stared at me, his eyes hard and cold. "You come in, shoot up my crib, kill my boys, and—"

Shorty hit him across the face with a forearm, knocking him to the floor.

"That's for my partner," he said, pointing to Mikey who was sitting, propped up against the wall across the hallway.

Frankie was pulling Mikey's jacket off to get to the wound. He turned around when Shorty hit Juan and nodded. "Hit him again," he said.

So Shorty did, kicking him again and then again as Juan curled up in a fetal position and tried to crawl away.

"Hey. Enough," I said finally, grabbing Shorty's arm and pulling him away.

Juan didn't move. He was just lying there all curled up and braced, like he was expecting more.

"Hey, you're still alive," I said, leaning down and whispering in his ear. He heard me. I knew he did, because he flinched. "You're lucky. I should've killed you," and I was thinking of how he shot little Darly, and how he put Louise and me in the hospital, and that he probably killed Crane, and maybe even Ethan and Tamara. And I was sorry I had stopped Shorty. Sorry I had stopped him.

So I kicked him. "That's for shooting *my* partner." And I kicked him again, "And that's for Crane." Juan groaned and blood began oozing from his mouth. So I stopped. That was enough. And I was breathing hard, and for the first time, I felt the heat of the rat-infested, stinking Hole.

Casto spoke up. "We didn't kill nobody at the center."

I looked at him. He flinched. "And if we did, he deserve it. *Pendejos* act like they so good. Fact is they all *chulos*!"

Juan coughed then strained to look up at me. "You surprise, huh? You ask the priest. He knows. He's part of it." He paused. "Believe it." And he doubled over again. The pain.

And I thought of Trujillo. What the hell? Pimps?

"How's Mikey?" I said, turning to Frankie who was helping Mikey to his feet.

"He's okay. Took one in the shoulder. Gonna have to get him to a doc." He paused. "You and Richie clean up this mess?"

I said yeah and held out my hand. "Thanks."

"Fuggedaboutit." Then, "Come on Shorty. Let's get Mikey outta this hole before the son of a bitch bleeds to death."

It was quiet when Frankie and Shorty left, hauling Mikey between them. Juan and Casto stared at me—as they had been the whole time. Never taking their eyes off me.

"I won't forget this, cabrón," said Juan, talking over his pain, his eyes narrow and angry. "Te mataré a ti ya tus hijos ya tu amiga colombiana." His eyes locked onto mine. *I will kill you and your Colombian girlfriend.* And I didn't blink. Remembering, *The first one who blinks.*

"I'm gonna talk to the priest." And I paused, letting that sink in.

"I'll be back. Count on it."

And that was that. A battle always seems to last forever and yet, like this one, it all takes place in just a few bloody seconds.

And silence settled on the building once again and I stood there for a few moments. Richie picked up all the guns and folded them into an old shirt that was lying with the rest of the garbage. He tied the arms together and threw it over his shoulder.

"Just in case," he said, turning toward Juan.

The smell of death drifted over the dust and trash in the hallway. I wondered if someone would pick up the bodies and dispose of them or would they just lie there and become part of the garbage and eventually be hauled outside, pushed into a bin to be picked up by a waste management truck. But I figured one hadn't been around here for a while.

So Richie and I left, Richie with the shirt full of guns slung over his shoulder, the gangbangers and the girl staring after us. I looked back. There was enough killing for one day.

CHAPTER 58

What's Up?

Late Sunday Morning, October 31

We left Gangland in worse shape than we found it—if that was possible. No cops would come there to check out the gunfire. That was part of the scenery of the place. Father Trujillo was just leaving the chapel in the student center and walking to the rectory when we got there. Richie and I were the only ones who got out of the limo.

Trujillo stopped when he saw us and waited for us to come over. There was nobody around him. So I just got to it and told him what Juan had told us and asked him to explain. He stared at me in disbelief for a few moments, like *What are you talking about?* Eventually he motioned for us to follow him into the rectory.

It was dark in the entryway until he turned on some lights. The building is a reconditioned old community center built like a rectangular box with one hallway running down its center and rooms on each side. He led us into a den situated at the end of the hall with a fireplace rising against the far wall. Florida does get cold in the winter, so fireplaces, though not common, can be found in some homes and hotels. Sometimes they're just decorative. This one wasn't.

"I hate being a priest," Trujillo said as he leaned against the mantle. "Everybody thinks we're some kind of special human being. A supernatural superstar. How are you supposed to handle that?" He doesn't wait for an answer. "Then this kind of stuff, from a gangbanger like Juan. And you believe him? A *pandillero?*…over me? He's the kind of person we're trying to help."

We waited for a moment while he settled into a chair that snuggled up near the fireplace. A large bay window to his right looked out over the church grounds. He motioned for us to sit on a couch across from him. The light in the room settled like a haze over an old-fashioned movie set—like it was done in sepia. Trujillo didn't seem nervous and he didn't say anything. He just looked tired. Neither Richie nor I said anything either. Kind of like a stalemate after a short chess game.

It was confession time, but he wasn't confessing to anything. He just stared at the floor. Then he looked up, his eyes hard and unblinking.

I repeated what I had told him outside. "Juan said we should talk to the priest about the murders, Father." Silence. More staring.

"Said to ask me?"

"Not quite. He just said, *the priest.*"

"Then he didn't say me." A statement.

"Yeah. But who else?" I said.

"How would I know?"

"We ain't the cops, Father," said Richie. "The cops get into this, it's another story. When you talk to us, you ain't talkin' to the cops."

"You don't talk to us, you will be talking to the cops, Father," I added, "if what Juan says is true."

And then I asked him again, "What other priest could he have been talking about?" thinking back over what Juan had said. I guess I had just assumed he meant Trujillo.

Trujillo turned so that he was staring out the big bay window. We stared with him. It overlooked a picnic area with a barbeque grill, tables, and benches. A sago palm hung over the table allowing for a modicum of shade. There was nobody there now. Just the sun trying to warm things up.

Trujillo finally broke out of his reverie and began to talk about the seminarians, about how the center was the perfect place for them to serve as interns. Help him with his ministry to the poor Hispanics in south Florida. Maybe rescue some of them from the gangs. Almost like he was preparing a statement for the cops. Almost like he was going to confess. I waited.

"I don't know who killed Justin. The cops think it was some *pandilleros*," the priest said.

"What do *you* think, Father?" I said, pushing him.

He looked at me, like *I'm supposed to know?* But he continued anyway.

"Hector I never trusted. I told the rector I didn't like him. I told him he's a mean one."

"Casto is from Cartagena," he said, "just like Hector. They grew up in the same neighborhood.

"Hector was five years older," he went on, "got Casto into the gang. Juan was recruited by Casto when he was thirteen," he droned on, back in his reflective state.

And then he added that Louise knew them all, reminding me that her father was a major force in trying to destroy the cartels in Cartagena and was ultimately assassinated by them, and that's the reason she left and came to this country. Get away from the memories.

He told the story almost like there was no one there, just him and his thoughts drifting out into the late morning air. It was already warming up in Oceanside; the threat of hurricanes was over at the end of November; the rainy season was done, with only the warm breezes of the fall to contend with. There was more going on in his head than the mere recitation of facts. He was struggling with his thoughts, the pain manifesting itself in his eyes as he focused on whatever he saw through the window, which was nothing I was sure. What he was struggling with rose from within—like a bad dinner. Whatever it was registered on his brow like furrows in a field. And it must have it hurt like hell. I was still looking for a confession.

Then out of the silence: "I never trusted Hector. Said that already, didn't I?" And not waiting for an answer, he went on. "I saw him meeting with Casto and Juan about two weeks ago—here at the center," he added looking over at me. Then as though back to his thoughts, "They looked like they were fighting. Hector mad and Casto pointing a finger at Hector, like he had done something wrong..." his voice dying out.

"Uh huh," I said, breaking in. "So Hector's tied into Casto and

Juan," repeating it to reinforce it in my own mind.

"Yeah, of course. As I said, they all came from the same neighborhood—in Colombia. And grew up together. Hector is older, of course. Kind of a big brother. When he came to this country and entered the seminary, Casto and Juan contacted him. Let him know they were here too. One of the reasons Hector is working here. He told me he wanted to keep them away from the gangs. So I told the rector it would be a good internship for Hector. Help out his own."

"Okay, Father, that's all fine and good. But we need to know why Juan told us to talk to you about the killings. Help me with that one."

"I think Hector was doing something that Casto and Juan didn't like. You have to talk to Hector about that. Maybe Crane was involved also."

"Somebody delivering a message, Padre?" Richie said.

"Maybe somebody delivering a message," he repeated, nodding.

"Maybe Juan and Casto?" I said.

"I don't know. Have you talked to the rector yet?"

Then it hit me like a bolt of lightening. Juan's priest. The rector.

I looked at Richie and motioned that we needed to go. I thanked Father Trujillo and was out the door. I heard Richie telling the priest to call us if he had any more information. "You have any trouble— with anybody—just call. We'll come over and talk with them about it." I could picture that talk. Richie and his baseball bat.

CHAPTER 59

Murphy

Late Sunday Afternoon, October 31 (All Hallows' Eve)

The sun was high in the sky when we headed west and then north on Midnight Drive; the road runs east and west and then takes a northerly route when it reaches the Everglades and heads towards Shark Valley. The mornings never get cold in late October as they do in the north when it's Halloween Eve. Sometimes in Ohio during this time of the year, you can feel the beginnings of winter and sense the coming frosts that warn of early snow. But not here in south Florida, near the Great Swamp, where the tropics loom just forty miles or so south and mosquitoes infest the land all year long. But you do feel a slight change of weather, almost like the breath of a child that floats across your face when you stoop down to pick him up. It was that sense of changing seasons and a sense of impending darkness that lurked about me as I made my way to the seminary.

I punched in Murphy from my contacts and got the main switchboard. I asked for Monsignor Murphy. She connected me.

I told the secretary I wanted to speak with the monsignor.

She said, "Certainly, Mr. Cooper, and let me see if the monsignor is in." He would be in, of course, if he wanted to see me, and out if he was in no mood. Playing golf, maybe, or leading the rosary at some women's club.

He was in.

"Yes, Cooper, what can I do for you?" Murphy.

"I need to talk to Hector," I said.

No reply. "I'll be there in about ten minutes. And I want a few minutes with you also."

Silence.

Then, "Why Hector may I ask?"

"It's about Crane's murder. A few questions."

Silence again.

"I don't understand. Why Hector? You can talk with me about anything you need to know."

"I understand," trying not to alarm him. "It's just that I have a question for both of you." I paused. "Is that a problem?" Testing him.

Another silence. Maybe this is what it's like being in the monastery. You say something, then the other person says something about a half hour later. Damn, that would drive me crazy.

"I don't know, Cooper. This is very unusual. I am trying to run a school and I can't have my seminarians being called out for anybody and everybody who comes along."

"Like for solving a murder case that involves one of your boys? Father Trujillo seems to think he knows something about the murder. This is what you hired me to do. Right?"

He was quiet. Then, "Okay. I guess you're right. Where are you now?"

"Just pulling in."

It wasn't snowing, but we got a chilly response from the receptionist when we walked into the office. Murphy was standing at his window, his back to me. Hector was sitting in a chair off to the side next to one of the heavy, red velvet drapes that hung over a tall window. I was waiting for someone to ask about Richie. After all he doesn't fade into anybody's background.

"Hector, Mr. Cooper has a few questions for you, specifically about Justin's death."

"Murder," I said.

Richie cleared his throat. Murphy turned around and stared at him.

"Sorry. Yes, murder," he said, and he was still looking at Richie.

"What's he doing here?" he demanded, turning to me.

"I'm the bodyguard, remember?" said Richie, shooting his cufflinks.

"You told me a man by the name of Crow was going to take his place," said Murphy, waving at Richie like he was a piece of unwanted furniture.

"They work together," I said. "We need two men to give you adequate around-the-clock protection."

Hector shifted in his chair and Richie turned toward him and held him in his gaze. Hector wasn't intimidated.

I caught Hector's attention. "We had a discussion with one of your friends this morning." Hector looked puzzled.

"Juan." I paused. Hector's lips tightened around his teeth. "He called you a pimp. Why would he say that?" I stared him down. "Fact is he called you all pimps."

Hector's face got red. "What he doesn't like is somebody taking his homeboys away from him. And Crane was a lesson," pausing to wet his lips and then continuing to rant. "And that's the business we're in—getting kids away from the gangs—his gang. That's what we're doing, got it?" No question. Just a threat. "And you know how that works, Cooper. You mess around with a gang, they get you back. That's what they did. Question is, what're *you* going to do about it? We hired you to protect us, not question us."

I looked at Hector as he was talking. Was he telling the truth? Was this just some gangbangers retaliating against some holy Joes taking away their homeboys. Maybe. Murphy looked nervous. What was that about, I wondered? Then I thought about Juan's *priest.*

Gunner came through the open door and stared at us. He didn't say it, but *What's going on here?* was on his mind. "Why didn't you call me?" turning to Murphy.

I jumped in. "Juan said..." I hesitated for a moment—Gunner looking around the room, confused—"that you holy boys are in the business of selling kids."

"What?" he screamed. "You're nuts. Tell him, Monsignor," his eyes angry, like a bull's who had just seen red. But Murphy just stood there. Quiet.

Then, "You better leave now, Cooper. My secretary has called the police."

I heard sirens as we pulled out of the parking lot. They were growing more distinct as I passed the seminary.

"Fuckin' cops," Richie said.

CHAPTER 60

Pacholewski

We rode in silence pondering what had just happened. I stared at the trees that lined the boulevard. They were maples, planted there to make the area look like a northern college town. It worked in some ways. The trees provided shade. They hovered over manicured lawns maintained by landscaping crews. They were working now along the street, their rigs parked on either side of the road. The crews were mostly Hispanic, the case with most of south Florida. To see a black man doing landscaping was as unusual as seeing a caucasian.

"So now what?" said Richie.

"Extract a confession from somebody," I said.

"Uh huh. And how are we gonna do that, smart guy?"

"We're going to use your persuasive influence."

"Persuasive influence, huh?"

"Yeah, persuasive."

"So then I can use my ball bat."

"As long as it's persuasive."

Richie nodded.

"So we're not going to take the philosophical approach. Fool him into a confession by logic and trickery." Richie could be so literate.

"Right. That would take more time. And we don't have time. So using sophistry won't work here. The priest boys are trained in detecting fallacious arguments. They're smarter than us."

"Yeah, but you got a Ph.D."

"I'm out of practice, Richie. Got only you and DeFelice to practice on. And you two guys aren't that sophisticated," I said, turning to him. "No offense."

"No offense taken, Coop. But your smarts ain't worth crap on the street." Richie was offended.

"So we're going to use your methods. Quicker and more effective," I said.

"So who we gonna do our sophistication on?"

"Sophistry—no sophistication about it."

"Yeah, who we gonna do that on?"

"Joe Pacholewski."

My cell phone rang out its new tune: Frampton on his electric guitar.

"You had it right, Coop," said DeFelice. "I just told Louise. Those prints...," Richie watching me now, "match the prints of a Hector Ramirez in Cartagena. Her contact did a DNA check too. Another match. Hector in Colombia and Hector here—bingo—same guy. And..." pausing for effect, "Hector has a sheet long as your arm! So what the hell's this guy doing in a seminary?"

"What?" said, Richie, watching me.

I waved him off and focused on Tony's call.

"Louise is gonna report this to Oceanside," he continued. "Though we don't got much on him—just his experience in prostitution. But it all makes him a good candidate for a sit-down, don't it?"

said DeFelice. "By the way, I'm following up. Not you, Cooper. Remember you ain't a cop no more." Then, after a pause, "Where are you?"

I told him Richie and I were following up on some things. He said *Yeah I bet, and don't forget what I just told you.* I told him no problems, thanked him and promised a cut of the lottery when I win the big one and he said, yeah, sure, keep me in the loop, and blah, blah, blah. Richie was staring at me under his salt and pepper eyebrows.

So I filled Richie in on Louise's story about a guy back in Cartagena with the same name as Hector, about the Interpol match on the prints and the DNA, and about Hector's prostitution ring back in Colombia.

The trees slid by quickly as Richie went quiet. "Shoulda beat the son-of-a bitch to death," he muttered.

The work of getting a confession is not always neat. But you've got do what you've go to do. Joe was our man. I called Trujillo.

"When is Pacholewski scheduled to come to the center, Father?"

Silence. Then, "He's here now. Scared. What's going on?"

Before I could answer, he continued. "In fact he came here because he was afraid of you," he added quickly.

"Is he with you now?"

"No, he's in a classroom, working with some kids. Should I tell him you're coming?"

"No. We'll be there in a few minutes. Don't tell him anything," and I hurried through the Sunday drivers.

CHAPTER 61

Go-Fast Boats

My cell buzzed.

"Shouldn't talk and drive," Richie said.

I answered," Richie leaning over to see who it was.

"Got some news for you, Kemo Sabe." No question about who it was.

"I'm listening," I said.

"Those fast boats. You wanted to know who owns them." Huck likes to bait me. I was in no mood.

"Yeah, I would like to know, Huck. And I'll bet you're going to tell me."

"I went to City Hall and introduced myself—told them I was working in the capacity of a private investigator—"

"You what?" I said. "You're not a private investigator and you can get into trouble impersonating one."

"They were good with it, Coop. Not a problem. You know, the moon is in its full phase—it's the Hunter's Moon," he reminded me. "And this month, boss, there are two full moons—the second one is tonight. And tonight is..." and he paused for effect.

"Is what, Tonto?" I said running low on patience.

"What only occurs once in a Blue Moon?" he said.

"A Blue Moon?"

"And that means that the spirits are with us tonight, Kemo Sabe. And it's why I have been able to bring you this information."

"Which you are about to give me." I couldn't believe it.

"Okay, here's what happened," he continued. "Some fancy boys came in about four in the a.m., motors trimmed down to real quiet, parked their ponies, a coupla Baias, over by the Watson store, hauled their asses out—"

"Uh huh," I urged. "Keep going."

"So, they come in, park and open up the store—"

"How'd they do that? That's a museum," I said.

"Got me," he said. "Went around the back and just left their-selves in. Don't know what they did there. But I snuck down to the boats whilst they was inside and got the numbers off the Baias and their licenses."

"That's great. How in the hell did you know when they were coming in?"

"Surveillance, Coop. Surveillance. If you want to catch gators, you gotta get your flashlight out. Look for eyes in the water."

Richie was holding his hands up, like *What the hell?* I summarized for him.

"What'd they look like?" I said.

"Colombians. One hombre real tall, skinny dude, handgun strapped on. Other'un, medium height, big hat, long fur hangin' off his shoulder. It was dark, Kemo Sabe, too dark to see much; no light except for the moon."

"Did you find out who owns the boats?" I said.

Silence. "You're not gonna believe it."

"Try me."

"Fella by the name of Murphy."

"Murphy!" I said out loud and Richie jumped at the word. "First name?" I said.

"Em Ess Gee Ar." He paused. "Strange name."

"That stands for monsignor," I said.

"What's that?" he said.

"Never mind. You got an address?"

"Right near to where you live."

CHAPTER 62

The Confession

I couldn't stop thinking about what Huck had told me. Murphy owned two Baias. Everybody knows what they're used for in the Everglades: drugs, illegals, trafficking. Maybe the cops are looking the other way because the owner is a holy man.

I filled Richie in as I pulled into the center parking lot. Joe was already headed for his car, a big black Chevy. Trujillo must have warned him. I pulled in behind him and blocked his way. Richie and I both jumped out of the car. He was rolling down his window as I approached.

"What's the problem?" he said, like a motorist pulled over by a state cop. Innocence pouring from his eyes.

"We need to talk, Joe," I said, Joe looking nervously over at Richie who standing behind me holding his Louisville Slugger.

"What's he dong here?" Joe said.

"He's your bodyguard, remember? Let's head back to the center. Get a private place."

We found an office just inside the entrance to the center. Trujillo's name was on the desk. We sat—the three of us—Joe facing Richie and me. He was trying to look confused, but I had the sense he knew exactly why we were there.

267

I told Joe what I had told Trujillo, and the rector, and Gunner and Hector, and about what Juan had said. I asked him about it.

He looked panicked. Then Trujillo came in the door and sat down next to Joe. "Tell them what you know," the priest said, leaning into Joe like he was hearing his confession. I think that did it because...

"I didn't have anything to do with those kids who were killed," he said, looking at Trujillo.

The priest stared at him. His face wasn't any more that twelve inches from Joe's face. "What are you talking about?" he said. I leaned in wanting to know the same thing. Was he giving up the people who killed Miller and Dougherty?

Joe started to cry. "I'm saying I didn't kill those kids or kidnap anybody. It was never my idea to do anything wrong!" and he paused to wipe his eyes.

The priest put his arm around Joe's shoulders and asked him to tell him about it—like a father to his son. "Go ahead," he continued. "Get it off your conscience."

And Joe started. He told us the most bizarre story I had ever heard—about how Hector had explained how they could help the kids in the neighborhood, get them off the street and away from the gangs, people like Casto and Juan, about how they could help them make some money, *Break the cycle of poverty,* and how the monsignor said the same thing, how they could place the kids with a person who could support them, maybe some priests, maybe some important people in the community, maybe some families, and these people would eventually adopt them.

And Joe talked about how that didn't work out and what really happened was that the person who was supposed to take care of them was really looking for sex, and the kids were being sold for sex, yes even to some priests, and some important public figures—*People in the news—and we started to take money in trade for the kids, and I tried to stop them,* Joe said, *but I couldn't,* and *Ethan Miller was one of those kids,* and he did know about Tamara—*she was Ethan's girlfriend—and maybe they got to know too much—I don't know—and Eddie Dougherty?* he didn't recognize that name—but he did hear Gunner and Hector talk about a young boy that they had gotten hold of and maybe that was him—he didn't know—and many of the kids were nameless so maybe he was one of them...

And I slipped away in silence, maybe not wanting to hear this gruesome story anymore, not wanting to think of Maxie as one of those kids who got sold as sex slaves, or as workers, or as walking sources of body parts, or God knows what else, so I didn't listen any longer, but that was okay because Joe had stopped talking now, and Father Trujillo was giving him a blessing and telling him to confess all this to the police and that he was good to do what he had done today.

It was the beginning of All Hallows' Eve and the first fingers of sundown were beginning to work their way into the center. It wouldn't be long before the ghosts of All Souls' Day would infuse the darkness that was spreading. Part of that darkness had already closed over the priest and Joe.

Richie sighed so deeply I thought he wouldn't breathe again. "Jesus Christ," he said, "this is a freaking nightmare," and he was fingering the bat he had carried into the office.

Father Trujillo noticed and shook his head *No*.

And then, "You son of a bitch whore of a semitarian," he said, misusing the word, but maybe it fit here. "What have yous guys done?" And his face showed his fury like a storm shows with lightning.

I grabbed his shoulder to calm him and he just kept muttering what he had already said, Joe and Trujillo watching him for an eruption. But nothing happened.

You live in Florida long enough and you see plenty of violence. Storms grow from small disturbances in the Caribbean into tropical storms and sometimes into hurricanes. You haven't lived until you survive one of those storms.

Richie was that storm and Joe was waiting for it to explode. But it didn't and we left the center with a confession and with Joe in the hands of Trujillo who promised he would call the police. I wasn't sure I believed him.

But Richie and I had business to take care of at the seminary and I would have to trust Trujillo on that one.

CHAPTER 63

All Hallows' Eve

Sunday Evening, 6:30 p.m.

The sun was sinking quickly as we left the center and headed back to the seminary to look for Hector and Gunner. I didn't expect to find them there. When we pounded on the door, a young man answered. He asked what we wanted. I told him and he told me that everyone was in the dining hall for supper and that included the two guys we were looking for.

The early evening left bright splashes of red on the darkening lawn that spread under the maples lining the campus. We were watching the last remnants of a falling sun.

"Cooper!" cried a voice from my left. "What the hell you doing here?"

And then I saw the origin of the color. The splashes were emanating from a globe atop an unmarked parked on the street with two cops climbing out on either side: Detectives Sandy Neumann and Randall Flagg.

"What are *you* doing here?" I asked Neumann.

"I ask the questions, Cooper," said Neumann, limping as he crossed the walk. Flagg was shoulder to shoulder with him.

"You stay the hell away from the monsignor, Cooper. That goes for you too, stubby," he said, looking at Richie. Richie glared at him. I grabbed Richie's arm. Neumann noticed and retreated a few feet. Then, "You screw with me, Cooper, and I will mess up your life."

I nodded. "You're going to want to hear what I've got."

He studied me for a moment and then looked over at Flagg. Flagg shrugged.

"Okay, whaddya got?" he said finally. "But this better be good," like an old-time movie threat. And he pulled up his pants that were slipping down below his stomach, making him look fatter than he was—if that was possible.

They both watched with suspicion at first then curiosity as I explained what we had learned so far: about the DNA and fingerprint match on Hector, about what Trujillo told us about him, about what Joe confessed to, and right about then they both got serious.

"You gotta be kidding," Flagg said, screwing up his face—already ugly from the acne that was festering there. "You want us to believe that a couple of future priests are in the black market—pawning off kids to perverts? That's crazy."

"Suit yourself," I said. "That's what Pacholewski told us just an hour or so ago—in front of the priest. Hell, ask the padre yourself."

"So where's this Joe Pachoski?" said the fat cop.

"Pacholewski. He's with the priest at the center," I said, hoping he was still there. "Trujillo should be calling the station even as we speak." And like a well-timed line in a play, a voice came over their radio about Joe.

They looked at each other. "Looks like we need to have a talk with Pacha—whatever the hell his name is—whoski." said Neumann looking over at Flagg.

The night was beginning to assert itself, making good camouflage for the ghosts that had begun to file down the sidewalk fronting the seminary. The streetlights were just starting to come on. The creatures of All Hallows' Eve were in all sizes—even some adults dressed up in kids clothing, hoping for some treats—oh, what games we play.

And they would knock on doors warning the residents in their safe homes that no home was really safe without a treat—because 'no treat' meant a trick. And the shadows followed them, these small groups of young ghosts, dressed as skeletons—their bones glowing in the dark—or witches in high pointed hats, and they were all giggling, these scary creatures of All Hallows' Eve, and they would pass skeletons hung from doors, and jack-o-lanterns with the light from a burning candle shining through their teeth and eyes, and scarecrows stuffed with hay. And I thought how ironic it was on this night before All Saints when the spirits of the dead are allowed to wander without interruption—or suspicion—that evil resided in a building where saints should be and that the darkness of this night was nothing like the blackness of the world we were about to enter.

I turned back to the main entrance and knocked. The tires on the cop car squealed away from the curb. The same young man came to the door again, looked through the now dark streets as though to check for alien vehicles, and then turned back to me. I said the police were gone and asked again where the men I had asked for earlier were. He told me Gunner was there and would be out but that Hector was gone. I asked him where he had gone and he said that he had to drive the monsignor somewhere.

When someone says 'somewhere', that means they don't want to tell you. So I asked him where 'somewhere' was. He said he didn't know—which means he wouldn't tell me. I told him he was a damn good liar. I think I scared him because he backed away, but that may have been because he saw Richie staring at him like only Richie can. And then Gunner appeared behind him.

I nodded for Gunner to come out into the yard and he did, gingerly at first, like he had hurt his knee, but I could see that it was only hesitation. A big man, slump-shouldered now—like a weight was there. I could smell the fear. Shadows played around his face, creating lines where there probably were none. They filled cavities in his cheeks in such a way that the skeletal structure of his face emerged. Just like the gremlins prowling the street tonight.

He said, trying to play the tough guy, "What do you want, Cooper? You know the cops are looking for you."

"Yeah. They've gone to pick up Joe."

The fear I talked about earlier—there it was. He didn't know what to say.

"So, Gunner, you want to be the last one standing or do you want to tell us what happened?" I continued before he could answer, "We've talked to Joe. He's told us the whole story. Mostly your fault—his words. So, either you jump in here and help us or you can wait for Hector to join Joe and leave you out in the cold. Your decision. Mainly we need to know about the kids you kidnapped."

Gunner seemed to shrink as if trying to pull the cloak of evening around his body. Across the street a group of kids carrying flashlights were heading up the walk to a house hidden behind some maple trees. They were wearing sheets. One of them was dressed like a witch. A slight breeze caught the trees as Gunner turned back. He had been staring at them.

"It was just a business at first," he said.

The Confession

"It all happened this way." he began. As Eogan droned on I thought of the Doughertys, of the fear on their faces as they told me about their missing son, I thought of Hannah Miller and the pain in her eyes trying to cope with her son's murder, and I thought of the millions of other parents, friends and family members who had missing loved ones—they would be haunted for the rest of their lives until they were found—dead or alive—and the chances of alive were not great as days slipped by. Clues disappear early on. And so does hope. And so does the chance of finding someone—barring a damn miracle—or a confession out of the blue...

But that's what we were getting here. Gunner was rambling on. About how he was not guilty of anything—it was Hector's idea all along. You know, the usual self-exoneration that people who confess

275

engage in. *I'm innocent, I swear!* It makes me sick to hear it, his voice drifting into the evening, and I watched the kids in sheets coming back down the walk from the house where they had scared the residents into giving them treats, counting what they had gotten, and one of them looked our way and waived, *Hey Father*, and I wondered what he would have thought if he only knew what tricks were being played out in this holy place, and I could picture one of them as a victim, and I watched the children walk away from us to the next house as Gunner continued.

"Hector had this idea: make a little money from sems and priests, supply them with companions. An escort service. *Hey, we're all human*, he told me. And besides, the kids will make some money." Gunner's face was backlit by the moon.

I shook my head. "So this was all Hector's idea?"

Gunner looked relieved, like I had given him an out.

"Hector had just come to the sem. I was in first theology. He was older. Always with Murph..." he hesitated, "the rector."

"Uh huh. You call him Murph?"

"Uh, no. Behind his back," he said, looking unsure about where this was going.

"Yeah, so go on…about Hector," I said.

"You're pissed off with me," he replied. "Why?"

"Because you're a son of a bitch liar," I said as coolly as I could.

"I'm not a liar. I'm tellin' you the truth. Hector recruited me. Recruited all of us. Then he threatened us if we got cold feet."

He paused, and watched some specters draped in white sheets

and chalked faces pass. One of them waved. A friendly ghost. Gunner waved back, distracted for the moment.

"Hector took a liking to me too right off. I don't know why. So we became friends, hung out, had some beers; that's how it happened," he said, looking like he wanted me to believe. I didn't say anything.

"So I got to know him, about his family back in Colombia. The tough times he had there. He wanted to know about me. I told him about my family back in Ireland. Nine of us in all, four boys and three girls, me the youngest. My da was killed by a bomb. Ma trying to raise us with no money.

"So Ma gets money for a ticket to the U.S. from the local priest. For all of us. That was ten years ago. And that's all we had. Money for a ticket to Miami. So the boys got jobs to keep the home fires burning. The girls stayed home with Ma and took in laundry, cleaned houses."

I nodded. I don't know why I even listened. I knew what he had done. I guess I just wanted to hear it from him.

"I got a job running bets for a bookie in Hialeah. Brought some good money home. But the local priest pulled me aside and told me I needed to start going to church. So I did. Became an altar boy and here I am," he said, holding his arms out as if he were embracing the buildings around him.

I said, "I'm still listening."

Richie was ignoring him, watching the goblins filling up their baskets. One group started toward us. He waved them away.

Eogan continued. "So one day Hector pulls me aside and tells me he has an idea about how we both could make some money for the family and help ourselves as well. So I said okay, let's have it. And that's how it all began. And it's a long and crazy story, Coop," telling me like we were buddies in a bar and having pints in our fists.

"I got all night," I said.

"Okay then…" he hesitated. "I'm telling it just like it is. The truth."

I didn't say anything.

He continued his confession—*Bless me father for I have sinned*—under the soft lights that overhung the dark street.

"So Hector said, you know how money is made, don't you? I said, no I don't. He said by two things: greed and sex. And he said both are part of human nature and that priests and sems are just human, no? So I told him yeah, that's true and what does that have to do with us. He said, we're going to make some money off both and, funny thing, we're gonna make it off the good guys: priests, other seminarians and the like. I tell him, he's crazy and asked him what the hell he was talking about."

"And you had no idea?" I said.

"No. So I asked him to clarify."

"That was real smart," says Richie. "Your ma would be real proud of you."

"So he tells me how he ran this thing in Cartagena and made a bundle, no problems, nobody gets hurt, about how he was a supplier of local talent to businessmen and how everybody was good with it, I mean, the politicians, big shots, even the talent. Big money for everybody."

"Local talent?"

"That's how he put it. I figured he was supplying local businesses with, you know, whatever. What the hell did I know—?"

"That's real smart, Gunner, you bein' a college grad and all. You think we're gonna believe this story, you slimy piece of shit!" said Richie, raising his bat.

Gunner cringed as he eyed it.

"I swear I didn't know anything about what he had in mind when he first told me. I swear on my ma's grave."

"I thought you said your ma was alive and you were going to send her money," I said.

"Yeah, she is. It's just a manner of speaking."

"Liar," muttered Richie.

"So go on," I said.

"So I told him it sounded interesting and he said let's talk about it some more later. I said fine. Then about two weeks later—this was about a year and a half ago—he tells me he has a kid—he calls him talent and the kid's gonna be a companion for a padre. I asked him what kind of companion. And he told me."

"Sex, huh?"

"Yes. Sex. So I told him, *no.* And he said, *what?* You told me you were in, so you're in. I tell him no way, and he said, oh yeah? and to get my lazy Mick butt moving 'cause we were gonna deliver the kid today. I'm quoting, you know. So I tell him, no way and then he pushes me up against the wall and tells me I'm in and the only way out is...you know...dead. Just like that. Dead. And he asks if I understand—I mean he's choking me! So I nod and then he lets me go and says let's get the hell out of here. I mean he was mad. And I swear to God I thought he was going to kill me!" and he paced toward the street and looked up the sidewalk at the backs of kids who had just passed.

"So maybe you can grab some of those kids and sell them," I said.

He jerked around, angry.

"So then what did you do?"

"So I went with him, of course! What the heck do you think I would do?"

"And...?"

"So he takes me to this place down in Oceanside, big deserted apartment building, falling down, couldn't believe it didn't collapse when we went in. A couple of guys who looked like gangbangers were inside the door waiting for us. They led us upstairs to a room at the end of a hall. I remember the number on the door, 336, third floor. Filthy place, dead rats, garbage. So Hector knocks and we go in. A big room, couches, chairs, a bed, kids in there, some on the bed, some on the floor, ten, twelve, thirteen years old. Two guys and a woman were with them. I didn't recognize anybody. The kids looked clean—but their eyes...a hungry look, like they hadn't eaten in days," and he dwelled on what he had just said. "I figured I could make like

I was 'in' and then grab some kids, when I had the chance, and get them out of there."

But I knew that was a lie.

And the scene he described got into my brain: the mattress— it had to be filthy—and the odors from the young bodies crowded onto it and the stench that arises from fear and the two men and the woman—I struggled to picture them—and the eyes of the children, red from no sleep and worry...

"Where is this room?" I said, my stomach burning like an ulcer was eating away.

"Oceanside. Place they call the Hole."

"So how does this thing work?"

"All you have to do is grab a kid and sell him. You usually get fifty to a hundred thousand for a kid, easy. Quick money. Hector sells to his contacts here in Miami who transport the kids out of the country and sell them to brokers who have buyers waiting for delivery. The kids are used for all kinds of things: sex, work, body parts, you name it. Which is why I told him I didn't want any part of it. I thought he was talking about selling real talent, kids who wanted to make it in show business. I didn't know...until I got to that room. Then I knew," and he started for the sidewalk again.

"Don't even think of it," I said.

"What?" holding out his hands like he was being crucified.

"Richie can run faster than you. And he will break your legs when he catches you." Gunner shrugged and walked back.

"Where did the kids come from?" I said, feeling a sickness seep into my skin.

I tried to chase the images of the children in that room from my mind, wondering what was happening to them now, wondering if we could save some of them, wondering if Eddie was one of them.

"I don't know. He just said that he had his sources. Maybe he picks them up on the street or buys them from some poor families who need the money. Not as though this doesn't happen every day. Hell, Cooper, hundreds of thousands of kids are taken every year, and many of them are glad to work—most of them being dirt poor."

It was all I could do to keep from hitting him.

"Do you think the kids are still in the apartment building?"

"I don't think so. Hector moves them pretty fast. For instance, the kid he was delivering that day went out with one of the Hispanic guys. Hector said he was headed for the Everglades. I assume they were going to ship him out through the Caribbean."

He must have read my thoughts because he continued. "Murphy has a house near Everglades City. He and Hector use it as a holding place before they ship them out. That's how it works, see? Someone gets the kids, brings them to the Hole then they go from there, depending on who's buying."

"You are some sick son of a bitch," I said. "You're gonna pay for this."

Gunner didn't say anything. He just stared out over the street now empty of the spirits that had haunted it earlier.

"Why do you think Hector took you to the Oceanside apartment?" I said.

"To tie me in so I couldn't get out. That way I'm part of the whole operation. Then who's to say I wasn't part of it from the beginning?"

"Yeah, who's to say?" I said. "So Murphy is part of this whole mess?"

"That's right," he said. "What I'm telling you is that I am a victim of a maniac Colombian and his buddy, Murphy. You've never been in the seminary. If you had been, you'd know that the rector is the man. Nobody crosses him. And I gotta tell you, he's a monster."

"And what are you?" I said, shaking my head. "What about Joe and Justin? How were they involved?" I said.

"From the beginning. That's why Justin's dead. Juan and Casto must have killed him. They warned us," he said.

So Juan *was* sending a message.

"What about the two kids who are dead?" I said.

"What kids?" he said.

"Don't screw with me. Ethan Miller and the Thompson girl. You have anything to do with their murders?" I was just about done with this whole conversation.

"I don't know what you're talkin' about. I told you, I'm a victim here. I told you everything because I want to see that bastard brought to justice," he said, his voice rising and falling at the end like an Irishman.

"You can drop the phony Irish brogue crap. I want to know what you had to do with those kids. Did you kill them?"

He looked down. Tears began to appear at the edge of his eyes as he struggled to answer. Then, "Honestly, Cooper, I didn't have anything to do with those kids. What happened to them was terrible. Person that killed them should be…"

At that moment I saw an explosion of movement as Richie came hurtling out of the blackness and descended on Gunner like a rhino. Eogan grunted, collapsing under Richie's pounding, his arms flailing as the steady rhythm of fists hitting flesh were the only sounds in the night. And then Richie paused, sweating and bleeding, and Gunner, who was holding his hands over his face, groaned, begging him to stop.

"Enough," I said. But as I pulled Richie off, he jerked away and kicked Gunner one last time, and I heard a crack, like a limb breaking, and Gunner drew into a fetal position and hugged his body tightly. And then Richie stopped. I looked at my hands. They were wet from the sweat, tinged red, that came from Richie's body.

We both stared at Gunner. He didn't move.

"Is the bastard dead?" said Richie. He obviously didn't care.

What makes Richie dangerous is his violent temper, and he is so cold when he's violent. At one time he worked as an enforcer for a Cleveland mafia boss. One night he was 'recruiting' clients in a suburb of Cleveland on the east side, a place near Collinwood. It was out of The Family's territory. It was a blue-collar bar in the steel production part of the city. A wise guy who was muscle for a competitor saw Richie talking to the bartender and the guy asked Richie what he was doing. Richie said, *Whaddya think I'm doin'? Havin' a drink here. Got a problem?* And the guy said *Yeah, and I think you need to stay outta my territory.* And Richie said, *Uh huh, and you know what you can do with that thought.* And the guy said, *Yeah? and I know your sister, you dumb goombah. I hear she's a good fuck.*

Richie turned on that guy, no questions asked, and in a fury beat the life out of him. In about two minutes. Blood all over his hands and clothes, Richie turned to the bartender and said, *Any questions?* and went home. End of story. Beginning of the legend. Cleveland Johnny put Richie on hold for a while, telling him, *You gotta use a little restraint, Richie. We ain't living in the 1920s here. We're inna civilized period of history. You unnerstand?"*

Richie said *Yeah and sorry for any inconvenience.*

Johnny said *No problem, Richie, and whyn't you go home and get a little R and R, okay? And don't worry, I'll take care of the cops.* Richie told him, *Why should I be worried? I got this,* holding up his bat.

See that's the Richie I know. He's dangerous but he's good. Gives you a little insight into me also.

Gunner was still not moving. I felt his pulse. He was definitely alive.

"He alive?" asked Richie.

"Yeah, no thanks to you. You beat the hell out of him."

"Uh huh. Shoulda killed the bastard."

"How're you doing?" I asked, staring at his nose. "What's the matter with your nose?"

"I don't know," feeling for it. He tried to move it. It moved. "Must be broken." He reached into his pocket and pulled out a handkerchief and held it to his nose to stop the bleeding.

"We gotta get you to a hospital."

He shook his head. "I'll be all right," then looked over at Gunner. "I say we take this pervert into the Glades and dump him off somewheres. I'm sure somebody'll come along and have him for lunch. That prick don't deserve to live."

"No. We need him. We're taking him with us."

"Where we goin'?"

"To Everglades City."

CHAPTER 64

The Swamp

A trip through the Everglades always creates an unease in me. No, I should say it scares the hell out of me—especially at night. Why? Because I have nightmares about the Great Swamp. Those dreams are never very clear. They take place in the depths of the mangrove jungles, somewhere among the Ten Thousand Islands. The waters that flow through the Glades seem to run forever, so making an exit seems futile to someone caught up in a dream, the soft bottom of the Glades pulling at your ankles and the splashing of gators sliding into the water. And snakes: pythons—thirty to forty thousand of them—and coral snakes, and moccasins, and rattlesnakes, and the panther. And you wonder why I have nightmares. And you probably wonder why I would live on the edge of a wilderness that harbors so much danger. And I don't know why. Probably why so many people live on rivers that overflow every year and flood them out, or why Californians live on a fault line, or Kansans live in the path of tornadoes, or Floridians with hurricanes. Crazy, isn't it?

We left Oceanside around 7:30 p.m., heading for Route 997 which takes a northerly direction past fields of sawgrass. But it was dark and I couldn't see the grass clearly, just an outline, and if I could take my finger and trace a path through those fields, the line left by my tracing would stretch for almost sixty miles across southern Florida. It's why one writer described this great tract of sawgrass and mangrove forests as the River of Grass—the water that flows t hrough i t c onstantly m oving—an a rea o f m ore t han t hree thousand square miles, as large as the states of Delaware and Rhode Island combined.

"How far we got to go to get to this place?" asked Richie, staring into the darkness.

"About an hour I figure."

Gunner was silent in the back seat, watching me in the rear-view mirror. His face was swollen and still bloody, though we had cleaned him up at a gas station at the entrance to Route 41. It turned out he had suffered a laceration to his ear, a broken nose, and some broken ribs. I had wrapped his torn ear in close to his head with a sterile cloth I had in a first aid kit I carried in my car. I couldn't do much with his broken ribs—or the nose. I told him the ribs would heal by themselves. Actually, I didn't care one way or the other.

"Never heard of Chokoloskee Island, Cooper. You think this kid's tellin' us the truth?" Richie said, turning and looking back at Gunner. Then, "If you're lyin' to us kid, you'll wish you was already in jail. Not that you ain't goin' there anyways."

We left State Route 997 and headed west Tamiami Trail, also known as U.S. Route 41, an old highway that runs from the center of Miami, beginning at Highway 1, through the Everglades and up the west coast of Florida through Fort Myers and Sarasota to Tampa. Hence the Tamiami Trail. But tonight we would travel only about forty miles of this historic highway to the westerly end of the Everglades and to a small Florida town called Everglades City.

The night was dark as we entered 41, the southernmost route through the Everglades. It used to be the only way through the swamp until Alligator Alley opened in 1969. Now it's the scenic route. And scenic means it's dark. And it's hard to describe the depth of the darkness on this highway as it threads its way through the Everglades—one lane each way—and no berm to speak of, just a fall-off on each side into the swamp itself. Not fun at night. And once you enter the road you can kiss the lights goodbye—except for the two lonely beams that penetrate the darkness from your car's headlamps. And there was no traffic either way to help illuminate the road ahead or behind. It's like travelling in a cocoon.

And no gas—for sixty miles—and no stores, only tall barren trees jutting out over the River of Grass like skeletons to the left and right of the road and jammed up against each other like toothpicks in a dispenser, barely visible in the night sky. The soft lights of Miami hung behind us like the last rays of a westering sun. But the sun had disappeared hours ago.

The denseness of the Great Swamp swallowed up Route 41, and tonight it was the loneliest road in America. So we rode in silence, Gunner lost in his pain and his thoughts, Richie in his anger, and I in my lost son. As the highway straightened out ahead I'd hoped we would see Murphy's Mercedes in the distance. I checked the glove compartment for my .38. Richie pulled out his Glock, checked it and then replaced it in his shoulder holster.

And so we sped on through the night on the narrowing highway, past big signs like Cooperstown, Population 5, and another that read, The Oldest Air Boat Rides in the Everglades, in Business for 60 Years, and further up the road another that read Buffalo Bob's Air Boat Rides. There were several of those—airboat signs that is. I stopped off at a diner in Cooperstown to see if anyone had passed through. The town has one establishment, that diner. It was still open. A waitress who must have driven a truck to work was closing up. I asked if anyone had come by. She said no. I asked if there were any houses in the Glades that she knew of. She said not that she knew of but then again she didn't live "out here," she lived over there, and she pointed toward Miami. I smelled coffee and asked if it was fresh. She said she was closing but she had part of a pot left. I said thanks and I'd like a cup of decaf. She did a double take.

"Decaf? Mister we ain't had decaf here since this place came into existence way back in 1950. People who come in here want real coffee," she said, turning back to finish closing. I said thanks and wondered if she knew DeFelice.

We got back on the road, passed another sign that advertised airboat rides: Captain Joe's Tour of the Everglades. See alligators up close. Live. Exciting.

Gunner was still sitting quietly in the back, holding a rag to his nose. Blood had seeped through.

"So, what do you know about the two dead kids, Gunner. And don't bullshit me any more. I've got no more patience for you."

He didn't reply right away.

"The Miller kid was working for Hector," he said.

The road seemed to narrow ahead when I heard the news.

"The Miller kid was working for Hector? Are you crazy?" I paused to catch my breath. "You really expect me to believe that crap!" and I turned around to let loose at him.

"Watch out!" yelled Richie.

The car skirted a ditch running along the highway, riding the slope that curved down to a trench that separated 41 from the Everglades. I struggled to keep the wheel steady, fighting against the car's urge to plunge us into the trench below, then suddenly the front wheels caught the road and I was able to swing the car back up onto the berm and came to a stop.

Sometimes there is nothing to say or do. Sometimes there is no way to distinguish lies from truth. Sometimes I don't give a damn anymore. This was one of those times. So I just pulled out on Route 41 and let the blackness of the night swallow me up and the whole sorry mess. I tried to picture Ethan Miller working for Hector. I hoped to God it wasn't true.

CHAPTER 65

Everglades City

It was 8:30 p.m. when we turned off Highway 41 onto Route 29 and headed toward Everglades City. In five miles we were there. Gunner shifted nervously in his seat as we pulled into town. A few lights hung from posts situated almost randomly in what might be called a town square. There were a few restaurants scattered around the square. But my favorite place is The Oyster House. To get there you have to leave the square and head south on 29. The Oyster House overlooks the waters that lead into the Everglades. I pulled into the restaurant's lot and parked near the water. If we had stayed on 29, we would have come to Chokoloskee, a small island village at the end of the road and in the middle of the Ten Thousand Islands. But this was as far as we were going for the time being.

I called Huxter.

"You ready?" I asked.

"You in town?" he said.

I told him where we were and he said he would meet us in the bar. His house was just a few hundred yards away.

I left Richie in the car with Gunner and walked up the stairs to the restaurant. The first thing you see when you go into The Oyster House is a large u-shaped bar that covers a lot of the floor space.

About a half dozen tables were scattered around the bar, more people sitting there than at the tables.

The bartender, with dirty blond hair and a mullet hanging over his shoulders, nodded to me when I walked in.

"Welcome," he said and began cleaning a space at the bar for me to sit.

"Whaddya have?" he said.

"I'm looking for some directions and some information."

"We give directions. We don't give information," he said, polishing the bar without looking up.

I asked if he knew about a priest's house in the town.

He said he didn't know nothing about that and did I want a drink or not—a little testy.

I told him no and climbed off the stool to leave when someone behind me cleared his throat.

I turned around. "There's a padre owns a house down by Choko-loskee," said a man sitting alone at a table. The guy at the bar glared at him. The man ignored him and waved me over.

"Can I buy you a drink?" I said. His face was weathered from too much sun and sea.

"Hank ain't too friendly, especially to outsiders," the man said.

I was glad I wasn't from some foreign country, like Hawaii. I said thanks but no thanks to the beer since I was driving, but another time.

"Where's this house?" I asked

"What's your business with the priest?" the weathered man said.

"Just a friend," I said.

"Like I said, it's down in Chokoloskee. When you git there, you'll find it. Just ask anybody."

I thanked him and headed for the door.

"Hey fella," the man behind the bar said. "If you got business with the padre, keep it friendly."

"Sure thing," I said.

"Folks here look out for their own. You know what I'm sayin'?"

"Heard you the first time," I said and the door swung into me as I left. Friendly people. Friendly door.

Huxter almost ran into me coming in.

"Leavin' so soon? You hardly got here. Come on back in and meet my friends."

"Some kind of friends," I said.

"Hold on," he said, stopping me on the steps. He opened the door ahead of me.

"Hank, pour me and my friend a couple of cold ones," he said as I came back through the door.

"This here's a friend of yours?" Hank said, like he had to verify my credentials. Then, without waiting for an answer, "Sorry mister," and he filled two glasses from the tap.

Huxter winked at me. Grabbed my arm and headed for a table.

"Who's the guy with Richie?" he said as he pulled out a chair and waited for me to sit.

I filled him in on Gunner and Murphy.

Huxter shook his head. "This is bad stuff, Kemo Sabe." At least he didn't say *bad medicine*.

I nodded then asked him if he knew about a house that a priest owned in Chokoloskee.

"You talking about Murphy—the rev who owns the fast boats?"

"Yeah. I'm talking about him."

"Don't know, but can find out. But let's finish our beers, okay?"

So we drank the beer in silence, Huck's leg bouncing like he was ready for a marathon.

I downed the last of the beer, and hit the table. "Time to go," I said and went to the bar to pay.

"On the house," Hank said. I nodded and told him thanks.

"No hard feelin's?" he said.

"None," I said.

Then Huck and I headed for the door. This time it didn't hit me in the back. When we got to the car, Richie was already pulling himself out.

"About time,'" he said, glaring at Huck. "This guy's getting on my nerves," motioning to Gunner who was barely visible through the back window.

"He tell you where the house is?" I said.

"No. If you want, I can beat it out of him," grinning that Richie grin, distorted by the shadows.

"So you got your Indian getup on, huh?" eyeing Huck in his fur hat, matching deer-skin pants and shirt and looking like a grizzled, sixty-year-old Daniel Boone.

Huck ignored him. He was staring at Gunner who was almost invisible in the darkness.

"We've got some work to do," I said, motioning Richie into the front seat. Huck was already getting into his pick-up.

Richie struggled his large frame into the front seat. "Sure make these cars small, don't they," he said, mumbling.

Chokoloskee is part of old Florida, just like Everglades City. Population 359 at last count—120 people more than its area code which is 239. It's the last outpost at the westernmost end of the Everglades and a good jumping off point for drugs, smuggling, and illegal immigration. Modern America hasn't discovered it as yet and isn't likely to for several hundred more years. The road there is a narrow two-lane one, lined by stretches of water and open land. At night it is unlit and unwelcoming. It's Route 29, the only road into the heart of the Ten Thousand Islands.

So we headed south on 29, the four of us, Richie, Gunner and I in the Volvo, and Huxter in his pick-up close behind. Route 29, also called Copeland Avenue in Everglades City, became Smallwood Drive as we neared Chokoloskee Island. We headed for the End O' The World Cafe that faces Smallwood Drive and sits at the end of South Lopez Lane. Richie went in with me this time and pushed Gunner in ahead of him. Silence as we came through the door. No wonder. Gunner looked like hell and the rest of us looked like we had just chased a gator through the swamp. Huck followed last. A few people at the counter were having coffee. A man, a woman and two kids were sitting at one of the tables. They interrupted their hamburger and fries to stare. Some older guys—by that I mean sixty-five, seventy and looking a lot like steady customers—were huddled at a table in the corner. One of them yelled out Huck's name. Huck smiled, gave a nod and pointed his finger at the table. The lady behind the counter looked up, studied us briefly and looked down again.

"Howdy, Huck," she said without looking up.

"Need a little information, Mattie," said Huck.

"Hmmm," she said, now looking up. "What happened to your friends? You been fightin' again?"

Huck shook his head. "Nope. I quit fightin' when the white man chased us out of our home." Huck never missed a chance to remind us of his heritage.

"You weren't never chased out of any home," Mattie said. She was staring at Gunner.

"Hank tells me there's a padre has a house on the water somewheres around here. You know about it?"

She continued staring at Gunner.

"Your friend's ear is bleeding," she said still staring at Gunner. "Haven't I seen you before?" She paused. "You sure do look familiar."

Gunner looked away like he was trying to find a place to hide. He shook his head. She seemed unsure.

"Ma'am?" I said. Reminding her of Huck's question.

"The house is down the road a piece, on the east side of the Island. Kinda out in the water," and she pointed east like we should be able to see it from here. "You can't miss it. There's a boat dock just beyond. I think it's his." Then she thought for a moment. "Don't ever see him much. Comes in ever once in a while to get some coffee." She paused. "Why're you interested?"

"Just a friend. Anybody else out there with him?" I said.

That was probably one too many questions. She looked at me, eyes narrowing.

"You a cop?" she said, looking from me to Richie and then to Gunner.

I shook my head. "No. The padre's a friend. We we're hoping to surprise him." And let me tell you, that wasn't very convincing because she continued to stare and shake her head.

"We don't talk about folks to strangers…no offense, Huck," she said, looking his way.

"I know, Mattie," he said, apologetically. "Trust me on this one. We just want to surprise the padre. He's our friend." Gunner snickered.

By this time the people at the counter had turned and were staring at us. I could see we were done here.

"Thanks for your help, Mattie," I said, everyone still staring. Somebody yelled "Good to see you Huck!" as the door banged behind us. We were making progress but no friends.

I stared back at the End O' The World Cafe and wondered what planet it had come from. Huck noticed.

"These are island people," he said. "Many of them from families that have dwelt in this land for a hundred years or more. If your name ain't Brown, or Smallwood, or Futch, you won't get much information. This is a closed town, Coop. And you ain't part of it."

"But you are," I said. "And I bet you can get us to that house from what Mattie told you."

"You betchum, Kemo Sabe," he said.

"I'm not the Lone Ranger, Huck."

"Nope. And I'm not Tonto. But that there's an expression that my people have used for a century," and I just shut up after that. What was the use of fussing.

CHAPTER 66

The Dark Road

"So where is this house?" I said.

"Follow me," he said, climbing into his truck. His tires squealed as he led the way out of the parking lot of the End O' The World Cafe and into the darkness of Smallwood Drive. We followed his taillights as he turned off the main road onto a side road, Richie in the back with Gunner.

A small child in shorts, no shoes, was walking toward us on the berm of the road. She stopped and watched us. There were a few isolated houses in the shadows behind her. There were no lights in any of them. I wondered how safe it was for her to be out this time of night. I waved to her. She stared back and then ran into the darkness.

About a half mile east of the café, Huck swung left off the road into what looked like a black hole. No mailboxes, no houses, just an old dirt trail that led through the swamp. We took it, the Volvo picking its way carefully through ruts, potholes, and overgrowth that blocked whatever light emanated from the rising moon, leaving only the taillights of Huck's pick-up now well ahead of us.

"Where the hell's he takin' us?" said Richie. "Can't see a damn thing." I forgot to mention Richie's one fear: the water. He can't swim.

Gunner continued his silence. After a few minutes of darkness, penetrated only by the bouncing headlights of the Volvo as it heaved forward and Huck's taillights far ahead, a field of sawgrass emerged. And then the road ended suddenly. There was a small turn-around where a Mercedes sedan and a Land Rover were parked. Huck's pick-up sat next to them, Huck leaning against the hood, holding a rifle across his chest.

My headlights lit up a wooden walkway lined with handrails that led into the sawgrass. I killed the lights. I sat there a few minutes trying to get accustomed to the dark.

"It's blacker than hell out there," whispered Richie, leaning forward.

"You still with us?" I said, turning to Gunner.

No response. Then, "Yeah, I'm still here."

"Have you ever been here?"

"No."

I didn't believe him.

"Okay, now here's what were going to do," and even as I said it I noticed a light blink through the swamp—maybe a football field or two away—beyond the walkway. I turned back to Gunner. "You make any noise, I'll knock you senseless and leave you for the gators. Okay?" thinking I should do that anyway.

"I'm already dead," he muttered. But I saw him nod in the darkness.

Richie got out of the car, opened the trunk and pulled out his Remington 12 gauge and a Winchester 1894 model that loads .30-.30 ammo. He pumped the shotgun once and checked the load. Gunner jumped and hit his head on the car roof when he heard the noise.

I checked the load of the .357 Magnum I was carrying in a shoulder holster. Then I pulled the Glock out of the glove compartment and stuck it in my belt—behind my back so an accidental discharge wouldn't hit me in the groin. There's no safety on the Glock.

Richie pushed a Kel-tec PF9, 9-millimeter semi-automatic pistol into his shoulder holster, grabbed the rifle, and handed the shotgun to me. I guess he didn't need the ball bat since he left it in the car. Then he opened the passenger door and told Gunner to get out. He did, slowly, groaning as he inched his long body through the door.

"So let's do this," I said, nodding for Gunner to lead the way. "Remember what I said," I whispered as he started out into the swamp. Richie fell in behind me, with Huxter right behind him, cradling his old gator gun, a .223 Remington, and a fearsome hunting knife he had just sharpened on his buckskins.

CHAPTER 67

The House on Chokoloskee Island

A light mist was settling over the swamp as we made our way over the wooden path, the only thing guiding us, a rail on each side. The distant light that I had seen earlier was growing more distinct. Then an outline of a house began to emerge over the marsh grass. It had a peaked roof with gables that looked ominous in the fog. I pushed Gunner ahead. He stumbled then regained his balance against the rail, muttering under his breath. I reiterated my warning.

The night air was cool, a dampness accompanying it. And I became aware of the sounds of the walkway as we neared the house—it creaked and moaned more than I had noticed. Voices muffled by the distance were more distinct now as we approached dry land. I stepped off the walkway about a hundred yards from the house, Richie and Huck right behind me. The structure loomed in front of us like something out of a Halloween set. It was raised above the swamp on pilings, resting like a spider about to move. In the middle of the pilings a wooden stairway ascended into the floor of the house.

"What's the plan?" whispered Richie.

"Don't have one," I said. "Let's wait and see what they do."

"Good plan," said Richie. And we waited.

Lights blinked on and off as forms passed by open windows. I crawled up the embankment to get a better look. Then a door opened beneath the house and two adults came down the narrow stairway pushing two kids in front of them. The kids struggled to keep their balance. Then two more children appeared followed by several more adults barking at them in Spanish. The kids hurried against each other trying to get down.

We had crawled to within thirty yards of the house. Our cover was a pile of brush.

I counted four adults so far. Then two more children appeared on the steps with two more adults behind them, pushing them ahead and down the stairs. One of them was tall, his body angled against the meager light of the moon as he descended. Hector, I thought. One of the children was crying. I heard a sharp slap, skin against skin, and the crying stopped. I wondered if Eddie was one of those kids.

Then a large man emerged behind him and hesitated on the stairs as if he were surveying the whole operation, talking the whole time in tones too low to decipher and pointing at the children who were standing in a group. And I knew I was watching Murphy.

I pulled my Glock and took aim, at his center body, and held my arm steady, knowing all along that it was a long shot. An impossible shot. And I muttered 'click' under my breath. And I lowered the gun.

CHAPTER 68

Into the Darkness

And so Murphy would live another day. Lucky him—or maybe not. And he urged the children away from us toward a growth of mangroves south of the house. And the small forms stumbled and struggled as they went, and the men pushed, and the night air was cold, and the moon hardly lit their way as they moved—and all of this on All Hallows' Eve. And I realized that these orphans of the night might never put on Halloween masks again— unless we rescued them. Tonight. And I thought of Maxie and that drove me harder.

Up ahead, toward Chokoloskee Bay, I heard the sudden roar of an inboard motor.

"What the hell...?" whispered Richie. Gunner froze next to me.

I looked around for Huxter but he had split off and was creeping through sawgrass on our right, carrying his rifle high and heading toward the bay. He shook his gun to indicate that he had heard the noise.

Chokoloskee Bay is a large body of water that begins at the town of Chokoloskee and extends southward into the Ten Thousand Islands which stretch across the southwestern edge of the Everglades. The waters from the bay flow through the Islands into the Gulf of Mexico and from there into the Atlantic. Once a boat gets into the open waters of the Gulf, it's hard to catch, especially a go-fast boat, the choice of smugglers. And they're faster than anything the Coast Guard has.

And it was toward this bay—and the boat docked there—that the kidnappers drove their captives. And the children, slumped forward as though bracing against the wind and prodded like cattle, pushed on slowly to the boathouse that overlooked Chokoloskee Bay. And there a go-fast boat was roaring out its welcome, churning the water hard and throwing it against the dock.

So here's what we had. There were six adults plus the boat driver. There were only three of us. Forget Gunner. They had at least one go-fast boat. We didn't have any. So I called 911. The operator asked me my location. I told her Chokoloskee Island in the Everglades. She said, where? I repeated what I had told her. She asked me what was our emergency. I told her there was a kidnapping going on and we needed help. She fell silent. I asked her if she was still there.

She said, "Yes sir. One moment please. I'm connecting you to the Collier County Sheriff's Office."

The children were now close to the boathouse, the roar of the engines from the go-fast boat building as we got nearer. Richie, Gunner and I were only about a hundred feet behind them but they hadn't seen us yet. Huxter was closer, having circled in from the right. He was concealed by overgrowth near the water's edge.

"I have someone from the Collier County Sheriff's Department on the line, sir," the 911 operator said. "Can you hear me? There's a lot of noise on your end."

I told her I could.

A woman came on the line.

"What's your name and location, sir?"

I told her.

"What seems to be the trouble?" Matter-of-fact.

Another boat fired up. The noise was deafening. I told her what was happening and that I needed to get off. She told me not to do anything, that she would call the Coast Guard and asked me if this was the number where they could reach me. I yelled yeah and hung up. The adults were loading the children into two boats—one the fast boat and the other a larger boat parked next to it. Their motors churned the water like a hurricane and made a hellish noise.

Huck suddenly stood up and yelled, waving his rifle high over his head. But the roar of the boats screamed over his voice, the motors throwing water five to ten feet high, making it impossible to distinguish the good guys from the bad guys. So I closed the distance between me and the boats and Huck fired a warning shot into the air.

"Careful!" I screamed. "The kids.

Both boats cleared the dock, leaped out of the water, and headed with a roar into the center of the bay.

The average go-fast boat is built out of fiberglass and is anywhere from thirty to fifty feet long. The larger one was closer to fifty.

Both boats were equipped with three engines, probably 350s, and capable of generating speeds over ninety miles per hour, fast enough to outrun even the Coast Guard's chaser boat.

They were disappearing quickly into the bay. Panicked, I looked back at the boathouse. There was a boat moored inside. A triple-engine Grady White, its motors were in the water and ready to go. I boarded and headed for the captain's chair. Richie and Huck were right behind me. Huck cast off while Richie pushed Gunner into a seat in the cockpit.

I hit the starter button, throttled forward, and eased the boat out of its mooring, trying to search the bay for the lights of the two renegade boats. All I could hear was the drone of their motors in the distance. No lights. I had driven this water many times over the last six years, first with a fishing guide but always entering from the Gulf side. Never from here. I knew to watch out for logs, sea grass, and shallow water. The open waters of the bay were easy to maneuver. No problem—in the day. But at night...? That's a different story. And the killer would be to follow the kidnappers through the maze of channels and slim waterways that weave in and out of the islands—ten thousand of them—literally—and the chances of getting lost are great, even for the seasoned sailors that live around the bay—especially at night. And tonight the moon was caught behind some clouds. But I threw the throttle ahead full anyway and the Grady White leaped out of the water like it was just as anxious as I was to find those children.

"Keep this thing in the middle and stay away from the mangroves when we hit the islands, Coop," Huck yelled over the roar of the motors. I nodded.

One of the boats was relatively small, like a Baia 40 Outlaw, the favorite of smugglers. Baias are inboards and so there is less chance of getting hung up, whereas the boat I was driving is a fishing boat with outboard motors, easier to get caught in sea grass, oyster beds, or the shallows. But the good thing is the Grady White is fast, almost as fast as the Baia.

The other boat was larger, able to carry eight to ten passengers, and yet just as fast as the Baia, its hull camouflaged like a military landing craft. The wide stern of the larger lead boat accommodated at least three, maybe four inboards. When it had left the dock they had let out a low and menacing rumble.

In the end, it all came down to one thing: We couldn't let them get to the Gulf and into the Caribbean. Even the Coast Guard would have a tough time finding them in the open sea. And if they crossed into Cuban waters, they would be out of reach.

The roar of our own motors made it impossible to hear the fast boats. And they were apparently running without lights. So I cut the motors to idle and we sat in the silence listening. I heard the whine of the fast boats off starboard. I had an idea of where they were headed or at least should be. So I pushed the throttle full ahead and the Mercurys sent us flying into the direction of the Ten Thousand Islands and the pass where I figured they were headed.

"You want me to take the wheel?" Huck said, hanging over my shoulder. "We're in the Indian hunting grounds."

I gave him the wheel and went below deck to look for treasures. I found what I was looking for. A pair of night glasses. Made sense for them to be on board—especially for bad guys who run in darkness. I came back topside. Richie was sitting behind Huck on the long seat in the cockpit, Gunner beside him. I was suspicious of Gunner's long silence. He had a brooding, angry look.

The night sped by quickly as we crossed the bay and approached the first of the islands that lay directly south of Chokoloskee. Huck pointed over the prow at lights in the distance—running lights from a boat.

"They're headin' for Sandfly Island," Huck said, pulling back on the throttle.We had caught up to them more quickly than I thought we would. My guess, they didn't know we were tracking them. But then what they didn't know is we had the best tracker in the Everglades: Huxter Crow.

"Figure they're about two hundred yards ahead," he said, peering into the darkness of the swamp. It was almost impenetrable.

"Hear that?" he whispered.

"They're slowing," I said, their motors winding down from a steady whine to the mutter of idle speed.

"Uh huh. They're crossin' the shallows around Sandfly." The going would be slow through there.

Huck entered the islands north of Sandfly, following the lights of the fast boats in the distance. The Ten Thousand Islands were all around us now, their shorelines serving as the edges of the waters that flowed among them. Navigating any water at night is treacherous, but the Ten Thousand Islands pose additional problems: sand bars, and the tangled roots of mangroves reaching out from the shore, and alligators and crocodiles— there's always the chance of running into one of them if we drifted too close to the shore. The American alligator can jump six feet vertically into the air. I didn't want to tell Richie that. So the only safe passage was to stay in the center of the waterway. Even there we could get hung up on a sandbar or oyster bed.

Huck was steady at the wheel as I strained to find the shoreline and looked for debris that might have drifted into the water. I told Richie and Gunner to split up, one on each side of the boat to help spot the random log lying in wait or for oyster beds that would tear the bottom of the Grady to shreds. Not easy without running lights. So I switched on a searchlight mounted on the deck.

"Why don't you use the night glasses," said Huck, pulling back on the throttle as he steered away from a log that had drifted into our path. "That searchlight's like sending up smoke signals."

I shut it off and picked up the night glasses from the cockpit. The shore lit up like it was midday.

"What's our speed?" I asked, looking down at the speedometer and getting the answer before Huck told me.

"We're below ten knots," he said. "Better to be..."

"...safe than sorry," I said.

"'White man reads minds," he said.

"On the port," I said, the glasses tight against my eyes. "Maybe a..."

"Sandbar," Huck finished. " Then, he poked me and pointed directly ahead.

"Lights," he said, whispering over the motors now at idle. He edged the throttle ahead.

"You see something?" said Richie entering the cockpit and straining into the darkness. Gunner was still standing at the gunnels at starboard, looking for debris I supposed. I wondered if he considered jumping overboard. There wouldn't be much we could do if he did. Good riddance maybe, I thought.

"Richie noticed me eyeing Gunner. "Let that dumb goombah jump. A gator would have him some good Irish stew." I cringed at the image.

The lights from the boats skittered in and out of the darkness as we slowly gained ground on the fast boats. Huck guided the Grady White carefully through a channel crowded on both sides by mangrove islands. I didn't breathe until we were in open water again. We had lost their lights for a short time while we were in the channel, but they flickered on again, bouncing over the water like tiny stars. Then just as suddenly, they disappeared.

"Listen," said Huck. And he turned his ear into the Great Swamp's cool night air.

I could hear a hum of motors—like bumble bees swarming over a field of flowers. Gunner had left his post on starboard and joined us in the cockpit. He was staring at the lights and I could almost see his mind working on an escape plan—wait until we get close then drop over the side and swim like hell.

Clouds slid away from the moon. And there it was, low in the sky, reflecting off the water and illuminating the shore like a great lantern hanging over fields at harvest time.

We were drifting now, the outboards at idle, and ahead I could hear the muffled roar of the fast boats. Their running lights had disappeared again. They were probably in a narrow channel. Plenty of logs and sandbars there to sink their boats. I guessed they were lost and poring over maps to see where they were.

I told Huck to kill the motors. I wasn't surprised when I heard voices in the near distance. Then through the mangroves and over the otherwise quiet waters, I heard the sound of someone revving a motor, like an angry NASCAR racer trying to get out of the pit and back on the track. Like someone hung up on a sandbar. We had them.

CHAPTER 69

Over the Side

"Where the hell's Gunner?" said Richie turning around in a panic. I was so focused on the fast boats that I hadn't been watching him. I figured he would try to jump. I just didn't think it would happen until we got closer to the boats. He's crazy, I thought. The damn water is full of gators. And moccasins. And Burmese Pythons. But I didn't care about catching him. His use to us was over—we had our prey and they were just a few hundred yards away.

I still couldn't see the boats. But the voices rode distinctly over the water, interrupted now and then by the revving of a motor. Because they were busy, we were able to draw near. I could now see the boats, both close to the shore and off our starboard. One boat was hung up on what was probably a sandbar. They clearly didn't know these waters. The currents that flow to and from the Gulf of Mexico carry the sand as the tides work their way through the islands and wash up against the shore, depositing the sand in the narrow channels that run between the islands. And so a sandbar develops, much like what you see along any Florida beach where the ocean has washed up against the shore and gathered sand in its lap, carrying it into the deep so that when the tide goes out the wader can cross shallow water to a sand bar—a temporary island that will disappear again when the tide comes in and re-deposits the sand onto the shore.

I was leaning against the gunnel and pressing the Steiner binoculars against my eyes. The moon hung just above the boats like a lantern overseeing their work. The boat that was gunning its motors was trying to dislodge the other from its sandy prison, staying far enough away to avoid the same fate.

No one had seen us as yet. Figures moved back and forth on the boat that was hung up. They were gesturing and shouting over the noise. I didn't see the children. Probably huddling on the boat's floor.

I heard splashing on the port side. I turned my glasses toward the sound and saw a swimmer pushing hard for the fast boats and waving to get their attention. Someone in the boat stood up and fired a shot, hitting the water near the swimmer. He screamed.

"Must be Gunner," said Huck, idling the boat around in his direction. "Loco men are shooting at him!"

The swimmer screamed again at the man in the boat, then the shooter dropped his rifle and waved him in. Several men reached over the side and pulled him aboard. When he stood his tall frame hunched against the moon. Then he pointed in our direction. It was Gunner.

"They've got us," I said, watching through my glasses.

Richie grabbed Huck's Remington and fired at the boat, missing it by yards. A young girl screamed. I grabbed the gun out of his hands. "What the hell are you doing?" I whispered—loudly.

"I missed deliberately," he said, angry with my interference.

"We don't need to be killing any of the kids," I warned him.

'Bastards," is all he said as he let go of the gun.

I handed it back to Huck who grabbed it and glared at Richie. "You don't light a prairie fire when there's papooses around," he said.

Gunfire flashed from the big boat spraying shells into the water around us, none of them hitting the Grady White. I took the wheel, pushed the throttle forward, and swung the boat around to put distance between us, then pulled into an inlet downstream from the two boats. I let the boat drift as we watched bodies, small and large, clamber out of the stranded boat and move from the sandbar into deeper water where the larger boat was waiting. I wondered how much room there was—six kids and eight adults, including Gunner and the driver. They moved in slow motion—the children—herded like the captives they were into the channel where they waded through water lit only by the reflection of the moon. We couldn't fire, of course. The kids.

So on this Halloween Eve all the ghosts were out. The mangroves and palms moved in unison with the forms in the river, mimicking their motion as they struggled with the current. A procession of the dead—or soon to be dead if we couldn't save them. Before this night was over I feared some of them might be counted among the lost souls that we would celebrate on the eve of All Souls' Day—that would be tomorrow—a day when the souls of the dead wait to be freed by prayer and to be counted among the saints. Tonight the saints and sinners were intermingled.

And so we sat in the water, motors idling, helpless to act, the children so close and yet so far away. Our only hope was to follow them until the Coast Guard caught up with us, sooner than later I hoped.

Richie was getting restless. "We gotta do something."

"What we can do is follow."

"Us following ain't gonna get us nowheres," Richie said and raised his rifle.

"Put that thing away," I said, pushing away the Winchester. "We'll wait for the Coast Guard."

Richie was not happy with me. We didn't talk for a while, just watched the scene continue to unfold in the river. One of the children was crying, the sobbing low and constant.

A last few shadowy forms stood up in the shallows, in the moonlight, and then hurried and pushed through the last few yards to the fast boat. We were less than a hundred yards away from them now, with a clear view from the inlet. I wondered why they didn't fire at us. Too anxious to get the hell out, I supposed.

As soon as the last person boarded, the pilot gunned the engine, sending the boat recklessly into the center of the waterway with the inboards churning up great heaps of spray in their wake. They would never learn. I pushed the throttle full ahead and followed in the middle of their wake, figuring if there was any trouble ahead—as I was sure there would be—they would hit it first. Then we would have them.

The night screamed past as we raced down the waters separating the islands. They were never built for this kind of traffic. The driver of the fast boat took a sharp right and headed west past the north end of Sandfly Island. They were taking us deeper into the islands and away from the waters I was familiar with. I tried to picture the maze of waterways as we followed. But without a chart, it was hopeless.

I lost their wake as they pulled ahead and disappeared into the darkness. Huck had the night goggles on. "Watch out!" he yelled. "A sandbar."

I swung hard to the port side and felt the stern dig into sand. A scraping sound sent chills down my spine.

"Let me see what we've got," he said and jumped overboard.

As I heard him splash around in front of the boat, I wondered about the creatures that lurked in those dark waters. Richie was leaning over the side with me as I tried to locate him.

Then out of the darkness, "We're hung up," came Huck's voice from beneath the boat. "I need some help."

I looked at Richie. He looked back at me, like *are you kidding?* I shrugged and explained that I had to tend the wheel. He shook his head and with what I know must have taken an ocean of resolve, grabbed a life vest from the deck, strapped it on, held his nose and jumped in. He immediately came up coughing and sputtering like a drowning man.

"You're standing on a sandbar," I yelled. "It's shallow there."

Once he realized it he blew the water out of his nose, cursed me, Huck, and the water, and then waded the few feet to where Huck was standing. I turned on the deck lights so we could see what we were doing. Huck had his hands on his hips—the water was only waist high. He was shaking his head.

Once they got positioned on either side of the bow, Huck yelled for me to slowly reverse the engines, which I did. I felt the boat grind its way off the sand as Huck and Richie leaned into it, Richie cursing and yelling until the sandbar suddenly lost its hold and the boat floated free. I eased the motors to idle again and waited for Richie and Huck to climb back on board.

In the meantime the kidnappers and the children were long gone.

CHAPTER 70

Racing the Moon

The moon stayed with us as we rushed past overhanging mangroves, their roots stretching into the water, some just below the surface. The right side of the boat caught a branch that ripped off some hardware on the boat's deck cover. And oyster beds were everywhere. No way to see them. Luckily we hadn't hit any yet. Then, I picked up the sound of the fast boat again.

The moon helped us navigate the treacherous waters that wove like a spider web through the mangrove islands as I tried to follow the sound. The high pitch of their motors indicated that they were speeding. Probably confident that they had lost us. And probably trying to make up for lost time. And probably meeting a larger ship in the Caribbean where they would make a transfer of cargo—I'm talking about the kids of course. A valuable cargo—each one worth hundreds of thousands of dollars on the black market—each one with no idea of what lie ahead—and each one with a different ending: maybe sold into slavery, maybe used as prostitutes, maybe sold for body parts, or maybe all of the above. I've said enough.

But the driver was pushing through the islets that make up the mangrove forests of the Ten Thousand Islands too quickly. No one, no matter how well they knew these waters, could possibly see all the traps in these back waters in the moonlight. I was just waiting for the sound of a hull scraping against the sharp edges of a bed of oysters. So I slowed down so I could back off when I heard it.

Then it came—a crunching of fiberglass against sharpened shells and the whine of angry engines fighting for deep water. They were done. I throttled back and brought the Grady White to a stop. We were about a hundred yards away from them.

Someone screamed: "Don't come any closer or we'll kill these kids."

I looked at Richie.

"What the hell, Cooper. We can't sit here and do nothing. I say we go after the bastards."

I called out Murphy's name, hoping to reason with him. No answer. Then I thought I heard someone call out. A child?

"Might as well give it up," I yelled back. "The Coast Guard's on its way."

At least I hoped they were. I hadn't heard anything since we left the dock on Chokoloskee Island.

The boat was stationary. There was no movement on board. No sounds. Just the waves from the water washing up against the hull. Our two boats sat facing each other in the dimness of the moon, in the quiet of the swamp—like two sides in the trenches on a battlefield, the first one moving loses.

Then there was a disturbance in the silence—like the sound of a gator slipping into the water—only it didn't come from the shore. *Someone's making the first move,* I thought.

I let Huck take the wheel so I could focus on the water. "Back it up," I said, knowing that we would be firing in the direction of the children if we stayed where we were.

And so he did and headed for a mangrove island off starboard about a hundred feet from where we were. Huck tucked the Grady White into a dark inlet where the moon didn't shine. I scanned the water for waders. I saw two heads bobbing in the deep, apparently not seeing where we had gone. The moon disappeared behind cloud cover and darkness concealed everything.

Richie picked up his Winchester and the night goggles.

"I got this," he said. I nodded.

It was tricky. Richie used the gunnel as support as I placed the night goggles on the barrel.

"This working?" I said.

"You got it, boss," he said and fired four quick rounds into the dark. Someone screamed.

"Got one!" Richie said. "Keep that damn thing steady," he continued, his right eye still glued to the night sights. He fired again. No sound, just the report of the Winchester ripping through the quiet.

"Two down," he said, lifting his head from the rifle.

I heard the boat start up again. It was trying to break free from the oyster bed. Amazingly the big boat surged ahead, and there was a loud scraping sound as the motors whined like an injured animal. It finally broke loose and headed into open waters. I heard children scream as the boat's powerful engines sent a wake that rocked our boat. I knew they wouldn't get far. And so Huck followed their wake, easing the

Grady White forward while staying well away from the oyster bed.

Then our boat hit something. Huck cut the motors. I scanned the waters with the spotlight. A log. Floating like a dead body. I thought of the two we had just killed and wondered where their bodies were. They would have a quick burial, I thought, as I heard something slide into the water from the shore. Gators.

CHAPTER 71

The Children's Hour

If you would check a boater's map of this region, you would see that the Chokoloskee Bay empties into the Ten Thousand Islands like water into a sieve. It pours through the mangrove swamps that comprise the Islands, forming a network of waterways that flow eventually into the Gulf of Mexico. The trick is to find your way through that maze and into the waters of the open sea. You can get lost in the islands in the daylight, let alone at night. I used to fish among the islands in my eighteen foot Boston Whaler. But that was always in daylight. And even then I usually stayed to the south of Chokoloskee, crossing the one and a half miles of the Bay toward Chokoloskee Pass which lies south/southwest of the island. From there I would follow the Pass all the way to Rabbit Key and then into the Gulf of Mexico. I never entered the islands the way we did tonight, nor did I ever explore that area.

The fast boats had initially gone into the Islands north of Chokoloskee Pass through Sandfly Pass, and now they were trying to find their way out of the maze of mangrove swamps and into deeper waters. They were clearly lost. By following them we had a good chance of getting lost as well. The passes offer relatively safe passage to careful boaters in the daylight since the coral beds that line the waterways are usually marked with white PC pipes clearly visible in the sun. Driving these waters at night is kind of like feeling one's way along an Afghan road trying to avoid IEDs and other roadside traps.

The sound of their motors echoed over the swamp. I took over the wheel so Huck could stand in the front of the boat with the night vision glasses and look for sand bars and oyster beds and maybe pick up traces of their wake. We weren't that far behind them. I strained to see the shoreline of the islands that seemed to rise randomly on every side. We were in the maze of islands somewhere between Sandfly Pass to the north and Chokoloskee Pass to the south. I knew that much. But without maps, maneuvering the big Grady through oyster beds was like feeling my way through a dark basement with glass strewn across the floor. There was the light of the moon, to be sure. And we had sonar. But that didn't help much since the oyster beds would be on us too quickly to stop the boat. Suddenly the night was still once again, except for the sound of our own boat.

Huck was pointing at a clearing about two hundred yards ahead.

I could see the outline of the fast boat in the reflected light of October's moon. It wasn't moving. Hung up again, I was betting, on an oyster bed. I spotted activity in the waters near their boat. So I idled the Grady White slowly ahead as Huck scanned the water for sand bars and oyster beds.

There were swimmers in the water. Several of them spotted us and began crying for help. I turned the boat toward the nearest swimmer. He was splashing erratically. We were within a few feet of him in seconds, close enough for Huck to jump off the boat and grab him. I cut the engines so Richie could open the small hatch at the stern. Huck handed the boy to Richie. Water was pouring from his clothes and he was coughing and sputtering like a drowning man. He collapsed on the deck and then after a few moments pulled himself up against the gunnels where he rested, his head in his hands. Then he looked around to see where he was and finally locked on me.

"You're safe now," I said, sitting down next to him and putting my arm around him. He was thin and shaking. He was about twelve years old, I figured, and the 'old' showed in his face.

Then Huck jumped overboard and swam away to rescue another kid. Richie had gone below to find something warm for the boy to throw over his shoulders. I took the wheel and idled the boat toward Huck, watching carefully so as not to run over a swimmer.

And so it went under the Hunter's Moon, hands reaching out, Richie and I grabbing arms of swimmers, pulling them out of the water into the safety of the boat, and Huxter muttering to himself as he swam back for another. By the time we were done, we had five kids sprawled out on the deck, coughing and crying, and looking at us, their eyes wide with fear. I wondered what horrors each one had experienced, and I wondered how long it had been—their captivity. Days? Weeks? Months? And I wondered what goes through the mind of a child who has been taken. And I drove that thought from my mind. My advice. Don't try to understand. It will take you to a very bad place.

Huck finally climbed back on board, water pouring off his bare back and leathers. His hair gray, but looking black in the darkness, was matted against his head and down over his eyes. He shook the water off like a big dog who has just climbed out of a lake.

"I think we got 'em all," he announced. "And I've gotta get dried out before the night chills my bones," and he turned to go below.

"But mister," a young girl said, standing up and grabbing my arm, tears running down her face and mixing with the water from the swamp, "there were six of us."

"Okay," I said, a sudden fear hitting me as I thought of a drowning child. And I looked quickly out over the water, trying not to alarm her. "Okay." And what I saw when I looked into the face of this young girl, her hair wet against her cheeks, was a mother duck leading her little ones across a very dangerous highway. She was a tough and brave girl.

"We're missing one," I said turning around and halting Huck's trip below. "Let's give it one more try." So Richie threw the boat into gear and began to circle the area once more.

CHAPTER 72

One Missing—
One Found

We circled the area where the stranded boat still lay. It was caught in an oyster bed and gradually sinking into its own grave. But the waters of the swamp were still. No sign of anyone swimming. No floating bodies. The kidnappers had apparently abandoned the children and off-loaded themselves at an island near where the boat was stranded. So I gave up the search. We needed to tend to the kids.

You have to picture this. Five soaked children, huddling against each other, trying to get warm. It was time to do something. So I took the wheel from Richie and told him to get Huck. He disappeared below and came back almost immediately with Huck trailing behind, still in wet clothes but looking like he had toweled off.

"No dry clothes?" I asked.

"Negative, Kemo Sabe," he said. "Some towels though. You want me to take the wheel?"

"Roger that," I said. "I'll help Richie get these kids below and dried out." I paused and studied Huck. He had to be worn out from the rescue. "You all right?"

He nodded, then motioned at the kids. "They need you more

right now."

For the first time I was able to survey the kids, the moon providing a little light.

"Let's go," I said, waving for them to follow Richie and me down the ladder.

Below deck was a small kitchen, a shower, and a single bunk tucked into the prow. A leather-covered bench huddled against the starboard side. It faced a sink and several storage cabinets. The toilet was in a closet next to the shower, a TV inserted into the hull over the sink. Three of the children had squeezed onto the bunk. The girl and one of the boys took the bench, all of them still shivering. And they were a mess, faces dirty from sand and sediment from the swamp, hair plastered against their faces, eyes filled with questions, and deep down in each one of them—I could sense it—a lingering fear of what was next. Even now, even in their rescue. And why not? They didn't know us from the men they had just escaped from—except we were being nicer to them. Still, doubt rode in their eyes as I studied this shivering bunch, lips pale from the cold, arms and legs huddled against their bodies.

I studied them all. And no. Not one of them was my son. But the boy sitting next to the girl, a lanky kid, thin face, his hair so messed and wet it could have been any color...I studied his face, and he looked back at me and then away, as if he were possibly in trouble, and I thought of the picture I had taken from Ned Dougherty, and wondered...

"Eddie?" I said, my heart jumping at the name, shaking my head at the foolishness of it. What were the chances that...? out of the hundreds of thousands of kids that go missing every year, Eddie Dougherty would be sitting in front of me in the middle of the Everglades staring at me now, like I had just posed a riddle for him to solve rather than simply what his name was, and besides how many Eddies are there? I mean there must be hundreds of thousands of Eddies, so I quickly added, hoping against every hope, thinking of how happy Ned and Catherine Dougherty would be if this just happened to be their son, but no, I thought, it isn't possible...

"Eddie Dougherty?"

And I think I caught the slightest sign of recognition there, somewhere in those eyes—eyes that had seen what I would nev-er want my own son to see, what I hoped my own son had never seen—a semblance of hope there, a breakthrough, a sign of trust perhaps, out here in Chokoloskee Bay, on the way to being sold into slavery, and...

"Yeah," is all he said, is all he had to say, and my insides jumped with that simple 'yeah' and I grabbed his hands and wanted to hug him, but I could still see the doubt, the suspicion, and then the girl next to him cried, "Yes!" and she hugged Eddie and both began to cry.

And then I told him who I was.

CHAPTER 73

Eddie

"I'm Cooper, Eddie," I said, trying to be calm. He stared at me. "Your mother and father," I began, "hired me to find you. "And so I'm a friend and I'm glad that you're okay," squeezing his hands to assure him.

He said nothing, his thin body still shaking.

"What were they going to do with us?" he asked. Wow. Out of the blue.

I looked around at the others, the girl, and the three other boys who were sitting up on the bunk. Their faces were turned to me, blank in some ways but, underneath it all, full of anxiety, the kind that you see in an animal that isn't sure about a stranger.

I had no idea of how to answer that question. So I didn't.

"Jesus," said Richie, leaning over my shoulder, "these damn kids are freaked!"

"Watch your language," I whispered. "Kids."

But it had been a hellish night and it wasn't over yet. We still had five kids to get to a safe place, one still unaccounted for. And of course there were the bastards who got away.

The girl pulled at my arm and asked, "Are you gonna keep looking for...?" and she hesitated. "I don't know his name..." She looked embarrassed. Then added, "I really don't know anybody's name," like she was responsible for them. "They wouldn't let us talk," she continued, watching me all the time to see if I understood. I nodded that I did.

Then, "What's your name, honey?"

She looked at me, as if to process the question, then said, "Ana."

"I think they may have taken the other boy with them as a hostage." I was hoping. Otherwise... "So we'll have to find the people who had kidnapped you to find him. Okay?"

And she nodded. Then I told her we had to prepare for the trip back and would she help me get the others settled down since they needed sleep, and it was at least a three hour trip back to the mainland, assuming we found the way out. I didn't tell her that. And I didn't tell her about the side trip we would have to take to find the sixth kid. She didn't need to know that. She didn't need to know we might have to kill them—the bad guys—the ones who tried to sell them like goods on the open market.

I looked over at Eddie one more time. Fear still lingered in his eyes. So I bent down, put my arm around him, pulled him close, and told him he was safe and that he was going home. He was still afraid, but I saw the smallest trace of a smile—maybe it was hope. The kids on the bunk watched with their mouths wide open when I told them *We're all going home.* They nodded collectively, but were still staring at me as I went topside.

It would be a long time before the memories of this nightmare would fade into the distance for them. I could only think of my son and wished he were here with me now, and that both of us were going home.

Richie was with Huck who was holding the boat steady until we developed a plan. I asked Richie to make sure the kids got out of their wet clothes and dried off. Uncle Richie. He nodded.

"There are blankets in the holding bins," I said. "They can sleep in those until their clothes dry."

"What am I the babysitter?" I heard him mutter as he headed below. But then I heard him yell, "Now listen up," as he poked his head below, and I knew he was good with it.

Huck guided the boat slowly through the water as I watched the sonar for depths. No one in the water that I could see. I took the wheel while Huck went below for night glasses. In the meantime I turned on the floodlight and searched the shore in the vicinity of where we had picked up the swimmers, hoping to find the missing kid waiting there. Hope beyond hope.

Mangroves crowded the shoreline, their branches reaching out over the water and hiding the dry land. Their roots twisted into the water making a landing difficult if not impossible.

"Over there," Huck said, pointing to a clearing about a hundred yards on port.

I angled the boat to the clearing and throttled back to idle about ten yards off shore while Huck used his glasses to search the dense overgrowth for signs of life. Nobody visible. And no sound except for the murmur of the motors and Richie's voice urging the kids asleep. There was no way to effectively search with a bunch of cold and weary kids below. They would be asleep soon, if they weren't already. And I had the responsibility to get them back to safety as soon as possible.

And yet, the kidnappers were still out there...and one of the kids...and I couldn't let that go.

CHAPTER 74

Murphy

On a chance, I tried 911 again. No signal. I hoped to hell the Coast Guard would come along quickly.

Huxter had his glasses on the fast boat that had drifted into its grave near the oyster bed. The upper deck was still above water. An American flag was flying off the stern. I'm sure they hoped that would show they were patriotic Americans in any run-in with the National Forest police.

I swung the boat toward the fast boat, anchoring a safe distance away from the oyster beds. Richie and Huck had pulled up a raft that was stored below and inflated it. Richie stayed with the boat, keeping it at idle so it wouldn't drift into the oyster bed. Once Huck and I pushed the raft overboard, we had about twenty feet of paddling to reach the sunken vessel. The oyster bed was only about five feet below the raft, but only several feet below the surface where the keel of the fast boat met the bed. The formation of the oysters had cut into the boat's bottom like a fishing knife slicing through an unwitting hand. As we got closer, I could see that the entire area below deck had taken water.

As I climbed aboard, I felt the boat shift under me. Then it stabilized itself as I found my balance. The deck was littered with trash:

shoes, kid sized; paper; charts that had fallen from the cockpit and were now soaked—I assumed Murphy knew how to read them; and the remnants of uneaten food.

I directed the beam of the flashlight below deck: cushions floated randomly, boxes of food, a jacket—or a shirt, I couldn't tell—and a rifle lying against the ladder.

It was late and the night was threatening to take away our chances of escaping the swamp. So I climbed over the side to slip back into the raft, Huck steadying it and holding a flashlight. It was a Torch, and the powerful beam of the light hit the water just under me as I stepped back into our boat. And I thought I saw something in the water below me. A shadow.

"Hey. Down there," I said, pointing to a moving form.

And Huck aimed the beam at where I was pointing.

The light hit the water like the brights on a car. The Torch puts out about 4100 lumens. Almost enough to fry an egg.

"Where did you find that thing?" I said.

"Below deck. It's strong enough to search for my ancestors in the stars," he said.

The lamp cut through the darkness of the water like a knife and lit up the eyes of the man who lay below us, mouth open wide, the side of his head torn away.

"Ey, eyy, ayy," said Huck. I stared at him. "Indian talk," he said.

I didn't ask him what it meant. I was riveted by the eyes. *Death, the great equalizer.*

"It's Murphy." I wondered who killed him.

"Hmmm. Whassup, chebon?" Huck said, staring into Murphy's torn face. "This the chebon who owned the boats?"

"What are you talking about?" I said.

"Is he the dude who owned the boats?"

He is," I said, studying Murphy's torn face. Yeah, somebody killed him, I figured.

"He don't own them any more, does he?" A statement more than a question. "What're we gonna do with this chebon?"

"Leave him. Let the Coast Guard deal with him. This is a good place for him to lie; he made his bed, let him…"

I never finished it, Huxter shaking his head like *Okay I got it.* The moon hung over the mangroves like a lantern in a graveyard.

CHAPTER 75

The Search

"So?" said Richie as he helped me through the hatch on the boat's stern. "Murphy," I said, looking back at the dark grave. "He's sleeping with the oysters."

"We kill him?"

"I don't know. Maybe one of them did. Whatever. He took the secret with him."

"How are the kids?" I said.

"Asleep like the dead..." then he stopped. "Sleeping," he said, correcting himself.

The chill of the swamp was beginning to set in.

"We got enough blankets to keep them warm," he continued. "But they're still in their same old wet clothes." Mother Richie.

"Yeah," I mused, feeling the dampness of the night crowding in around me. "Whatever we're gonna do, we better do it quickly. I don't know how much more those kids can stand."

The three of us stood in the cockpit as the boat idled. I shook my head then urged the boat from idle to a slow roar. The Mercurys pushed us away from Murphy and the stranded boat and I angled the Grady White toward an island that lay about forty yards from where the fast boat was hung up. We still had a missing child to find and I was thinking of the pain on Ana's face when she told me about him. And there was Gunner. And Hector. And the men who were with them. And they were there—somewhere—in the darkness of the mangroves—and they would have to pay. I would make sure of it.

CHAPTER 76

One of Ten Thousand

"One of us has to stay on board with the kids," I said, looking sidewise at Richie.

He shrugged. "Damn babysitter." But I suspected he liked it—the protection business. Then..."Hell yeah. I'm good. Yous guys get into trouble, just yell. Richie'll be there," and he looked toward the ladder where the kids were tucked away below. They had a new father now, a hit man turned babysitter. They didn't know how lucky they were.

Huck and I prepared to go ashore. Richie steadied the boat as Huck and I stepped through the hatch and back onto the raft. He passed the guns over the side: Huck's alligator rifle and my Glock.

"Better take this too," he said, handing me the Mossberg. Like I said, Mother Richie.

I pushed away and we headed for the island closest to the stranded boat.

The Ten Thousand Islands is a name that was given to the area because of the number of small islands that populate the region from Marco Island to Flamingo. I don't think anyone actually counted them. Kind of like saying there are hundreds of thousands of stars on the night sky. But when you're navigating the islands, it feels like at least that many. And without a good guide, a map, or a GPS you could easily get lost—for days, weeks, or forever for that matter. I was glad Huck was with us. He's like an Indian tracker. Matter of fact, he is exactly that.

The island that we targeted seemed like the most likely place the kidnappers would head for. It's the closest piece of land in the area. Many of the islands are simply marshes overgrown with mangroves, no land to build a shack on. Generally one would need a canoe to explore the islands and paddle down the canals that run through the marshes. Navigating those waters takes daring and know-how. They are teeming with alligators, crocodiles, and Burmese Pythons, and then there are the panthers, coyotes, and wild dogs on dry land. In short, the great marsh is a zoo without walls. In this case we're the ones looking out. The animals are watching us.

Some of the islands have sandy beaches where it's possible to put-in and explore. Most of those are small. Several islands—like Tiger Key, about six and a half miles from the ranger station—have camping areas for overnights. We were nowhere near Tiger Key.

I heard something slide into the water as we pulled the raft up onto a sandy shore relatively free of mangroves. I knew what that was.

We headed inland, listening for sounds of human activity. As I mentioned, Huck is a skilled tracker. So he moved ahead of me, his light poking a hole into the darkness of the interior.

He used his hunting knife to hack through some dense under-brush and then suddenly we were in a field of sawgrass where the moon, now free of the mangrove forest, illuminated a savannah that stretched for maybe a hundred yards. Beyond that was a wall of darkness, probably another mangrove forest. So far there was no sign of life anywhere.

Huck surveyed the open field for a few minutes. A breeze—ever so slight—brushed against the grass. It moved in rhythm with the night—peaceful and silent—as though there were nothing evil in its presence. We stood there for a few moments transfixed by the motion and by the moon, this Hunter's Moon. The first moon after the Harvest Moon, so named because the American Indian used its light to stalk his prey as he hunted to store up food for the winter. And tonight it hung low over the field like a lamp, creating a path across the sawgrass, like a road with indistinct berms whose surface moved gently in the wind.

Huck had been studying the scene before us. Then he crouched, pointing straight ahead like an Indian scout in a James Stewart western.

"Cooper," he whispered, "see that bent grass?" directing my attention to the open field.

I nodded.

"That's where they went," and so I followed him into the meadow, spongy and wet from recent rains.

The night was quiet except for the sounds we created making our way to the tree line. I heard a rustling in the underbrush ahead: a coyote or wolf, or maybe a panther. Then a sudden explosion of sound as birds came flying out of the tangle of grass and branches. I must have jumped several feet because I heard Huck whisper, "Christ, chebon, you ever been in the woods before? It's just some birds."

Then he was out ahead again, at times either waving me on or holding me up with hand signals. I was checking everywhere for the sounds of an alligator. No use in worrying about the python. He doesn't make sounds.

We were almost at the dense mangrove forest when Huck waved vigorously for me to disappear. I dropped down below the level of the sawgrass. Voices, like whispers, floated in the wind. I froze. They weren't far away.

Huck came back and pointed straight ahead into the trees. I nodded. Then, suddenly, the sky lit up like the Fourth of July. A flare. It arced overhead. We were exposed for a few moments like players on a well-lit football field. I buried myself into the sawgrass, the dampness of the ground working its way quickly into my body. I didn't breath. Then the flare dove gradually for the treetops. There was no sound of alarm from the trees. They hadn't seen us.

They also didn't see the twelve-foot gator that had appeared briefly in the flare's light as it disappeared into the darkness. It was sitting on high ground near the tree line. I nudged Huck. He nodded, held up his alligator gun and smiled as if to say *no problem.*

Then, "What now, Kemo Sabe?" he whispered.

"Try to get as close as we can."

And I began to move slowly through the high grass and away from the gator to the far left of the tree line and away from the voices.

"Come on, Huck," I whispered, looking around. He wasn't there. He was heading straight for the trees on my right. I scrabbled ahead quickly, grabbed at his pant leg and stopped him.

"Where the hell are you going?" I said, keeping my voice low. "We're not charging into their camp. Besides they may have one of the kids with them. Let's see how many there are and exactly where they are, first. Besides there's a gator over there!" I whispered hoarsely.

He pulled back reluctantly. "Okay," he said. "Then what?" I knew he wanted to get near that gator.

"We're not hunting gators, Huck. And they're not in season," I added.

"That's funny, chebon," he said. But I knew he had plans for that gator.

Another flare went up, turning the sky into shades of red and orange. Then the moon spilled its light over the swamp once again as the flare died out, casting shadows where there were none minutes before and transforming the tree line into a dense and impenetrable wall of darkness.

"They must be trying to signal a boat out in the water," I whispered to Huck.

"Think so, pardner," he said, sitting up and laying the rifle across his lap.

The voices continued like the murmurs of ghosts on this the last night of October. I strained to hear what they were saying. But they would not give up their secrets. We were out of the high grass now and crawling toward the tree line. I could hear the wash of water against land. I figured we were close to the shoreline on the other side of the island. We entered the tree line east of where I had spotted the gator. I was hoping he wasn't tracking us. What we crawled into was a dense collection of pines and cypress where the ground was damp and marshy. Finally we came to where the mangroves met the waters of the swamp which flowed among their roots feeding them like mother's milk. Beyond the mangroves and to our left was the shore.

I reached for Huck's night vision glasses.

There were three adults and a boy standing near the edge of the mangroves looking out over the water. Perhaps waiting for a boat. And then I heard engines in the distance and they slowly grew more distinct. Not a fast boat.

"They're getting help," I said, handing the glasses back to Huck so he could have a look.

"I see four adults and a boy. Here," he said, handing them back, "see if you can identify them." Musical chairs.

It was difficult even with the help of the glasses. Their backs were turned to us. There were two tall men standing together and talking. I figured I was looking at Hector and Eogan because the other two men were much shorter. Finally one of the tall men turned and looked in our direction. I pushed my body into the wet ground further, hoping he hadn't seen us. Then he turned back and continued talking. It was Hector. I figured the other man was Eogan.

They were both standing next to two other men, both shorter, and a boy who was book-shelved between them. Each had a hand on the boy's shoulder. Both had long rifles slung over their backs. I dropped the glasses and tried to think of a plan.

The sound of the motors grew louder. A big boat. Coast Guard? Couldn't be. Not that quickly. I knew we needed to do something before the boat arrived.

I fired a warning shot over their heads. "Let go of the boy!" I yelled, rising to a kneeling position. I was about fifty yards away.

Huck stood up and leveled his alligator gun at them. "That's a warning," he said.

The men hesitated for a moment. Then one of the men flanking the boy fired at us. He couldn't have seen us very clearly because of the dark wall of pines behind us. I fired back. I missed. Huck fired and hit him and the man jerked backward and fell. The others scattered, one of them pulling the boy with him into the mangroves.

One of them had run into the pines far to my right for cover. I fired into the trees. I heard a man scream, sudden and shrill, and then a noise like a rhino crashing through underbrush. Then that scream again. Huck raised his night vision glasses toward the noise.

"You gotta see this," he said, handing the glasses to me. I saw a man struggling against a huge gator just this side of the pines, its jaws locked on one of his legs and dragging him back toward the shore. It was Gunner. And I fired—at thirty feet—too far away to penetrate the animal's armor—but I fired again anyway, emptying my Glock, but the creature kept dragging him, his back against the sand and his leg in the gator's mouth, through the mangroves and toward the water, and I looked over at Huck who had his rifle raised—the classic Winchester 9422 with a night scope mounted—and he aimed at the gator—or was it at Gunner—and then he said, "Ain't never gonna kill that animal. That boy's a goner," and he fired four quick rounds using the lever action of the Winchester, a true Florida cowboy, into the animal—one hitting Gunner. I watched through the night glasses. And Gunner never moved, his face had that look of a man being dragged into hell, but I can tell you this, he was dead before he got there.

And I wondered if I ever really wanted to save that son of a bitch. Huck stood there as well, his rifle resting on the ground. Then he looked up at the moon that had just reappeared and said, "The earth has claimed her own, Kemo Sabe."

CHAPTER 77

The Children

In the meantime Hector had fled with the boy. And near where he had been standing, the Colombian I had shot was lying with his head stuck between his shoulder and the ground. A deadly position. Then I heard a boat roar away beyond the mangroves.

The kids! I thought. And I screamed loud enough—I was hoping—to alert Richie who was babysitting them on the Grady White. So I turned and ran back through the marsh, the gator a worry in the back of my mind, and pushed through the marsh grass toward the line of trees and the field of sawgrass. Huck was right behind me crashing through the underbrush. He fired in the air hoping Richie would hear, I guessed.

In a few minutes we were back at the shoreline where the Grady White was facing off against a larger boat in the middle of the water. Richie fired several bursts in their direction. That was followed by a rain of shots that pelted the water short of his boat. Were they warning us or just shooting badly? Richie idled the Grady White around a tangle of mangrove roots and into a small spray of sand. He did it like a true captain—in the dark, away from the catch of mangrove roots, and up onto the strand where he finally grounded the boat.

Huck pulled in a bowline as Richie jumped off and helped bring the Grady White further up onto the shore. The kids lined up on the side of the boat like they were waiting to get off a bus. They jumped one by one, Richie, Huck and I taking turns catching them. And they screamed as bullets peppered the water. As soon as they were all on land, we pulled back into the tree line. Shells continued to pelt the side of the boat.

"Bastards," said Richie, emptying his Mossberg at the boat, but too far away to be effective. The kids started to cry again.

I laid a hand on his barrel. "Enough," I said. "Save it for when we're closer." He grunted under his breath.

"Hey, you're shot!" said Huck.

I didn't feel anything, but I saw blood starting to ooze from my shoulder. Huck ran back into the clearing, boarded the boat and disappeared below. No shots. He leaped over the side gripping a first aid box with a red cross on it. When he got to me he stripped off my shirt like a medic and searched for the wound.

The bullet had sliced through the flesh on the top side of my shoulder, missing bone, but leaving a bloody crease. He cleaned up the wound with some alcohol, plastered a heavy bandage over it, and sealed it tight with adhesive tape.

"That'll do," he said, patting the wound.

"Medic?" I said.

"Vietnam," he said. "End of the conflict."

Another volley of shots rang out, slamming into the gunnels of the Grady White. Richie fired back, using Huck's Winchester this time. The shooting stopped. And then the boat moved behind the Grady White so it was away from our field of vision. But I could hear it idling in closer to us and I realized we had to get the children to safety.

The moon was so bright now I hardly needed the night glasses. I noticed an imperfection in its surface. A large black dot in the center, growing larger as I stared at it.

Sometimes the night plays tricks. We imagine things that aren't there: creatures in the closet, sounds in the basement late at night. That's the root of fear, you know: things we cannot see.

The dot kept growing, and a sound grew with it. I was caught up in its magic. Then the boat in the river edged around the Grady White and the men on board fired as we scrambled into the trees.

"Get the kids out of here," I told Richie. "Find a safe place away from the shoreline."

I looked at the faces of the kids. They were terrified. Several were wiping their eyes and sniffling away runny noses. Ana looked brave but uncertain. She pulled at my arm and asked if I would go with them. Water crept from the edges of her eyes. I put my arm around her and told her not to worry—that we would all be okay. She looked at me doubtfully. I wondered if it was worse to lie to kids than to adults.

So Richie and Huck and I led the children away from the shore and into a field of sawgrass. I called them around me with Richie looking on like a concerned father, all the while the sounds of shells ripped through the trees. I heard Huck firing back. He had stayed near the shore to give us a few minutes of safety.

I bent over the first kid. "You're?"

"Julio," he said, his eyes cast down. Then he looked up and met my eyes. Anxiety there.

"And you?" bending toward the next boy.

"Ernesto, but they call me Ernie."

"And you?" the boy who looked like the youngest, big eyes, black hair falling over his face, looked like he had just finished crying... "and you?" I repeated.

"My name is Victor," he said, finding his English. "Victor Huego."

"Victor Hugo, eh?" I said. "You will be a writer." He didn't move or smile. "Huego," he said. I patted him on the shoulder.

Finally I turned to Eddie. He was trembling—from fear or from the cold I couldn't tell. And I felt the sadness that his eyes carried, and my stomach felt it, and I knew I would have to kill the monsters who preyed on these children.

"Are we going to be okay?" Eddie said, and it was hard to handle his worry.

"We're going to be okay," I said, holding his shoulders firmly. He tried to smile but gunshots stole that from him quickly.

Then thunder rocked the air around us. I looked past the trees that sheltered the island from the water and the dot in the moon had grown to a full sized copter roaring overhead now, buzzing the boats like an angry bee—a metal monster.

"What the hell," yelled Richie over the noise. "Who's that?"

"The Coast Guard," I think. "I believe we are about to be saved."

The copter swung over the river once again and the smugglers fired at it. The Coastguardsmen fired back and then the chopper swung away from the river and out over the Everglades. They were leaving? Hopefully a boat wasn't far behind.

"We need to find a place for these kids," I said again. The children were watching me—the night air putting a chill to my words.

Huck had pointed out an old shack, inland, about a hundred feet past the tree line. I told Richie to keep his eyes on the kidnappers' boat while Huck and I found a haven for the kids.

It was a lonely procession into the trees, the kids struggling with the mangrove roots, several tripping, and then the mangroves turned into pines and cypress, and then the woods gave away to a field of sawgrass, and I walked behind as Huck led the way to the shack, and the moon stayed steady overhead, still low on the horizon and it cast a pale light over our procession of bowed heads, Ana's head bobbing in front of the other four as they trailed behind Huck—Ana, the mother duck.

It was an old trapper's shack, some cans and trash scattered around the floor, a musty sleeping bag in one corner. A table made out of logs that looked like they had been scrounged from cast-off lumber was pushed up against a wall, some rifle shells that looked relatively new scattered on top. An old crossbow hung on the wall, a rack of arrows just beneath it. Maybe someone was still using the camp. Maybe even living there.

Huck was holding his nose. "No Indian would live here," he said. "Our tents are clean."

I told the kids they would be safe and promised we would be back soon.

As we set out, Ana watched me closely. I gave her a nod to reassure her. She nodded back, nervous but trusting. When we got back to the beach, Richie pointed to the smugglers' boat. It was now back out in the middle of the river.

"They're waiting for us," Richie said, unholstering his Browning and raising it to the light of the moon. He checked the rounds. Thirteen in all.

"I didn't know you brought it," I said.

"My baby," he said. "You don't leave your baby at home," and he polished the barrel against his shirt.

I ejected the empty cartridge from my Glock and jammed another into the handle. Huck was checking his alligator gun and feeding shells into its chamber. I felt like asking him why he didn't just shoot the damned gator between the eyes while it was dragging Gunner into the water. But I knew why. He could have killed it easily. Gunner was better off where he was. So were we.

"So what's the plan?" said Richie. Then, "Why'm I asking you? You ain't got no plan."

"Exactly," I said. "No plan's the best plan." And he's right, I didn't have any plan. "Let's go get the bastards," I said, holstering the Glock and heading for the boat.

We had to wade a few feet from the beach into the water to get to the hatch near the motors. I pulled it open as quietly as I could but every movement of fiberglass on fiberglass sounded like a shot in the quiet night. Still no movement on the smugglers' boat. It was silent in the water. I headed for the wheel as soon as I was on board, staying low beneath the gunnels. Richie was breathing heavily behind me. Huck slid onto the deck right behind him, his rifle slung over his shoulder. We waited for a few moments to see if the other boat had seen us. No activity at all there.

"I'm going to trim a little something off the front of their boat," I said, whispering. Water carries voices.

"You're what?" said Richie.

"You got a better idea?"

I started up the engines and moved the boat slowly away from shore. The bottom of the boat scraped against the sand and then finally broke away sending us out into the water toward the smugglers. They were about fifty yards away. Once I got the Grady White turned, I pushed the throttle forward,

Lights came on as the big boat came to life, its motors churning the water like a spooked horse rearing on its hind legs but unsure of where to go. Maybe because I was heading straight for them like a torpedo and was only about fifty feet from them—too late to turn and run. Nobody fired. But people started jumping overboard screaming, arms and legs flailing wildly, and in seconds I was on top of them and ducking away from the windshield as I steered the Grady White into the smugglers' boat, aiming to trim the prow that jutted out over the water. Just to trim it.

"Damn!" yelled Richie as we hit and the impact threw Richie, Huck, and me into the leather seats behind the helm where we struggled to untangle ourselves like the lines of three fishing poles. Huck was the first one free and he grabbed for the wheel, now spinning out of control, stabilized it, and swung hard to port, away from the smuggler's boat.

"Shut it down," I said to Huck. "Let's check out the damage," and I was looking for the smugglers' boat.

It was still afloat but probably not for long. It looked like Leviathan had risen from the deep, encircled it in its coils, and tore the prow away. The prow of the Grady White was crushed also but we weren't sinking—yet.

"Over here..." I heard a cry. It sounded like a boy.

I tried the spotlight that was mounted on the foredeck. I was amazed it still worked. And I spotted someone in the water about thirty yards from us, struggling to stay afloat. Huck stripped off his buckskin jacket and dove overboard. I watched as he disappeared into the water and then reappeared, his arms beating a path toward the boy. I shifted the spotlight toward the struggling kid again—he was fighting to stay above water. I called out for him to hang on. Then I saw two people swimming hard toward the boy from the smuggler's boat. I screamed at Huck to hurry.

Then I jumped in.

CHAPTER 78

My Name Is Samuel

Huck was about thirty feet in front of me. I strained to find the boy and then I heard him cry out again and saw him, splashing against the water and sinking, then coming to the surface, choking and gagging, and the two swimmers had reached him and grabbed the boy, but Huck was right on top of them now and suddenly Huck disappeared beneath the water and then one of the swimmers disappeared beneath the waves and I was just a few feet away and the other swimmer saw me and let loose of the boy and began to swim furiously toward the mangroves.

And the boy went under before I got to him, but he came up just as quickly, gasping and thrashing against the water and me and grabbed onto me in a panic, threatening to drown us both, so I grabbed his arm, turned him around forcibly and, hooking my right arm around his neck and across his chest, got him in a lifeguard hold leveraging his back against my side. He kicked and gasped for breath, hitting out wildly but I kept him on his back and swam like hell. When I reached the boat, exhausted from the struggle, I found Richie at the stern waiting. He had opened the hatch and reached down to grab the boy who had finally quit fighting.

"Where's Huck?" Richie said, looking out over the dark water while straining to pull the waterlogged kid onto the deck. The boy immediately collapsed, face down, coughing and spitting out water.

I had just pulled myself up onto the deck and turned around to see if I could find Huck when I saw a body thrashing the water toward us. It was Huck and he had a hunting knife locked in his teeth.

"Where's the other guy?" I said as he pulled himself up through the hatch, water streaming off his face and down over his body, bare but for the buckskin pants.

"Not in Happy Hunting Grounds," he said, removing the blade from his mouth. It was a deadly looking weapon. Maybe seven inches long, with a bone handle. After clearing off the excess water by wiping the blade over his soaked buckskins, he sheathed it carefully.

"When the Indian dies, his spirit wanders to the southwest where it takes up residence with his people." He paused. "This man will go to that place that the White Man calls hell." And then he looked down at the young boy who had sat up and was watching him. He was hugging himself against the dampness and cold of the night.

"What's your name?" Huck said, kneeling down and looking into the boy's eyes as if he saw something there.

"My name is Samuel," the boy said, watching Huck just as steadily.

Huck nodded and rose. "I'm freezing, Kemo Sabe," and he shook water from his body like a dog who had just climbed out of a lake. "That boy is too," nodding at Samuel who had begun to shake as well.

We couldn't take the boy below. The cabin was waist high in water. So I asked Richie to see if he could find some dry blankets that had escaped the water. He disappeared below. Then I lifted Samuel to his feet. His eyes were glazed—like someone about to go into shock. So Huck and I carried him to the cockpit where we settled him on the wide cushioned seat behind the wheel.

"It's okay, Samuel," the name sounding strange to me as I said it, "you'll see the other kids soon. You're safe now." He looked at me as if still unsure. But finally he nodded and dropped his head.

I started up the motors while Huck searched the water for survivors and dead bodies.

"I wonder where Hector is?" Huck said, passing his night glasses back and forth between the wreckage of the smugglers' boat and the islands on both sides of the waterway.

"My guess, he was the guy who headed for the nearest shore. Probably already there," I said, pointing to the island where we left the children just a few hours ago.

I turned the Grady White in that direction, passing over the remains of the smugglers' boat floating in pieces across the water. The stern—all that was visible above the water—had two words inscribed across the hull. I could barely make them out as the boat bounced in our wake and the words fell in and out of the moonlight. I finally made out *Mi Perro* in large black letters against the white hull.

"My dog." How strange. "Any sign of Hector?" I said, turning back to Huck. He was still scanning the mangroves along the shore.

He shook his head.

"We gonna make it to dry land?" said Richie, coming topside and carrying an armload of dry blankets. He laid them on the bench where he unfolded one and wrapped it around Samuel's shoulders. The boy shivered, whispered thanks, and pulled the blanket tightly around his body.

Richie looked over at me. "Well...?" Did I tell you he couldn't swim?

"Barely," I said, gradually pushing the throttle forward. I could hear water running into the boat below and the shore still two hundred yards ahead.

"Got lots of damage to the prow, bud," said Richie. "Looks like you flattened it with your crazy driving." He was nervous all right.

"I think we're going to make it, Richie," I said and pushed the engines a little harder.

We drifted into the shore near where we had landed the first time. I figured Hector had to have swum for there. It was the closest land.

I drove the Grady White as far as I could up onto the shore, the prow grinding into the sand with a loud scraping noise that told me the boat would need some major overhaul before it would be sea-worthy again.

Huck jumped overboard, his rifle raised over his head like a marine landing on Normandy. Richie grabbed Samuel and waited until the boat had settled into the shallows. Then he handed the boy down to Huck and eased himself over the side into about a foot of water. The stern of the boat was mostly under water as I shut down the engines. There was only one way back now and that was with the Coast Guard.

"You and Huck get the kids," I told Richie, "I'm going after Hector." And I dropped off the prow onto the shore.

They hurried into the trees in the direction of the shack, Samuel between them. The boy looked back at me, uncertain. I gave him a reassuring nod and headed into the grassy interior. I had brought a flashlight with me, hoping I could find a trail.

"There's no kids here!" Richie screamed from the darkness. "Where the...?"

My stomach turned. I had an idea of what happened and took off running for the shack. I heard noises in the distance, away from the shack, sounds of brush breaking away. I could picture it, Hector with two or three of the kids, the others running for their lives through the marsh. Huck and Richie were standing in front of the shack when I got there, Richie with his hands raised as if to say *What else!*

"Either Hector got here before us, or the kids ran away," I said. I was hoping for the second scenario but not really believing it.

"Fat chance of that, Coop," said Richie. "That son of a bitch took them, you can count on it."

Huck asked for my light, then bent down and studied the ground around the shack." There," he said, pointing into the darkness where I had just been and toward the noises I had just heard and in the same direction where we had chased Hector and Gunner just hours before. Then he handed the light back to me.

"You don't need it?" I said.

"The moon," he said. "The sky has given us her light."

Then he started across the field toward the forest of mangroves that lined the field of grass on our right.

I turned to Samuel, stooped down to meet him at eye level, and asked if he could stay in the shack until we got back. He began to cry. I said it was too dangerous to go with us and I really wished he could stay at the shack. He cried even more.

Richie punched me. "I'll watch him."

"You'll stay here?"

"Hell no, the kid comes with Uncle Richie. Do him some good, see his kidnapper get his friggin' head blown off," he whispered, trying to clean up his language—at least around the kids.

Samuel looked at me with big eyes, almost as though he had heard what Richie said. I shook my head, turned away, and stared into the trees where I knew the kids were. Putting one more kid in danger, I thought. But no arguing with Uncle Richie. And in this case, he had a point.

"Okay, but you guys stay close," I said.

Then I hurried ahead to catch up with our Native American tracker who was moving quickly across the open field. He must have heard me coming because he turned quickly, his rifle just inches from my belly.

"Jesus," he whispered harshly. "White man makes much noise!"

I shook my head. See, Huck is a college graduate. He knows how to speak proper English. But he loves to show off his Indian heritage. So he pulls this "white man" crap to remind me of his ancestry. I generally ignore it.

"Hand me the glasses," he said, reaching out for them. I handed them over. He scoured the mangroves then handed them back. "They're not in the mangroves anymore," he said. I had told him about the noises I had heard earlier.

So we turned back into the open field and followed the same path that we had taken earlier in the evening.

I heard voices, murmurs like the wind bothering the trees. Huck must have heard them also because he held up his hand and paused, bending his ear into the night. The voices stopped. Then he lowered his hand and started out again. Richie and Samuel were right behind me. We struggled over marshy ground. It sucked at our feet and grabbed hold of our shoes. Samuel let out an "ouch" now and then and I told him it was important that we be quiet because Hector wasn't far away. His eyes got bigger when I said that and I wondered what evil that son of a bitch had wrought on them.

Huck was finally at the point of entry in front of the tree line where we had been just hours before. The voices were back again— the children's voices. I heard *shut up*, as the four of us entered the tree line, Huck leading the way with his night glasses. I turned to make sure Richie and Samuel were behind me and that's when I stepped on a dry branch, the sound echoing like an exploding firecracker through the trees. I froze. Huck turned and gave me a look. I shrugged, like *I know. I'm a white man.*

I wondered where the gator was, half expecting the beast to come charging from the trees to finish his supper.

"That you, Cooper?" came a voice out of the dark. Hector.

Off to my right I heard a scrambling sound, like little feet in the woods, then small voices whispering to each other. The children, I thought, at least some of them. But strangely not anywhere near where Hector's voice had come from, but rather near where the gator had dragged Gunner into the swamp.

I turned to Richie. He had heard the same thing I had. "Why don't you check it out," I said. "If it *is* the kids, keep them away from the beach. And watch out for that gator," I whispered hoarsely.

He nodded. Richie crept silently away into the trees with Samuel hanging on to his shirt. Huck and I watched as they disappeared into the dark.

"Hector's in the mangroves near the beach," Huck said. "I'll circle around him and come in from the left." He paused. "Just like we did to Custer."

"Oh shut up," I whispered. "Those where northern tribe Indians, not Seminoles."

He nodded, smiling, and slid through the underbrush. The light he had taken from me earlier was stuck in his pocket and his alligator gun hung from his shoulder. He left the night glasses with me.

CHAPTER 79

Hector's Last Stand

As I lay and listened, I couldn't help but think back on the days when Maxie and Jillie and I picked up walnuts that had fallen on the side of the road and loaded our baskets with them, overripe and leaking black onto our hands; and on the days when we searched for blackberries in the late summer sun—in the woods behind our house—I couldn't help but think that these children, maybe Ana, maybe Eddie, maybe Samuel, had done the same thing, never dreaming that there might be bad men in those woods, or maybe in the house down the street, or outside their school, or at the city playground, men who might be planning on stealing them and selling them for money—and yet here we are...

I searched for Hector, staring into near blackness that the moon, hanging low behind the tree line, couldn't penetrate. The ground was damp, so I rolled to a kneeling position and swept the night glasses through the mangroves that lay about a hundred yards beyond the trees, and then I saw them—the children—a few shadows among the mangroves, and they were just inside the forest, where the clearing ended and the trees began, and they were watching someone, and he spoke in low whispers, threatening whispers, and I heard Ana, trying to calm him, the kidnapper of children, and I tried to locate the person behind the voice, but he was hidden behind the mangroves, and I wondered what he wanted out of all this, and I wondered how in the hell he planned to get away, I mean his boats had sunk, most of his men were dead, the others had disappeared into the Everglades. And then I understood...

It was the sound of a helicopter approaching—in the distance—the sound growing stronger by the moment—five miles away—maybe closer—and the children moved at the sound, restless maybe, and then I finally saw the man rise from the darkness of the mangroves and he had one of the children with him—and he started for the beach, pushing the kid ahead of him toward the sound of the helicopter and he was holding a gun in his right hand—and I was hoping Huck was near—and I got up and moved toward Hector—about thirty yards in front of me now—and almost at the beach, and finally he saw me and grabbed the kid—a boy—tighter, holding a gun to his head, and keeping the boy between us.

The copter roared over the swamp, its rotor blowing great billows of water into crazy circles and pushing it up onto the shore, and then began its descent into the water, stabilizing itself over the shallows between the river and the beach, and when the chopper finally hit the surface Hector grabbed the boy and began to wade toward it, and I raised my glasses so that I could see him clearly—I was only about thirty feet from him now—and he turned and saw me, but he was holding the boy in front of his body, and he smiled at my problem, a shot from a Glock at thirty feet would just as likely kill the boy as him, but I raised my gun anyway, sighting along the night-vision glasses, and I saw him clearly, and I saw an arrow pierce his neck, the arrowhead pushing through to the other side of his head, and I saw the surprise on his face when the arrow hit, and he dropped the boy and grabbed at the arrow, trying to pull it out by the feathers, and then another hit him in the chest, knocking him back with its force and he stumbled and tried to keep his balance, and then another in the stomach and that one pushed him into the water, and he looked up trying to find me, puzzled, and then down at the arrows in his chest and stomach, and he sank into the water still pulling at the arrow in his neck, but it wouldn't come out, and then I heard rifle shots from the shore as the copter tried to rise, and then a shotgun blast that blew away the passenger hatch, and the copter wobbled momentarily, then righted itself and angled down river, rushing into the cover of the darkness.

CHAPTER 80

The Stranger

I looked around quickly to see who was shooting. A man in buckskins walked out of the trees behind me, a crossbow in his hands. I remembered the bow on the wall in the shack where the kids had stayed. He came to my side without talking and stared at Hector who was now floating in the water—face down. Eddie was standing in knee-deep water near the body, staring dumbly at Hector. I went down to get him. The man with the bow followed me.

"He took the children from the hunting lodge," he said in broken English, as the two of us reached Eddie. I took the boy's hand and led him to shore. I wanted to ask him if he was okay. But that made no sense. He wasn't. So we headed up the sand toward the other children who had come out of the tree line and were waiting for us. Richie emerged behind them carrying his shotgun across his chest.

"They won't be back," said Richie. I almost expected to see him blow smoke out of the barrel of his gun.

I nodded and smiled. Then I turned and stared at the man with the bow. "It's your shack?" I said, remembering what Huck had said about Indians and the hunting lodge.

He nodded, looking back at the river and at Hector who was now an intimate part of it, his blood mixing with the water and gradually turning it red. The feathered end of the arrow was sticking straight up in the air.

"He stole the souls of children," the stranger said. "His spirit will not be welcome in the southwest." And I thought I was hearing Huck again.

"O'-Si-Yo', Sani," a voice coming out of the pine forest behind us. Huck.

"O'-Si-Yo', Huxter," said the Indian turning toward the voice.

"That your hunting lodge back there?" said Huck. He was carrying his rifle across his chest.

The stranger nodded. His face was lined and brown like well-worn leather.

"I'm Cooper," I said, extending my hand.

"Sani," said the stranger. "The boy will be okay," looking down at Eddie who was shoulder high to him.

"He's dead isn't he," the boy said, staring at Hector. The water was pushing him against the mangroves.

Sani nodded. "He is. When he comes to the village of his ances-tors, he will not be welcome." And the roots of the mangroves had Hector's head locked in a death grip.

"I'm glad," he said. "I'm glad he's dead," and he muttered it again several times.

Ana put her arms around Eddie. And then the others surround-ed him and talked about how brave he was. And that went on for a few minutes. But after that they were mostly quiet and just watched the beach and the water and Hector's body rising and falling with the tide. I knew that they would live with that memory for the rest of their lives.

After a few minutes I walked over to Eddie and put a hand on his shoulder. "You okay?" But I knew all along what his answer would be.

He nodded, but his eyes said differently. And I shook my head and pulled him into my arms and he held on like I was a life preserver. And slowly the other kids drifted away from the beach, each one of them, even Ana, their adopted mother, and one by one they came and put their arms around Eddie and around me and as Richie and Huck joined in, they hugged them as well.

CHAPTER 81

The Guardsmen

The night had worn out its welcome. The dampness of the swamp was seeping into our bones. The kids were shivering.

"How about we light a fire?" I said to Huck and Sani. "Think you can do it?"

They both grinned. "White man insults Indian," Huck said. They both turned and headed for the pines. I followed them. Uncle Richie volunteered to stay back with the kids.

So we gathered wood and piled it high on the beach. Sani started the fire by rapidly rubbing dried sticks together and lighting some dry pine needles. In minutes the flames filled the area with warmth and light. The six children crowded the fire like they were roasting marshmallows at summer camp. They shivered and held out their hands over the flames, trying to get close enough to dry their clothes.

I motioned for Richie and Huck to follow me, then looked around for Sani. I saw him loping toward the pines.

"He's Indian tribal police at the Rez," said Huck as he watched him disappear into the forest. "Better if he's not here when the Guard comes."

"Then who shot Hector?" I said, still watching the darkness into which Sani had disappeared.

"I did," said Huck, holding up Sani's cross bow.

I shook my head. "Okay," I said. "That'll work."

"Now we have to get these bodies out of here," I said. Hector was still caught in the mangroves. The guy I had shot earlier was still lying where he went down. The hole in his chest had leaked a lot of blood. Gator bait.

Around 5:00 a.m. in the morning, I heard the sound of the helicopter returning. There was another noise behind it. A boat. They must have seen our fire. The pines had burned all night and were still throwing off heat and fire. We rushed to the water line and yelled as loudly as we could, waving arms and jumping around. The shadows of our forms danced in the firelight like the phantom figures in Plato's cave over two thousand years ago.

It was a fast boat. One of the new Coast Guard Response-Mediums. About forty five feet long and fully equipped with life-saving equipment—thank God. A searchlight from the Response swept the beach as it slowed to anchor in the middle of the water. The helicopter roared overhead and finally settled in the water near a wide expanse of sand down the beach from where we were. Two men jumped out with their guns raised. They searched the trees as they waded ashore, a searchlight sweeping the beach in front of them.

"We're friendly," I yelled over the noise of the chopper, its blades beating a hole in the silence.

The Response anchored in the middle of the river. A rubber craft dropped over the side and three Guardsmen used a rope ladder to drop down into the boat. When they landed on the beach, two soldiers climbed out first, M-2s slung over their shoulders. The soldier behind them had bars on his shoulder.

"We're all friendly," I said again, reminding them, as they approached. "The bad guys are dead."

One of the Guardsmen noticed Hector floating in the center of the searchlight's beam. It captured him in all of his grisly glory.

"Captain Welder," said the officer, stepping around the other two and holding out his hand.

"Cooper," I replied. "These are the kids," I said— quietly—pointing to the huddled forms around the fire. They were staring at the soldiers as though they were invaders from Mars.

Welder shook his head in disbelief. "My God," he said under his breath. "What the hell have we come to?"

"So is this everybody?" he said looking around at the children, then at Huck and Richie.

"Yes," I said. I didn't tell him about Sani. "Except for the dead. We dragged their bodies away from here."

Weller looked puzzled.

"The kids," I said. "Had to get them away from the kids."

He nodded. "Where are the bodies?"

I told him. He said the Park Police would be along to clear the crime scene—*and the bodies,* he added. I told him an alligator had already helped to clear the scene.

The next hour was filled with Weller taking notes on what had happened and on deciding what to do with the children. Five of them, Victor, Samuel, Ana, Julio and Ernie would go with the Response. Eddie and I would fly back with Weller on the copter. I wanted to get the boy back to his parents before the morning sun turned hot.

Huck went with Richie and the kids. He was showing them the bow.

"He shot that guy with a bow?" Weller said, shaking his head. "How the hell did he do that?" He hesitated, looking at me with suspicion.

"He's one helluva hunter," I said. "Raised in the Everglades and still lives there." *Kind of,* I said to myself. "Indians," you know. "Bows and arrows."

Weller smiled. He knew who Huck was. "Sure there wasn't someone else here? My memory of Huck is with an alligator gun."

"I'm sure," I said. And I knew he didn't believe me.

And so Richie and Huck and Victor Huego, and mother Ana, and Ernesto (*they call me Ernie*) and Samuel (brave Samuel), and Julio all climbed aboard the Response. Weller gave Eddie a boost up through the copter's hatch.

"I will need you to fill in the spaces of your narrative about the events of the last few days, Cooper," he said as he pulled me up into the copter.

Weller told Eddie to take a seat near the pilot, then waited for the Response to leave before he signaled the pilot to take off. When we finally lifted off, I tried to clear my head of the hell we had been through for the last twenty-four hours. But as the island disappeared and the copter rose and angled toward Miami and the rising sun, the whole damned mess seemed to be part of another life—at least I tried to make it so. *Surely the world must be a better place,* I thought. *Surely it had to be.*

CHAPTER 82

The Reunion

Monday Morning, November 1, All Saints' Day

We made it back to Miami in less than an hour, landing at the U.S. Coast Guard Air Station in South Miami. It was 7:30 a.m. The Response would arrive at the Miami station a few miles north of us. But that would be later. They had a lot of waterway to cover. But I had a job to do before that. Deliver a young boy to his parents. I decided not to call them. It wouldn't be a long drive to their home.

Weller had given me his car to use. The ride was a quiet one. I looked over at Eddie. He was watching the early morning traffic. I wondered what he was thinking. What goes through the mind of a child who has been kidnapped? I couldn't imagine. He leaned his head against the window, staring at the city. Then his body relaxed against the seat and his eyes began to close. I wondered how long it had been since he had slept.

I tried to picture the faces of Ned and Catherine Dougherty when they would open the door. I tried to picture *my* reaction if someone—some cop maybe—brought Maxie to my door—in the early morning. Probably shock at first, then disbelief, then the dawning that this boy who was standing in front of me was actually my son, missing now for seven years, and I pictured how I would grab him up and squeeze him hard, so hard that the seven years of hell he had gone through would disappear in that single moment.

Then Eddie stirred, his mouth working its way through something—a dream perhaps—and I thought again of Ned and Catherine opening their door...

And now we were close and I watched the numbers on the houses, trying to remember where it was, and the only sound was the drone of tires against the street—no traffic here in this sleepy neighborhood, on this early Monday morning on the feast of All Saints. *One of the Saints is coming back to life*, I thought.

And then I saw their house, large and white in the morning sun, and my stomach jumped momentarily as I pulled into the driveway. I closed my door loudly so they might hear and walked around the car to open Eddie's door. He had been sleeping and he wiped his eyes as if to ask where he was, then noticed the house, and the first thing he did was jump out of the car and run to the front door, turning quickly before he got there to mouth a *thanks,* then yanked at the door, but it was locked, so he rang the bell and then pounded, yelling, *Mom! Dad!* And the door opened while I was still on the sidewalk just below the porch, and Ned stood there, dazed—like I knew he would—then he yelled so loud the whole neighborhood and all the Saints who were sleeping could hear him:

"My God! Eddie!"

And he grabbed him up—just like I pictured he would— and he cried and laughed and squeezed Eddie to death—not quite—and I laughed with him, and Eddie hung onto him like he would never let him go, like a boy who had seen a very bad place in the days he was gone, and he cried, and tears came to my eyes as I climbed the stairs and put a hand on Ned's shoulder—to reinforce his joy, I guess, or to share in it maybe—and then Ned yelled into the house, "Look who's here, Cathy!" and she was already rushing through the door, pulling a robe around her body and struggling to breathe, her hand covering her mouth, and she cried out and threw her arms around Eddie and Ned and sobbed like a woman who had lost a son forever—or so she thought—and now he was here. On her porch. Alive and kicking in their arms.

And then they noticed me.

"Oh my God, we're so sorry," said Ned, turning to me. "Please, come in and let's have some coffee so we can talk—about what happened," and he turned to Catherine and she was nodding her head eagerly, but Eddie was quiet. And Ned continued, "We can't tell you how happy we are and how grateful..." and he was shaking my hand and trying to lead me into the house when I stopped him.

I saw the look on Eddie's face. He was tired and nervous. And I said, "You've been a brave man, Eddie," squaring his shoulders with both of my hands. And then I turned to Ned and Catherine, "He has been through a nightmare these past days, and maybe someday he can tell you all about it. But for now..."

And they both nodded. And tears were in Catherine's eyes again. And I gave Eddie one last hug and turned to leave. And they thanked me and they thanked God for returning their son to them. And I thought that maybe God got too much credit for this one. And I could hardly see as I pulled into the street and headed home.

I was only sorry that Hannah Miller would never have this same experience. I would tell her later about her son's killer. But I would never tell her about what Eogan had told me. Maybe it was a lie anyway, I thought to myself.

Someone else would have to tell the Thompsons about what happened to their daughter. I was glad it wouldn't be me. There wouldn't be any happiness for either family in the telling of their stories—except for knowing the truth perhaps. But sometimes that's enough to bring peace.

CHAPTER 83

All Souls' Day

There was no sound in the Great Swamp as the sun began to chase the shadows of the night from the mangroves lining the shore behind my house. Just the indistinct whispers of an early morning breeze through the palms. It was 7:00 a.m., a full day after the events at Chokoloskee Island. DeFelice and Louise had come over and helped Richie, Huck, and me drink a case of Sam Adams lager. Nobody was driving, so no problems there.

Richie did most of the talking and DeFelice gave him a hard time with comments like, *Sure Richie, I'm sure that's just the way it happened,* and *Wow, you guys in Cleveland are really tough ain't you.* And Richie said, *What, and you ain't from Cleveland? Not lately,* Tony said back. *And I come from an uptown neighborhood, not where yous come from. People around me had some education. Could read and write.* Louise didn't say much. She was simply glad I wasn't dead and that the kids were back. Huck was having a hard time focusing on anything. Too many beers in his belly.

Delgado speculated that either Casto or Juan had killed Crane. "A contact in the neighborhood told me Crane had been spreading the word that Ethan Miller and Tamara Thompson were a gang killing. Said that's a death sentence for anybody spreading that kind of shit.

So, bingo, they aced him. Teach his buddies a lesson. My guess, the holy boys kidnapped them both, the girl escaped, they killed her, by accident or deliberately, take your choice, case closed."

"We catch Gunner and Hector in an afterlife, we'll be sure to ask them that question," I said.

The Coast Guard and two deputies from the Collier County Sheriff's Department found Murphy's body that same day. They also found several Colombians still alive on the island where the first boat had run into an oyster bed. They discovered the body of a white man, washed up in one of the mangrove swamps, partly eaten. He had ID on him: Eogan Clery. Hector was still pretty intact, less a few pieces of flesh that some birds had scrounged. The Coast Guard turned the Colombians over to the Collier County Sheriff's Department who, in turn, turned them over to the FBI.

The FBI had taken over the Pacholewski case. Word is he had given up Hector for both of the murders: Ethan's and Tamara's. They didn't have any information about whether Ethan and Tamara were working with Hector or for the motive behind the murders. The bottom line is they were both dead and that was no consolation to the parents.

In the end, nobody could believe that some holy boys had pulled this kind of horrendous crime. And that included me.

DeFelice, Richie, Huck, and Louise were still sleeping. I made a pot of coffee, real coffee this time. I usually can't stand the real stuff. Sends me through the ceiling. I'm a nice guy usually. But coffee turns me into a terrorist.

I took the coffee and two pieces of Jewish rye bread, buttered and topped with strawberry jelly, lots of it, out to the hammock that hangs between two mangroves in my backyard and listened to the quiet of the early morning. It had been a long time since I had any peace and for this brief time I felt neither depression nor anger about anything. I wanted to cherish the moment.

"Having a good time?" a voice behind me asked.

I turned and saw DeFelice stretching and yawning.

"You went through a lot of shit, Cooper. It's good to have you back in one piece. Next time how about you call for some backup. No need to be a hero."

We talked until early afternoon when Louise, Richie, and Huck appeared at the back door, looking like they had slept for days.

"It's late, Coop. Me and DeFelice gotta be going," Louise said. Then, "You gonna be all right?"

I nodded. "Sure." The feeling was hard to describe. Sadness at what the kids had gone through. Happiness that it was over.

So we said our goodbyes. DeFelice hugged me like an Italian father and told me to be safe. Louise gave me hug also, only it was more prolonged.

"Take care of yourself, Coop," she said. "Call me when you get back into town. Maybe we can get some coffee—and donuts."

I nodded. "A good cop," I said. She smiled and gave me one last hug. "For the road," she said.

Then she and DeFelice climbed into the Crown Vic, the staple of cops everywhere, and left the dust of my drive rising in their wake.

"I'm headin' back to the ranch," said Huck as he hiked up his buckskins. I wondered if he ever changed them. He grabbed another beer from the cooler.

"Be careful about drinking when you're driving," I said. He didn't need any more DUIs. Huck looked hurt.

"You think all Indians are alcoholics, white man," he said, taking a deep draw on the Sam Adams. "This is my first beer this morning." He paused. "Unless you call that shit you've got in the fridge beer. It's more like buffalo piss." Huck the poet.

"Yeah, well you be good," I said and I gave him a hug and pounded him on the back. He looked at me for what seemed like a full minute. I thought I saw water in his eyes.

"You were great, old buddy. Safe trip home," I said.

Then he climbed into his truck and headed out, leaning from the window and telling me not to forget about his P.I. badge. He's been hounding me about that for a while.

"Adios," he yelled to Richie from the road.

Richie waved back as he drove off my lawn. Then he walked to the porch, grabbed one more Sam Adams out of a cooler we had stuffed last night, twisted off the cap, came back and grabbed a lawn chair, pulling it around to face the water. We sat there for a couple of hours, not talking, just watching the sun make its way over the Everglades toward its westerly home. It was in its November position on this All Souls' Day, angled lower in the sky. The ghosts that had haunted us two evenings past were now gone, the rays of the sun soft on our skin.

"You comin' back to Cleveland, Cooper?" Richie asked, finally breaking the silence.

I didn't answer right away because it was tempting to think about it. I wasn't getting anywhere it seemed with my own son's disappearance now a little over seven years ago.

"Nah, I don't think so, Richie. I feel like I need to be here," leaving the thoughts of my son unspoken between us.

The afternoon wore on and the sun began its slow descent toward the Everglades. Richie rose, crossed to the back porch and went in to pack his bags.

I drove him to Miami International and got him there an hour and a half before his 8:00 p.m. flight. We said our goodbyes and I said thanks for everything. He said fuggedaboutit, punching me in the arm and telling me to take care of myself. It was sad seeing Richie off. I enjoyed having him here and I felt the loneliness of his being gone as I headed back to Oceanside.

The first thing I did when I pulled onto the scrub grass in front of my house—I don't have a drive—was head for the fridge and grab a bottle of Chardonnay, Colombia Crest Grand Estates. Some say it's the best white for about ten bucks. It's certainly better than the stuff I usually drink. When I opened the screen door, Sammy came out from under the porch, wandered up the steps, and rubbed against my leg. He looked up as if to say, *Where have you been, stranger?* I went back to the fridge and poured him a saucer of milk.

Then I carried the wine with a fresh glass out to the back yard, set it on a small table near the hammock, and poured. I eased into the hammock, carefully balancing the glass, and then I sipped wine in the cool of the early November evening.

The end of All Souls' Day was just hours away and I drifted off thinking of Ned and Catherine Dougherty, and Eddie, and Hannah Miller and her son Ethan, and Tamara, and Hector, and Gunner, and of Muskingum, Ohio where fields of wheat were waiting for harvest under this late autumn sky. And I looked up beyond the trees and past the few clouds that hung above them and at the whiteness of the Hunter's Moon, and thought, *This is my moon, really. Nobody else owns it. It's mine.*

And I liked the sound of it. Cooper's Moon.

Epilogue

A man is sitting with a boy in a skiff in the sawgrass near the boathouse on Chokoloskee Island. The man hands the boy a sandwich. The boy takes it. He puts an arm around the boy's shoulders as if to assure him that he is safe. He lights a cigarette; it burns brightly in the darkness, red against black, bright for only a moment then fading into the night. A motor catches and the boat moves slowly from the shore toward the web of waterways that enfold the Ten Thousand Islands. I can't see the boy's face clearly, nor the man's, but both are familiar to me, like I have known them well at one time. I strain to get a better look as the boat leaves the lights from the dock and heads for the open water. I must have leaned too far forward because I feel my body tumbling, as though tossed in the wind. The ground breaks my fall and a wetness spreads over me, smelling a lot like Chardonnay.

More nightmares. But it's two days past Halloween. All Souls' Day. So many ghosts this night. Did I see something at the boathouse when we pulled away? Sitting near a tangle of mangroves off to our left, near a river passageway that leads far into the Everglades, due north, and away from the islands? I couldn't remember; but my hand was shaking as I tried to find the bottle of wine, thinking once again of my son, his face, and the time we had those many years ago.

Acknowledgements

It's time for me to acknowledge the people who made it possible for me to write and publish this book.

First, let me thank my readers: Karyn Conrath, John Coburn, Ryan Conrath, Scott Nelson, Jane and Glenn Trout, James and Helen Conrath, Jack Conrath, Christine Bohanan, and Carrie Clark. Without their help my book would not be in its present form. I am indebted to them for their tireless input.

A special thanks to Jack Driscoll, author of one of my favorite books, *Lucky Man, Lucky Woman*. Jack gave me a detailed and frank evaluation of *Cooper's Moon* while it was still in its early form.

There are others to whom I owe a debt of gratitude. Randy Wayne White, a *New York Times* best selling author, has given me keen advice about the publishing world and how to survive in it. And thanks also to Captain Mark Futch, his friend, who helped me understand the mysteries of Everglades City and of the Everglades themselves. Let me also add the name of Tim Dorsey, a Florida best selling author, who has given me advice both about writing as well as suggestions for finding an agent.

Kathleen Donaldson, a former law enforcement officer, gave me invaluable input into the inner workings of police procedure. Any mistakes that are made in that regard are of my own making.

Tris Coburn, Tristram Coburn Literary Management, served as my agent for many years. It is due to his insights into the publishing world that I have rewritten this book (almost entirely) about five times—I've lost count. Thanks, Tris, for your hard work in shopping my manuscripts.

Cathleen Elliott is the designer par excellence of the marvelous book cover and of its contents. Cathleen is one of the top designers in New York City.

Martin Lipschultz is the photographer who rendered the picture of me on my website.

Ryan Conrath is the man who wrought the web page: www.coopersmoon.com. His perceptiveness and expertise have helped me through my journey.

And to Leonard Cohen, poet, singer, songwriter—I can only say that you spoiled me. I often wrote deep into the night listening to your voice. You took me through many painful rewrites. I will miss you.

And finally, I am indebted to my chief editor, muse, and inspiration: my wife, Karyn. Without her, this book would not be what it is today.

Author's Note

Cooper's Moon is a work of fiction. Some of the places exist only in the mind of the author. For instance, there is no city south of Miami that is called Oceanside. Nor is there an End-of-the-World Cafe in Everglades City, nor a town in Ohio named Muskingum nor a Concord College. I switched the names of town and college to protect the innocent. Other places, streets, and restaurants mentioned are for the most part real—though details may have been changed to suit the author's fancy. After all, this is a work of fiction.

We are trying to build a community of writer and readers. To become a part of that process, please feel free to offer feedback on my website: www.coopersmoon.com

If your comments are significant, I will consider giving you credit in my second book, Blood Moon Rising, which should be out later this year.

Coming soon! The second book in the Cooper's Moon
mystery series. Here is a preview of book two:

Blood Moon Rising
Prologue

It has been raining for five straight days now and the river is swollen, threatening to spill over the banks and inundate this small southern Ohio city. It's late autumn and this is what happens every fall. On the river. Rain, rising tides, flooded homes and people stranded on rooftops watching cars and animals floating down the river. People ask why don't they just move? The answer is because this is their home.

It's late, 3:00 a.m., and the waters of the Ohio are racing toward the Mississippi, the blood moon riding low in the sky now, watching the whole scene like a curious silver eye, casting its light on the waters and illuminating the flotsam that is beginning to jam the river and force it onto the shore. The people who were standing on its banks earlier in the evening have gone to sleep, hoping for a better day tomorrow, which means, of course, that the rain will stop.

What they aren't seeing now is a body, or should I say, parts of a body, washed against a pile of tree branches, bouncing like a rubber doll, one arm flopping as the waves from the torrent strike it. The other arm missing. Skin peeled back on the trunk. Her face, or what's left of it, is swollen and grotesque, the soft light of the moon unable to alter the fact that her body is decaying, the night breeze unable to hide the stench of rotting flesh. Her clothes are torn from the punishing waters, and her eyes, only holes now, stare into the night sky, as if anxious to release the secret of what had happened.

Author photographed by Ryan Cranmer Conrath

Cooper's Moon is Richard Conrath's first novel and part of a trilogy featuring Cooper, a private detective who looks for his kidnapped son while trying to track down missing people. Richard is a former Catholic priest who left to teach philosophy in a small college while freelancing for papers like the *Cleveland Plain Dealer* and *Sunday Magazine*. He left teaching in 1984 and began a series of three-year stints in administration as a college vice-president, president, and then as headmaster of an American school in Turkey. It was in Turkey, during the darkness of the winters there, that he began to write his first mystery.

Today he lives with his wife in south Florida and enjoys the peace that comes with the sun, the sand, and the slower pace set by island time.

29024879R00240

Made in the USA
Columbia, SC
27 October 2018